PATRICIA WENTWORTH

THE AMAZING CHANCE

PATRICIA WENTWORTH was born Dora Amy Elles in India in 1877 (not 1878 as has sometimes been stated). She was first educated privately in India, and later at Blackheath School for Girls. Her first husband was George Dillon, with whom she had her only child, a daughter. She also had two stepsons from her first marriage, one of whom died in the Somme during World War I.

Her first novel was published in 1910, but it wasn't until the 1920's that she embarked on her long career as a writer of mysteries. Her most famous creation was Miss Maud Silver, who appeared in 32 novels, though there were a further 33 full-length mysteries not featuring Miss Silver—the entire run of these is now reissued by Dean Street Press.

Patricia Wentworth died in 1961. She is recognized today as one of the pre-eminent exponents of the classic British golden age mystery novel.

By Patricia Wentworth

The Benbow Smith Mysteries
Fool Errant
Danger Calling
Walk with Care
Down Under

The Frank Garrett Mysteries
Dead or Alive
Rolling Stone

The Ernest Lamb Mysteries
The Blind Side
Who Pays the Piper?
Pursuit of a Parcel

Standalones
The Astonishing Adventure of Jane Smith
The Red Lacquer Case
The Annam Jewel
The Black Cabinet
The Dower House Mystery
The Amazing Chance
Hue and Cry
Anne Belinda
Will-o'-the-Wisp
Beggar's Choice
The Coldstone
Kingdom Lost
Nothing Venture
Red Shadow
Outrageous Fortune
Touch and Go
Fear by Night
Red Stefan
Blindfold
Hole and Corner
Mr. Zero
Run!
Weekend with Death
Silence in Court

PATRICIA WENTWORTH

THE AMAZING CHANCE

With an introduction by
Curtis Evans

DEAN STREET PRESS

Introduction

BRITISH AUTHOR Patricia Wentworth published her first novel, a gripping tale of desperate love during the French Revolution entitled *A Marriage under the Terror*, a little over a century ago, in 1910. The book won first prize in the Melrose Novel Competition and was a popular success in both the United States and the United Kingdom. Over the next five years Wentworth published five additional novels, the majority of them historical fiction, the best-known of which today is *The Devil's Wind* (1912), another sweeping period romance, this one set during the Sepoy Mutiny (1857-58) in India, a region with which the author, as we shall see, had extensive familiarity. Like *A Marriage under the Terror*, *The Devil's Wind* received much praise from reviewers for its sheer storytelling élan. One notice, for example, pronounced the novel "an achievement of some magnitude" on account of "the extraordinary vividness...the reality of the atmosphere...the scenes that shift and move with the swiftness of a moving picture...." (*The Bookman*, August 1912) With her knack for spinning a yarn, it perhaps should come as no surprise that Patricia Wentworth during the early years of the Golden Age of mystery fiction (roughly from 1920 into the 1940s) launched upon her own mystery-writing career, a course charted most successfully for nearly four decades by the prolific author, right up to the year of her death in 1961.

Considering that Patricia Wentworth belongs to the select company of Golden Age mystery writers with books which have remained in print in every decade for nearly a century now (the centenary of Agatha Christie's first mystery, *The Mysterious Affair at Styles*, is in 2020; the centenary of Wentworth's first mystery, *The Astonishing Adventure of Jane Smith*, follows merely three years later, in 2023), relatively little is known about the author herself. It appears, for example, that even the widely given year of Wentworth's birth, 1878, is incorrect. Yet it is sufficiently clear that Wentworth lived a varied and intriguing life that provided her ample inspiration for a writing career devoted to imaginative fiction.

It is usually stated that Patricia Wentworth was born Dora Amy Elles on 10 November 1878 in Mussoorie, India, during the heyday of the British Raj; however, her Indian birth and baptismal record states that she in fact was born on 15 October 1877 and was baptized on 26 November of that same year in Gwalior. Whatever doubts surround her actual birth year, however, unquestionably the future author came from a prominent Anglo-Indian military family. Her father, Edmond Roche Elles, a son of Malcolm Jamieson Elles, a Porto, Portugal wine merchant originally from Ardrossan, Scotland, entered the British Royal Artillery in 1867, a decade before Wentworth's birth, and first saw service in India during the Lushai Expedition of 1871-72. The next year Elles in India wed Clara Gertrude Rothney, daughter of Brigadier-General Octavius Edward Rothney, commander of the Gwalior District, and Maria (Dempster) Rothney, daughter of a surgeon in the Bengal Medical Service. Four children were born of the union of Edmond and Clara Elles, Wentworth being the only daughter.

Before his retirement from the army in 1908, Edmond Elles rose to the rank of lieutenant-general and was awarded the KCB (Knight Commander of the Order of Bath), as was the case with his elder brother, Wentworth's uncle, Lieutenant-General Sir William Kidston Elles, of the Bengal Command. Edmond Elles also served as Military Member to the Council of the Governor-General of India from 1901 to 1905. Two of Wentworth's brothers, Malcolm Rothney Elles and Edmond Claude Elles, served in the Indian Army as well, though both of them died young (Malcolm in 1906 drowned in the Ganges Canal while attempting to rescue his orderly, who had fallen into the water), while her youngest brother, Hugh Jamieson Elles, achieved great distinction in the British Army. During the First World War he catapulted, at the relatively youthful age of 37, to the rank of brigadier-general and the command of the British Tank Corps, at the Battle of Cambrai personally leading the advance of more than 350 tanks against the German line. Years later Hugh Elles also played a major role in British civil defense during the Second World War. In the event of a German invasion of Great Britain, something which seemed all too possible in 1940, he was tasked with leading the defense of southwestern England. Like Sir Edmond and Sir William, Hugh Elles attained the rank of lieutenant-general and was awarded the KCB.

Although she was born in India, Patricia Wentworth spent much of her childhood in England. In 1881 she with her mother and two younger brothers was at Tunbridge Wells, Kent, on what appears to have been a rather extended visit in her ancestral country; while a decade later the same family group resided at Blackheath, London at Lennox House, domicile of Wentworth's widowed maternal grandmother, Maria Rothney. (Her eldest brother, Malcolm, was in Bristol attending Clifton College.) During her years at Lennox House, Wentworth attended Blackheath High School for Girls, then only recently founded as "one of the first schools in the country to give girls a proper education" (*The London Encyclopaedia*, 3rd ed., p. 74). Lennox House was an ample Victorian villa with a great glassed-in conservatory running all along the back and a substantial garden--most happily, one presumes, for Wentworth, who resided there not only with her grandmother, mother and two brothers, but also five aunts (Maria Rothney's unmarried daughters, aged 26 to 42), one adult first cousin once removed and nine first cousins, adolescents like Wentworth herself, from no less than three different families (one Barrow, three Masons and five Dempsters); their parents, like Wentworth's father, presumably were living many miles away in various far-flung British dominions. Three servants--a cook, parlourmaid and housemaid--were tasked with serving this full score of individuals.

Sometime after graduating from Blackheath High School in the mid-1890s, Wentworth returned to India, where in a local British newspaper she is said to have published her first fiction. In 1901 the 23-year-old Wentworth married widower George Fredrick Horace Dillon, a 41-year-old lieutenant-colonel in the Indian Army with three sons from his prior marriage. Two years later Wentworth gave birth to her only child, a daughter named Clare Roche Dillon. (In some sources it is erroneously stated that Clare was the offspring of Wentworth's second marriage.) However in 1906, after just five years of marriage, George Dillon died suddenly on a sea voyage, leaving Wentworth with sole responsibly for her three teenaged stepsons and baby daughter. A very short span of years, 1904 to 1907, saw the deaths of Wentworth's husband, mother, grandmother and brothers Malcolm and Edmond, removing much of her support network. In 1908, however, her father, who was now sixty years old, retired from the army and returned to England, settling at Guildford, Surrey with an older unmarried sister named Dora (for whom his daughter presumably had been named). Wentworth joined this household as well, along with her daughter and her youngest stepson. Here in Surrey Wentworth, presumably with the goal of making herself financially independent for the first time in her life (she was now in her early thirties), wrote the novel that changed the course of her life, *A Marriage under the Terror*, for the first time we know of utilizing her famous *nom de plume*.

The burst of creative energy that resulted in Wentworth's publication of six novels in six years suddenly halted after the appearance of *Queen Anne Is Dead* in 1915. It seems not unlikely that the Great War impinged in various ways on her writing. One tragic episode was the death on the western front of one of her stepsons, George Charles Tracey Dillon. Mining in Colorado when war was declared, young Dillon worked his passage from Galveston, Texas to Bristol, England as a shipboard muleteer (mule-tender) and joined the Gloucestershire Regiment. In 1916 he died at the Somme at the age of 29 (about the age of Wentworth's two brothers when they had passed away in India).

A couple of years after the conflict's cessation in 1918, a happy event occurred in Wentworth's life when at Frimley, Surrey she wed George Oliver Turnbull, up to this time a lifelong bachelor who like the author's first husband was a lieutenant-colonel in the Indian Army. Like his bride now forty-two years old, George Turnbull as a younger man had distinguished himself for his athletic prowess, playing forward for eight years for the Scottish rugby team and while a student at the Royal Military Academy winning the medal awarded the best athlete of his term. It seems not unlikely that Turnbull played a role in his wife's turn toward writing mystery fiction, for he is said to have strongly supported Wentworth's career, even assisting her in preparing manuscripts for publication. In 1936 the couple in Camberley, Surrey built Heatherglade House, a large two-story structure on substantial grounds, where they resided until Wentworth's death a quarter of a century later. (George Turnbull survived his wife by nearly a decade, passing away in 1970 at the age of 92.) This highly successful middle-aged companionate marriage contrasts sharply with the more youthful yet rocky union of Agatha and Archie Christie, which was three years away from sundering when Wentworth published *The Astonishing Adventure of Jane Smith* (1923), the first of her sixty-five mystery novels.

Although Patricia Wentworth became best-known for her cozy tales of the criminal investigations of consulting detective Miss Maud Silver, one of the mystery genre's most prominent spinster sleuths, in truth the Miss Silver tales account for just under half of Wentworth's 65 mystery novels. Miss Silver did not make her debut until 1928 and she did not come to predominate in Wentworth's fictional criminous output until the 1940s. Between 1923 and 1945 Wentworth published 33 mystery novels without Miss Silver, a handsome and substantial legacy in and of itself to vintage crime fiction fans. Many of these books are standalone tales of mystery, but nine of them have series characters. Debuting in the novel *Fool Errant* in 1929, a year after Miss Silver first appeared in print, was the enigmatic, nautically-named *eminence grise* Benbow Collingwood Horatio Smith, owner of a most expressively opinionated parrot named Ananias (and quite a colorful character in his own right). Benbow Smith went on to appear in three additional Wentworth mysteries: *Danger Calling* (1931), *Walk with Care* (1933) and *Down Under* (1937). Working in tandem with Smith in the investigation of sinister affairs threatening the security of Great Britain in *Danger*

Calling and *Walk with Care* is Frank Garrett, Head of Intelligence for the Foreign Office, who also appears solo in *Dead or Alive* (1936) and *Rolling Stone* (1940) and collaborates with additional series characters, Scotland Yard's Inspector Ernest Lamb and Sergeant Frank Abbott, in *Pursuit of a Parcel* (1942). Inspector Lamb and Sergeant Abbott headlined a further pair of mysteries, *The Blind Side* (1939) and *Who Pays the Piper?* (1940), before they became absorbed, beginning with *Miss Silver Deals with Death* (1943), into the burgeoning Miss Silver canon. Lamb would make his farewell appearance in 1955 in *The Listening Eye*, while Abbott would take his final bow in mystery fiction with Wentworth's last published novel, *The Girl in the Cellar* (1961), which went into print the year of the author's death at the age of 83.

The remaining two dozen Wentworth mysteries, from the fantastical *The Astonishing Adventure of Jane Smith* in 1923 to the intense legal drama *Silence in Court* in 1945, are, like the author's series novels, highly imaginative and entertaining tales of mystery and adventure, told by a writer gifted with a consummate flair for storytelling. As one confirmed Patricia Wentworth mystery fiction addict, American Golden Age mystery writer Todd Downing, admiringly declared in the 1930s, "There's something about Miss Wentworth's yarns that is contagious." This attractive new series of Patricia Wentworth reissues by Dean Street Press provides modern fans of vintage mystery a splendid opportunity to catch the Wentworth fever.

Curtis Evans

Chapter One

ANTON BLUM was chopping wood. It had got very dark in the last half-hour; night came early here in the Königswald; the small clearing farmed by Josef Müller was ringed with trees which looked black long before sunset, and to-night there was no visible sun. The wind had been rising all day; trees groaned and strained against it.

Anton went on chopping steadily; he was so strong that he never got tired. Anna Blum had set him to chop wood, and he would go on chopping until she came out and said, "*Na*, Anton, that is enough. Come in."

Once, when she had been away all day, she came home to find him still washing the kitchen floor. She had told him to wash it, and then she had gone out; and when she came home, there was Anton on his hands and knees still washing the floor. But that was long ago, before they came to live in the Königswald. Tante Anna was more careful now.

Anton went on chopping wood. Down in the village they said "As strong as Anton Blum," where in other villages they might have said "As strong as an ox." To a naughty child one said "Take care, or Anton Blum will carry you off," and to a dull scholar, "You're as stupid as Anton Blum."

No one knew what Anton thought of it all. He lived with Anna Blum, who was his aunt, and Josef Müller, who was Anna's brother. He knew that. Anna was his aunt, and Josef was her brother. Anna was also a widow. The words aunt and widow belonged to Anna; and the word brother belonged to Josef. Anton did not get further than that. Since he had been wounded in the head, nine, ten years ago, he did not speak. From Josef he would take no orders. And he never went down into the village, because the children threw stones at him. But what Anna Blum told him to do, he did.

He went on chopping wood. If he heard the sound of storm in the rising wind, it did not trouble him. If he thought at all, he thought only of what he was doing. When the chips flew it pleased him. The swing of the hatchet pleased him too. Really his mind was very like the clearing in which he stood. There was a space that was clear, and all the rest was dark. In the midst of the clear space there was someone who was Anton Blum; he knew that that was his name; and he knew that he loved Tante Anna, and that he was afraid of the village children and of strangers. When Tante Anna spoke he could understand her well enough; but with strangers he became very easily confused, and then he did not know what was wanted of him.

Anna Blum came out into the yard, a square-built woman, very clean.

"Come then, Anton!" she called, and Anton stopped chopping and dropped his hatchet beside the pile of logs. Anna came a little nearer. "*Na*, Anton, the hatchet will rust. Pick it up and put it in the shed." She spoke as one speaks to a very small child, every word very distinct.

Anton did as he was told. He had the docility and gentleness of a large, house-trained dog. When he had hung up the hatchet, he followed Anna Blum into the house. They came into the kitchen, which was warm and smelt of paraffin because the lamp had just been lighted and the wick was still turned down. It was a cheap lamp with a tin reflector, and the light from it made a sort of yellow dusk in the room.

Josef Müller sat in his own chair taking off his boots. As Anna turned up the light, the likeness between them seemed stronger than it really was; the same square build, the same light brown hair, the same blue eyes. That was the first impression. Then in a flash it was gone, and one saw, instead, Josef's ill-tempered mouth and shifty gaze.

Josef threw his boots into the corner, where they fell with a clatter.

"There's a fine storm coming."

Anna looked over her shoulder at the unshuttered window.

"I must go down into the village," she said. "I must see Mina."

"*Dummes zeug!* Mina will do very well without you."

Anna looked across the lamp at him, and did not trouble to keep contempt out of look and voice.

"What an affectionate father you are! Your first grandchild a bare forty-eight hours old, and to you it is foolishness that I went to see Mina yesterday, and that I go again to-day! You, naturally, would not put yourself about to go—why should you?"

Josef scowled.

"When a girl marries, her husband can keep her," he grumbled. "What did you take with you when you went yesterday?—and what are you taking now? That is what I should like to know."

"Yesterday," said Anna composedly, "I took milk and six eggs. To-day I am taking milk. To-morrow I shall take eggs again."

Josef's scowl deepened. He swore under his breath; but his eyes shifted. His wife and his daughter had been afraid of him; but Anna was not afraid of him. He had struck her once, nearly three years ago now; and the moment that he struck her was nearly his last. Anna, standing between him and the frightened, cowering Mina, had seen his face change suddenly as Anton reached for his throat—Anton, whom they had all ignored in the heat of this family quarrel. There was a horrible moment of uncertainty, a moment in which Josef felt himself as weak as a new-born kitten in Anton's terrible grip; and then, in response to Anna's "No, no, Anton! No!", the grasp relaxed and Anton stood away with an inarticulate sound that was only half human.

Josef had never struck either his sister or his daughter again. Secretly, he went in fear of Anton. He turned in his chair as Anna crossed to the door.

"If you are going, you will at least take that lump with you. Do you hear?" He jerked his elbow in the direction of Anton, crouched on a stool in the chimney-corner, his hands spread out to the warmth.

"He has only just come in."

"What difference does that make? I won't be left with him."

"You are very brave!" said Anna with an ironic glance. Her eyes softened as she turned to Anton and called,

"Come then, Anton. I go out, and I have a basket to be carried."

He got up at once, stretched himself, and crossed the kitchen with an awkward, shuffling walk. Anna patted his shoulder, and they went out together.

Chapter Two

BY THE TIME that Anna Blum had paid her visit to Mina and admired Mina's baby, the threatened storm had broken. Out upon the Cologne road the rain ran like a river and the wind came in such gusts that Anna was glad enough of Anton's arm.

Anton, fortunately, did not mind the storm. The sudden flare of the lightning pleased him; and the crashing thunder that followed pleased him too. If he had been alone, he would have waved his arms and shouted, but he knew that he must hold Tante Anna steady and on no account drop the basket which she had given him to carry.

As they struggled against the wind, the wet road shone white for a moment in the glare of two powerful headlights, and a car went by them, heading for Cologne. Anna Blum clutched her old cloak about her, and felt the rain drive in her face.

"What a night!" she thought, and remembered another night of staring lightning and rending storm.

It was just as they came to the footpath which led from the main road to Josef's clearing that the lights of a car showed again, coming up this time from the darkness that hid Cologne. There was so much noise that the car seemed to be sliding towards them without any sound. Suddenly it stopped and a man called out "Hullo!"

Anna moved towards the car and said, "What is it?"

A man next the driver leaned out.

"Can you direct me to Josef Müller's farm?"

"Josef Müller?"

The men in the car were English officers. The little light on the dashboard showed the uniform coats and the faces. One bent over the wheel, young, handsome; the other, the older man, the one who had spoken, very ugly and dark.

Anna put her hand on the edge of the car and repeated, "Josef Müller?"

The man in the driver's seat spoke now in stumbling German.

"Yes, an old man upon the road told us to ask for Josef Müller."

Then the first man again:

"Dry up, Dugdale! No one can understand your German. I'll do the talking."

"What is it?" said Anna calmly.

"There's a tree down across the road. We were told we could get help to shift it at Josef Müller's."

It was at this moment that Anton shuffled into the glare of the headlights. They puzzled him because they were so bright, and yet when he went close to them they did not warm him.

"Who's that?" said Major Manning sharply.

"My nephew, Anton Blum."

"We want help to shift the tree; my friend and I can't quite manage alone. Your nephew looks strong. Will he give us a hand?"

"He's the strongest man in the Königswald. But"—she hesitated—"he is dumb."

Young Dugdale laughed.

"Well, we don't want him to make speeches," he said in his execrable German.

Anna took no notice of him. She leant on the door and spoke to the older man:

"He is as strong as an ox; but he is not like other people. I do not know if he will go with you."

Anton had left the headlights and come close up to them, drawn by the sound of the voices.

"Ask him," said Major Manning.

There was a lull in the extreme violence of the wind. Major Manning's words sounded unnaturally loud. Anna let go of the door, took Anton by the arm, and began to talk to him.

"There is a tree across the road. The carriage cannot go on because of the tree. It would be a fine play to lift the tree out of the road. Will you show the gentlemen how strong you are, and go with them to lift the tree? You will get a fine ride, and they will see how strong you are."

She turned suddenly and spoke to Major Manning:

"Is it far? I would not like him to go far. He is like a child; he gets confused."

"A mile and a half at the outside—not so much really."

"*Na*, that is nothing. Wilt thou go, Anton?"

To her surprise Anton stepped forward, nodding his shaggy head. Never for one instant had she supposed that he would go. A little, sharp stab of anger edged with fear went through her as Major Manning reached backwards to throw open the rear door.

"All right. Get in," he said; and Anton, stumbling at the step, knocked his forehead against the wet canvas hood, thrust awkwardly into the car, and sank sprawling on the back seat.

Anna Blum held her cloak about her with stiff hands. She watched the car back and turn, and she saw the tail light grow small and disappear in the darkness. Then she turned and went up the footpath towards the light that shone from the uncurtained kitchen window. There was nothing to be afraid of—but she was afraid.

As the car picked up speed, young Dugdale laughed.

"What's the matter?" snapped Major Manning.

"Well, we seem to have commandeered the village idiot; and I was thinking that the joke would be on us all right if we got him there and found he wouldn't play."

"You stop thinking and attend to business."

"We've some way to go yet."

"How d'you know? Half the Königswald may have come down since we turned. You keep your eyes skinned." Major Manning's voice rasped, his ugly face was very cross and puckered. Philip Dugdale took a glance at it, grinned, and dried up.

"No wonder they call him Monkey," he thought. "I wish I knew whether he's really shirty. That's the worst of it with the Major— you never can tell—always looks as if he was in a tearing temper, and you never know whether he's going to bite your head off or suddenly start ragging."

"Filthy night!" said Major Manning explosively. "Why did we ever come to this rotten country? Here, go dead slow—that damn tree is just round the next bend."

Anton, on the back seat, listened to the voices. This was a fine carriage. He was having a fine ride. He had none of his usual fear of strangers; he was quite content to do as Tante Anna had bid him and go with these men whose voices gave him a curious pleasure. Presently he was to show them how strong he was. That would be fine too. He was proud of being so strong. The strangers would praise him, and Tante Anna would praise him. It was all very fine indeed.

When the car stopped and the two men got out, Anton was ready enough to follow their example. The headlights of the car showed the block in the road very plainly. The bank on the right had slipped, bringing down with it a pine, which lay right across the wet road. Anton ran forward and kicked the tree with his foot. It was not large; but it was too large for him to lift alone. He turned, waving his arms, beckoning, a wild, uncouth figure with the rain streaming from his long, rough hair and beard. As Manning and Dugdale came up, he ran, still waving, to the head of the tree and began to tug at it. He had lifted it a couple of feet by the time they came up, and the three of them hauling together were able to drag it round so as to leave room for the car to pass. Rain was falling in sheets; their boots squelched in it; it beat into their eyes; and a raging, veering wind drove it first this way and then that. Every now and then wood and sky swam in a blue wave of lightning. The roll of the thunder never stopped.

Manning straightened himself.

"Good Lord, the fellow's strong!" he said, and pushed his wet hand down into his pocket, fumbling for his money. The fellow certainly deserved a good tip. "Where is he?" he called; and then one of those blue flares showed him Anton close in under the bank, staring up at the gap which the tree had left, at the matted roots, the raw, torn earth—and at something else.

The flare died, and suddenly Dugdale was shouting at the top of his voice:

"Come back! Here, you—oh, I say, come back!"

Even as he shouted, Manning had him by the arm and they were both running. There was a flash that was white, not blue, an intense and brilliant white, a molten light that showed them the falling, sliding bank, with the trees a-top of it tilting, falling too. Then with the darkness there came such a crack of thunder as neither of them had ever heard before. When it had passed into a long roll that echoed from every side at once, they found themselves close to the car, almost touching it. The rain had redoubled, and came sluicing down quite straight, for the wind seemed to be holding its breath.

"I say," said Dugdale, rather breathlessly. "That poor devil!" His voice sounded extraordinarily small and weak.

Major Manning summoned his parade voice and shouted back, "Have you got a torch?"

"There's one in the car."

"Get it!"

Dugdale was shaken by an unseemly gust of recollection: "Have you the pen of the gardener?"—"No, but my sister has the writing-case of her aunt." He rummaged for the torch, looking in every pocket but the right one; and in the end had it snatched from him by Manning, who at the same time cursed him for the slowest and stupidest young ass in the service.

As soon as he had snatched the torch and switched it on, he set off at a run, Dugdale, rather aggrieved, at his heels. It was not easy to see just what had happened; the darkness was very dark. The beam from the torch wavered in the rain-shot gloom, showing little enough. That more of the bank had fallen, bringing with it at least one other tree, was certain. Manning turned the light here and there, barked his shins on a boulder, floundered into a mess of leaves and branches, tripped, swore, and came sprawling, but as he fell saw the ray of the torch glance on an upturned hand. He was up again in a moment, shouting to Dugdale, climbing over the fallen tree.

Anton Blum lay on his back where a branch of the second tree had swept him down. The branch must have struck him on the head, for there was blood running from his forehead into the rain and mud of the road.

With an odd sense of irritation Manning reached for one of the great wrists, and felt the pulse beat strong.

Then the thing happened. The wind had fallen silent. Dugdale was coming up. He, Manning, had dropped the fellow's wrist and turned the light on to his face, when suddenly the thing happened. The man opened his eyes, blinked at the light, and pushed it away. The beam lit Manning's cross, anxious face, showed for an instant the little black eyes, the bottle-brush moustache, the numberless puckers, the white scar on the chin. Anton Blum looked up, laughed, and said:

"Hullo, Monkey, that was a bit of a crump—wasn't it?"

Chapter Three

THE DAZZLE of light in his eyes; the laugh; the unbelievable words! Manning felt as if he had been hit three times in rapid succession. The impact was terrific. In sudden, furious resentment he pushed with all his might against the iron strength that was keeping the light on his face. He pushed, and it was like pushing against a crowbar. And then all at once the arm, Anton Blum's arm, fell like a broken thing, and Manning lost his balance and came down with his face amongst pine needles, his hands clutching at bark and gravel. Next moment Dugdale was pulling him up. The torch had gone out. They were there in the dark, and Manning was gasping and spitting out pine needles.

Dugdale had a sense of catastrophe—beastly awkward if the man was dead.

"What's happened? Is he dead?" he asked, and was cursed for every sort of a fool and told to find the torch.

Found, it emitted a faint, expiring flash, and then declined to function. The flash had, however, shown them Anton Blum lying at their feet, one arm outstretched on the tangled branches, the other across his body; his eyes, the eyes that had looked at Manning with recognition, were shut.

Dugdale's sense of catastrophe increased. He had caught a glimpse of his Major's face before the light went out. There was something there that he had never seen there before. Afterwards, when they had got Anton into the car, it came to him that the Major had looked rattled—yes, that was it, rattled—Monkey Manning rattled.

"What in the world's up?" Philip Dugdale asked Philip Dugdale, and got no answer.

It wasn't a very easy business getting Anton into the car—the slosh of mud everywhere; the debris of the bank; and a regular entanglement of broken and twisted branches. They got him on to the back seat at last, a dead weight that had never moved as they shifted it. Then—

"I suppose there's room to turn here," said Dugdale rather doubtfully.

"You don't need to turn. We're going on."

Dugdale stared.

"Aren't you going to take him back to his people, Major?"

"I'm going to take him to my house." Manning got in at the back as he spoke. He settled himself to steady the unconscious figure. "Get in and drive for all you're worth!" And Dugdale obeyed.

It was a very odd drive. Manning sat on the back seat with one arm about Anton Blum. Every now and then the heavy head with its mass of wet hair came against his shoulder. He hardly noticed it. When they shaved another car whose tail-light had gone out, he did not notice it at all. Neither Dugdale's exclamation nor the swerve and lurch of the car reached him; his mind was entirely preoccupied with the amazing thing that had happened.

This was a half-witted German peasant. His name was Anton Blum. He had come to help them shift a tree. He had got knocked on the head. Then he had looked at him, Manning, and laughed and said "Hullo, Monkey!" But he was the half-witted German peasant called Anton Blum. And he was dumb—the woman had said that he was dumb. And he had laughed and said "Hullo, Monkey!"

When the car stopped, Manning woke up with a jerk. He was out on the wet pavement and in the house, shouting for Brooks, almost before the engine stopped running.

Brooks incontinently dropped the coat he was brushing and ran.

"The Major, 'e fair lifted the roof. 'Brooks,' 'e shouts, and I give you me word some of the plaster drops down from the ceiling." He confided the whole incident very frankly to Mrs Manning's maid next day. "Well, I took and dropped everything and run. And when I got down, there was 'im and Mr Dugdale, and the car sopping wet, and a 'ulking, great 'Un on the back seat. Well, miss, you could 'ave knocked me down with a gasper, straight you could."

"Lor!" said the maid. She was a middle-aged person, but not on that account averse to flirtation. "Lor! To think of us missing it, which we shouldn't have done if Mrs Manning had kept to her day. But there, that's a thing she's never done in her life, and not likely to start now."

Brooks resumed with a frown. Miss Possiter was an audience, and the sooner she tumbled to the fact the better. He hadn't the slightest desire to listen to her or to hear her opinions: he wanted to talk. He talked.

"Straight, you might have knocked me down. There was the Major 'opping about like the monkey they calls 'im, and making faces fit to bust 'isself, and damning us all into 'eaps because we wasn't quick enough. "Ere,' 'e says, 'carry 'im upstairs!' 'e says. And then, there was 'im, and me, and Mr Dugdale a-carrying that great, 'ulking 'Un up the stairs and into the spare bedroom. And I thinks to myself 'arf-way up that it was a good thing Mrs Manning wasn't 'ome to see the wet a-pouring down on the carpets, and the Major's boots fair caked with mud. Weighed about a ton the chap did, and you could 'ave wrung a river out of 'im. 'Get 'is clothes off 'im and get 'im to bed. And send for Major O'Neill,' says the Major. 'Get O'Neill on the telephone and tell 'im to come round at once and wait 'ere till I come back, because I wants to see 'im most pertickler!' 'e says to Mr Dugdale. Mr Dugdale, 'e looks as if 'e thought the Major 'ad gone batty. 'Where are you a-going of, Major?' 'e says; and the Major fair bites 'is 'ead off. 'Don't you let O'Neill go till I get back!' 'e says when 'e couldn't go on without repeating of 'imself. And then 'e bangs the door, and off 'e goes in the car. And Mr Dugdale, 'e goes to the telephone."

Chapter Four

ANNA BLUM SAT in the warm kitchen with her Bible open on her knee. Josef had gone to bed; and when Josef went to bed it was her custom to sit down and read a psalm. She had taken off her wet skirt and hung it over a chair to dry. A second chair was almost hidden in the folds of her cloak, a strange relic of the early nineties. The material had once been a gay plaid, and the garment itself a so-called golf-cape. Now the colours were all gone away to a dull, uneven drab.

Divested of cloak and skirt, Anna appeared in an old red flannel petticoat, very neatly mended, and a cross-over shawl of faded brown wool, which had been her grandmother's. She sat close up to the lamp with its tin reflector and read her psalm to the end.

Anton was late. He should have been back a long time since. The officers must have been mistaken in the distance. But if they took Anton too far along the road, perhaps he would get confused and not find his way back.

Anna jerked her head up and listened, then spoke aloud:

"Na, Anna—art a fool. Ja gewiss!"

She began to read the psalm over again; but half-way through she was listening.

"A hen with one chick, and a woman with one child—and if he is not my own son it is all the same. Mina lies there with her baby, and she thinks that I do not know what is in her heart, because I have never borne a child." She drew the back of her hand quickly across her eyes and stared down at the printed page. The letters swam in a dazzle of tears, and Anna called herself a fool again.

She was afraid. It all came back to that—she was afraid. Nothing to be afraid of; but she was afraid. The room seemed to be filled with her fear.

She read once more to the end of the psalm, and closed the book. As she laid it on the table, she heard at last what she had been straining her ears for—the sound of a footstep. She had left the window unshuttered, and ran now to the door, throwing it wide open so that the light should stream out in welcome.

As she stood on the threshold looking out, the first doubt came to her. She could hear the footsteps coming nearer. But—Anton walked more heavily than that; often he dragged his feet. This was a lighter, quicker step, the step of a different man. She drew back, and as she did so, some one came round the bend of the path into the light from the open door.

It wasn't Anton—she had known that it would not be Anton. It was one of the English officers who had taken Anton away. And that meant that something had happened.

Major Manning came up to the door, and found himself face to face with the woman he had come to find. She was silhouetted against the lighted room, and she spoke at once, breathlessly:

"Anton—*mein Herr*, what is it—why have you come—where is Anton?" Then, as Major Manning stepped across the threshold and the light showed his darkly frowning face, she said with a sickening catch in her voice, "Is he dead?"

"No, no—of course not."

Manning was really shocked. He had not expected—no one could have expected—any particular intensity of feeling over a dumb, half-witted creature, or—He refused to follow out that train of thought.

"What is it, then?" said Anna, her hand on the door. There was a shade of defiance in her tone.

"It's nothing—nothing to frighten you at all. A branch caught him on the head, and I took him on to my house to have the cut attended to."

"Why did you not bring him home?"

"I took him to my own house. I thought he ought to be attended to. And—I want to talk to you."

Anna's hand tightened on the door.

"Is he badly hurt?"

"No, he's only stunned—and a cut on the forehead. He's at my house. You've nothing to be frightened about. But I want to speak to you."

Anna collected herself. She shut the door. Her whole manner changed.

"*Gnädiger Herr* must forgive me. I was frightened."

She went to the hearth, caught up her wet things, and pulled forward Josef's chair. Manning looked at it, shook his head slightly, and sat down on the wooden chair from which she had taken her cloak, bestriding it and resting his arms on the back.

"Sit down, please."

Anna came back to her seat by the lamp. Manning looked at her over the back of the chair, frowning deeply. Now that he was here, he didn't know how to begin. The whole thing was unbelievable, absolutely. He saw Anna reach across the Bible at her elbow and pick up a half-knitted sock which lay on the table beyond it. He watched her settle the needles and begin to knit, all very quietly. No, he really did not know how to begin.

After a moment Anna lifted steady blue eyes to his.

"You wished to speak to me, *mein Herr*?"

"Yes," said Manning. "I did—about your nephew. He *is* your nephew?"

Anna nodded.

"Yes, certainly—my nephew, Anton Blum."

"And your name?"

"Anna Blum, widow, born Müller. Anton is the son of my husband's elder brother, Ludwig Blum."

"And he is dumb?" Manning shot the question at her.

"*Ach ja*. Since he was wounded he is dumb."

"Only since he was wounded?"

"Yes, *mein Herr*."

"How long ago?"

She let the knitting fall on her knees, and began to reckon on her fingers.

"It is eight—nine—nearly ten years—a long time."

Manning got up, crossed the room, and stood by the table. The lamp was between him and Anna now. When she spoke she must face the light. He pushed the lamp back a little to get it out of his eyes, and asked suddenly:

"Does he know English?"

Anna's eyes were on her knitting. He saw a line come in her forehead, just between the brows.

"English?" she asked, and then looked up with a puzzled expression. "He does not know very much at all. He understands what a child would understand. I speak to him as one speaks to a child."

Manning leaned on the table, his little eyes intent on her face.

"But before he was wounded—did he know any English before he was wounded?"

"I don't know," said Anna. "I only saw him twice before the war came. He was a forester on a big estate, and one of the sons was certainly married to an Englishwoman or an American. Anton spoke of it; he said there was an English groom—I remember that. It is possible that he learnt some words—I cannot tell."

She spoke in a quiet, considering manner above the gentle click of the needles. She did not look at Major Manning until she said "I cannot tell." It was on the last word that she lifted her eyes in a gaze of pure perplexity.

"Why do you ask that, *mein Herr*?"

"Because," said Manning, "when I went to pick him up, I thought that he spoke; and I thought that he spoke English."

Anna's face hardly changed. A faint shade of sadness crossed it. She bent her head and said:

"Ach so," And then, "Once—twice before, when he has been ill, it has happened like that—he has spoken as a man speaks in his

sleep; and afterwards he has been dumb again. The last time was four years ago."

Manning stood up straight.

"I suppose you've got all his papers—his discharge—all that sort of thing?"

"Ja gewiss," said Anna. "Would you like to see them, *mein Herr*?"

"Yes, I should."

Anna rose at once.

"They are upstairs," she said. And Manning waited whilst she went out of the door and up the narrow stair beyond.

Every sound was audible. He could hear her open a door and come into the room above the kitchen. He could hear the jingle of keys. He could hear her move a box and throw the lid back. In a minute she came down the stairs and into the kitchen. In a quiet, deliberate manner she laid out on the table under the lamp a metal disc and a couple of papers.

Manning picked up the disc first and saw Anton Blum's name on it, his regimental number, and the name of a regiment. He kept it in his hand and took up the papers—a birth certificate setting forth that Anton Blum was the son of Ludwig Blum, *Bauer*, and Elsa his wife, *geborene Platt*, etc., the date being July the 1st, 1894; and Anton Blum's discharge certificate, the reason for the said discharge being given as: "Dumbness and mental deficiency resulting from wounds."

Manning folded the papers, laid them carefully on the table, and put the identity disc down on the top of them. He did not know what to say to this quiet, friendly woman. To attempt to explain was an impossibility. But, having come so far in the direction of making a fool of himself, he meant to see it out to the bitter end.

"Your brother—Josef Müller is your brother, I believe—can I see him?"

"Yes, he is my brother. He has gone to bed, but—" She hesitated a little—"if you like, I will call him."

"No, I'll go up."

And go up he did, preceded by Anna and a lighted candle. At Josef's door he took the candle from her, banged on the panel, and went in, to find Josef snoring. It was not very easy to wake him; Josef, once asleep, was accustomed to sleep for ten hours at the least. He woke reluctantly to the very astonishing presence of an English officer who wanted to ask him questions about Anton. Drowsiness would certainly have passed into rage but for the timely recollection of what good customers the English were. To quarrel with them was certainly to cut one's own hand off. Josef loved his sleep; but he loved his pocket better still. He answered Manning's questions very readily, and certainly left the impression of having nothing in the world to conceal. Anton was his sister Anna's nephew, and an ill-conditioned, worthless lump into the bargain. Only Josef's good heart induced him to give the fellow food and shelter. Work? Oh, yes, he worked. But from beginning to end he was certainly more trouble than he was worth.

Manning went down the stair with the conviction that he had made a fool of himself—a first-class, out-size sort of fool.

Chapter Five

MAJOR O'NEILL looked up from cold beef and pickles as the dining-room door opened and his host came in.

"Hullo, Monkey!" he said, "Come and feed. I expect you want something. Where in the world have you been?"

Manning came up to the table, poured himself out a long drink, drank most of it at a draught, and sat down.

"Well, what do you make of the fellow?"

O'Neill was carving. He raised his eyebrows a little, and said coolly,

"There's nothing to make of him—had a crack on the head, and he's sleeping it off. And why, in the name of all that's unreasonable, you wanted to bring him here—" He broke off, pushed a plate of beef across the table, and added meaningly, "Just as well for you Mrs Manning's not back. Her spare room is likely to want a good deal more patching up than that fellow's head. Good Lord, Monkey, what possessed you?"

Manning finished his drink, put his elbows on the table, and produced the ferocious scowl which always meant that he was thinking hard.

"Look here, O'Neill, you've known me for getting on twenty years." He paused, and then rapped out, "Am I the sort of man who has hallucinations?"

"I don't know," said O'Neill thoughtfully. "Anyone may have an hallucination. As a matter of fact everyone does. You go to sleep, and you dream—"

"I don't dream."

"Lucky man!"

Manning rapped the table sharply.

"I'm not ragging. I want your opinion. Am I the sort of man who imagines things?"

O'Neill's rather quizzical manner altered. "No, you're not. What is it?"

"I'm going to tell you—seal of professional secrecy and all that."

"Of course."

"That fellow in there—of course you think I'm crazy to have brought him here and to have dragged you in to attend to him. I suppose Dugdale told you how we picked him up?"

"Dugdale said you'd commandeered the village idiot to help shift a tree."

Manning nodded.

"That was about the size of it. He's a half-witted peasant, and he's dumb into the bargain. We shifted the tree, and then some more of the bank fell, and he got knocked out. I went to pick him up, and I turned my torch on his face to see what the damage was."

O'Neill stared. Manning's voice, Manning's face suggested an extraordinary sense of strain. He wondered—and then Manning pushed back his chair with a jerk and stood up.

"Well?" said O'Neill.

Manning walked to the window and back before he answered.

"It sounds crazy," he said.

"What sounds crazy?"

"The whole thing. He—he opened his eyes, and the next thing I knew, he had hold of my wrist, turning it, you know, so as to throw the light on my face; and then he laughed—O'Neill, I swear he laughed—and he said, 'Hullo, Monkey! That was a bit of a crump—wasn't it?'"

O'Neill gave a long, soft whistle. Manning sat down and pulled his chair up to the table. He'd got it off his chest; the relief was amazing. He began to attack his plate of cold beef without troubling about O'Neill's scrutiny. After a moment O'Neill said,

"He spoke English?"

Manning nodded; his mouth was full.

"He called you Monkey? You're *sure*?"

"He said 'Hullo, Monkey! That was a bit of a crump—wasn't it?'—just like that."

O'Neill knitted his brows, and ran a hand through his fair, thin hair.

"It's incredible!"

Just for a fleeting instant Monkey Manning grinned.

"That's what I've been saying to myself ever since—quite a pleasant change to hear someone else say it."

"It's incredible!" said O'Neill again. "Who'd you got with you? If he'd heard someone call you Monkey, he might have just parroted it."

"I hadn't anyone with me except young Dugdale; and subalterns don't call me Monkey—not to my face anyway. The parrot theory's no good, old man—nor any other theory either. I've just come back from seeing his people. Devoted aunt—pleasant, honest-looking creature who showed me all his papers; and an uncle whom I'd have liked to kick—regular surly brute who talked as if the poor chap was an inconvenient animal, though I don't mind betting he's been getting about three men's work out of him."

With the last word the door opened. Brooks came in bearing cheese, biscuits and butter. He put them down on the sideboard, and with a deadly, careful slowness he changed Major O'Neill's plate, removed the beef, went out, came back, and vaguely marked time in the background.

Manning pushed his plate away impatiently.

"All right, Brooks. Put everything on the table, and don't come back."

"Though what on earth 'e and Major O'Neill, as sees each other every blessed day of the week, can 'ave to talk about so blooming private—well, I puts it to you, Miss Possiter—"

Miss Possiter bridled.

"Oh, don't put it to *me*!" she said. "I'm sure what gentlemen do or don't do isn't a thing that I should ever concern myself with." Here she chilled Brooks's young blood by a glance so undeniably flirtatious that he instantly heard the Major calling him.

In the dining-room the talk went on. Once, Manning and O'Neill went through the connecting door into the room beyond, and stood for five full minutes staring at the sleeping man in the spare room bed. There was a reading-lamp on the table by the head of the bed. O'Neill switched it on, tilted the shade, and let the light fall on the pillow. Anton Blum lay on his back, with the bed-clothes pulled up to his chin. They saw as much of his face as was to be seen in the twilight just outside the ray from the lamp. There was a bandage about his forehead. His eyes were shut; he appeared to be very deeply asleep. Between an uncommonly thick head of hair, a full square beard, and Major O'Neill's clean white bandage there really was not very much to see. After a moment O'Neill spoke in a quiet, low voice:

"Is he—is there any likeness, any look of anyone you ever knew?"

Manning made a frightful face.

"How can I say when he's simply smothered in hair? Take it off and I'll tell you."

"H'm," said O'Neill. He turned the shade down again. "Well, I'll come round in the morning, Monkey. He's pretty safe to sleep till then."

Anton Blum slept till the morning, and then went on sleeping. He drank a cup of Benger without waking, and O'Neill shrugged his shoulders and said, "Let him sleep." Even the stir and bustle of Lacy Manning's arrival did not rouse him.

Mrs Manning was what Brooks irreverently called a "houseful." She was a little person, but she certainly made herself felt. From the moment that she came inside the front door, silence was a thing of the past. There began instantly a clatter on the stairs, a banging of doors, a shifting of furniture, and above all, Lacy's sweet, very high-pitched voice: "Monkey! Monkey, darling! Brooks, where *is* the Major? Ada! *Ada!* Find Brooks at once! And ask him where the Major is. And, Ada—No, come back!"

Ada Possiter came reluctantly—Mrs Manning, who had travelled by air for the first time, had enjoyed the experience more than had her maid—Possiter looked gloomily resigned.

"Ada, I want my house-shoes—you've hidden them. And I want the Major at once. Oh, and tell the cook...." It never stopped; and the voice never varied from its flute-like sweetness.

"If she'd a 'undred servants, she'd find work for a 'undred and fifty of 'em," Brooks was moved to say in the interval between his twentieth and twenty-first errand.

Presently it was Manning who was receiving a fortnight's arrears of conjugal conversation. For the first ten minutes it concerned Don, and he had no difficulty in keeping his mind on it. Don, aged eight, had gone to his first prep. school after Christmas, and Lacy had been over to see how he was getting on. She considered herself an absolutely Spartan parent to have held out until mid-term.

Don, it appeared, was the most promising boy in the school.

"And he's going to be most frightfully good at games. I don't see why you should laugh, Monkey. He *is* clever, and he *is* good at games. Why, even when he was six months old, look how hard he could throw. You remember my diamond ring—right out of the window—and it never *was* found. So that just *shows*. Monkey, you're a pig to laugh." The bright, pink colour deepened in Lacy's cheeks. "You can ask Evelyn if you don't believe me. Oh, and that reminds me—" Her voice became eager; she ran to the bed, rummaged in one of the piles of odds and ends which seemed suddenly to have sprung up everywhere, and came back, fluttering the leaves of a magazine. "Monkey, darling, she's going to do it at last—I really do believe she is!"

"Who's going to do what?" asked Manning vaguely; his mind was still on Don. He laughed at Lacy, but he was really just as big a fool about Don as she was. "Who's going to do what?" he asked.

Lacy stopped by his chair to pinch him.

"Evelyn," she said. "Evelyn Laydon—going to do it at last, I do believe. What's that, Ada? Lunch? Oh, thank goodness! Monkey, come along and feed me. I can't even remember breakfast; it's such miles and miles, and hours and hours ago; and flying *does* make you hungry."

At lunch, when Brooks was out of the room, Monkey came back to Evelyn Laydon. He was really very fond of this cousin of Lacy's, who was more like a sister.

"What did you say Evelyn was going to do?"

"What everyone thought she'd have done years and years ago—not that there's anything settled, and I'm simply on tenterhooks till it's really come off. They've got a horrible, vulgar paragraph in the *Weekly Whisper*—I've brought it for you to see—and her photograph too, though I can't imagine how they got it. She'll be most frightfully angry; and I only hope and trust it won't rot the whole show."

"My dear child, if you'd tell me what you're talking about—"

"Evelyn—my cousin Evelyn—Evelyn Laydon—" Lacy's voice soared to even sweeter heights.

"Well, what about her?"

"Idiot!" said Lacy succinctly. She pushed the *Weekly Whisper* across the table. "Read it for yourself. I'm much too hungry to talk."

Manning picked up the magazine, and frowned at a blurred version of Evelyn Laydon's latest photograph. His frown deepened to a scowl as he read the paragraph beside it:

"We all know Mrs Jim Laydon. Some of us remember her pretty, tragic wedding, and poor Jim Laydon and his cousin Jack—the Inseparables as we used to call them. The name held to the end, for Jack Laydon was best man, and got his recall an hour after the ceremony, just as Jim did. And a week later they were both 'missing' and never heard of again. Well, well, that's old history, and all Mrs Jim's friends will be pleased if, as I hear, they are to have an opportunity very soon of wishing her joy and better luck next time."

Manning flung the paper across the room with a single explosive word. Lacy's eyebrows went up.

"Monkey, how can you!"

"What's it mean?" growled Manning.

"Well, there's nothing settled, but I believe, I *do* believe, she's going to take Chris Ellerslie at last. Goodness knows he's waited long enough."

Manning made a dreadful face.

"Man's about a mile high," he objected. "Pokes—wears glasses— writes *vers libres.*"

"He's *devoted* to Evelyn."

"Good Lord, my dear child, we're all devoted to Evelyn. If she married a tenth of the people who are devoted to her, she'd be put in prison. Let 'em be devoted; it does 'em good."

Lacy's colour rose becomingly.

"Monkey, I think it's because she's lonely—I do indeed. She came down with me to see Don, and—and she *looked* at him."

"My good girl, what else could she do?"

"Don't be an idiot! She—she—don't you see, Monkey? If Jim hadn't—if things had been different—" The tears came with a rush into the bright hazel eyes. "Evelyn ought to be going down to see her own boy at school, and—and I think it came over her. And I think that's what's going to give Chris Ellerslie his chance at last— Monkey, I can't find my handkerchief."

Manning had not been married nine years for nothing. He produced a bandanna, passed it over the table, and was rewarded by the instant cessation of Lacy's tears and an indignant:

"Monkey, how *can* you? Pouf! What *have* you been putting on it?"

Manning resumed his rejected offering.

"The petrol gauge leaked, that's all—perfectly clean, wholesome smell. I'd rather have it than half the scents you women use, any day of the week. But look here, Lacy—seriously—is Evelyn engaged to this Ellerslie chap? Has she told you anything? Or are you just going by that poisonous paragraph?"

"Of course I'm not." Lacy stuck her chin in the air. "No, she didn't exactly tell me, Evelyn doesn't—"

"Doesn't what?"

"Tell one things. And there's something about her—you can't *ask*. We've been like sisters all our lives, but sometimes I feel I don't really know a thing about her. When—when Jim was missing and she was breaking her heart—Monkey, I never was sure whether she was breaking it for Jim Laydon or—for Jack."

Manning moved impatiently.

"Jack? What Jack? What d'you mean?" His voice was very cross.

"Jim's cousin Jack, *of course*—Jack Laydon. Why *everyone* expected her to marry Jack; and they *were* engaged—I know they were; and then something happened—I never quite knew what, and it was all off. And then Jim got leave, and they were engaged and married all in a flash. Mary Prothero bet me ten bob Jack wouldn't have the nerve to be best man, and when she lost she said he did it to punish Evelyn. She was a cat; I just loathed being bridesmaid with her. She went round telling everyone that Evelyn *really* cared for Jack, but of course he was only the poor cousin without a bean, whereas Jim would have Laydon Manor. As a matter of fact, she'd have given her eyes to get Jim for herself."

Lacy was leaning forward, pleasantly flushed. Manning's black eyes rested on her for a moment with a sharply sarcastic expression.

Amazing how women loved to rake over old scandals. He was reminded of Vixen, his terrier, scratching to unearth a toothsome bone long buried. Lacy was enjoying herself very much. Enjoying the memory of Evelyn Laydon's broken heart? No, be fair—she did love Evelyn. Then what was it? Heaven knew! He looked away scowling. Lacy rippled on—

"Another thing I didn't know was how much Jim knew."

"Perhaps there wasn't anything to know, my dear."

Lacy tossed her head.

"Rubbish! There *was*. *I* saw Jack's face when Jim was saying 'I, James, take thee, Evelyn—' and all the rest of it, and it was—well—awful. And Evelyn was as white as her veil. She didn't look any whiter when the telegram came half an hour later and Jim and Jack went off together. Oh dear, it *was* a tragedy—recalled like that, and then a week later both of them missing on the same day. Well, Evelyn cared for one of them all right. I wonder how many men she's turned down in the last ten years."

"Why rake it all up now?" said Manning drumming irritably on the table. "For the Lord's sake—"

Lacy looked reproachful.

"Evelyn's like my very own sister. Of course, if you're not *interested*—"

At this moment Brooks came in with the pudding. Whilst he changed the plates Mrs Manning gave him three messages, recalled two of them and ended with:

"Tell Possiter that I'm going to lie down after lunch and I want her as soon as she's finished."

"Yes ma'am," said Brooks. He then came round to Manning's side of the table, lowered his voice in a manner which absolutely riveted Lacy's attention, and said,

"I give 'im some more Benger at one o'clock."

"Is he awake?" asked Manning sharply.

"No, sir, 'e is not, sir. Drunk it down like a baby with 'is eyes shut."

"Let him sleep then."

When the door had closed behind Brooks, words positively burst from Mrs Manning's lips.

"Monkey, what on *earth* was Brooks talking about?"

Manning began to explain, but was not allowed to proceed very far.

"You brought him *here*!"

"Well, yes, my dear. There—er, didn't seem to be anything else to do."

"*Monkey!* I suppose there are *hospitals*. You brought an awful, dirty tramp of a creature here, and put him to bed in the spare room?"

Manning jerked his chair back.

"Yes, I did."

From these preliminaries a very pretty quarrel emerged, proceeding briskly for some five minutes or so, at the end of which time the usual reconciliation was in sight. Manning had once in an unguarded moment assured Lacy that he knew the drill so well that he would back himself to go through with it by numbers in his sleep. The end was always the same—Lacy prettily tearful and injured; Manning, self-confessed a brute, with his tongue in his cheek; a kiss or two; and a final, "Monkey, I can't think *why* I married you."

On this particular occasion peace was restored at just about the time that Anna Blum, having finished her house-work and washed up after the mid-day meal, was setting out on the six-mile walk which lay between her and Anton in Cologne.

Half an hour later an unwonted silence had fallen upon the Mannings' house—the sort of silence which was only possible when its mistress was either out or fast asleep. Lacy was, in fact, slumbering comfortably and becomingly beneath a pink silk eider-down. Miss Possiter also slept—an uneasy sleep haunted by dreams in which she continually looped the loop. Manning was out; and Brooks had withdrawn himself to the seclusion of the basement. The house was extraordinarily quiet.

Chapter Six

IT WAS TO this quietness and stillness that the man in the spare room awoke. Lying on his back with his arms outside the coverlet, he stretched himself, yawned, and opened his eyes. A series of vague impressions presented themselves at once to his half - awakened consciousness—daylight,—nice room—very comfortable bed—rather too warm—oh Lord, yes! Much too warm—hot!

He pushed back the bed-clothes, sat up, and put his hands to his head with the instinctive movement of a man about to run his fingers through his hair. His hands touched a bandage, and at the touch he came broad awake. A bandage—there was certainly a bandage about his head. He felt it gingerly, and was reassured. His head felt all right, a little wobbly perhaps, but nothing more. Come to think of it, he remembered being hit. They had gone up, struck that beastly fog, and lost their bearings. The Lord knows where they had got to or who was firing. But he remembered being hit. His hand went up again and fingered the bandage over his right temple. That was all. He couldn't remember past that, except for an interminable, long dream in which he was always being ordered about and doing all sorts of things that he'd never really done in his life.

He drew his feet up and locked his arms about his knees. Very queer things dreams. You'd expect a man to dream about things he knew something about; and here he'd been dreaming miles and miles of an endless dream about hoeing roots and ploughing a long, narrow field set round with trees. Queerest of all, in his dream he had been a German. Crazy, absolutely. But there it was.

He began to remember all sorts of odd details out of the dream. Children throwing stones at him, and calling him *"Stummer Anton," "Dummer Anton"*—German children calling out at him with German words. But—*he didn't know any German*. All his muscles stiffened suddenly. For a moment he did not breathe. He did not know any German; but in his dream the children called him *"Dummer Anton" "Stummer Anton"—and he understood what they said.* They said "Stupid Anton," "Dumb Anton," and he understood them, just as he understood Tante Anna when she spoke kindly to him, and Josef when he grumbled. Tante Anna and Josef belonged to the dream, the long, long dream in which he was not himself at all, but Anton—Anton Blum. It was the very dickens of a queer start. Extraordinarily detailed the whole thing; nothing exciting about it; just an every-day dullness, going on, and on, and on. Why, he remembered the very clothes that he wore in the dream, the patches on his boots, and a neat, square darn on his left shirtsleeve—

He stretched and yawned again, then with a sudden movement pushed the bed-clothes right back and swung his legs out of bed. He sat on the edge of the bed, blinking hard and staring at his own bare knees. They had put him to bed in his shirt. He picked up the hem and fingered it—blue and white checked stuff, very old and faded. Good Lord! He'd never had a shirt like that in his life. *Yes, he had*—not really, but in the dream. Very, very slowly he lifted his right hand and felt for the darn on the other sleeve. It was there, neat and fine, just above the left elbow.

He sprang to his feet frowning. Where in the world was he? What was this house? Not a hospital, for there was a carpet on the floor and curtains at the windows. He must have been knocked out, and then someone had picked him up, carried him off to an expensively furnished house, and put him to bed in some other fellow's shirt. The whole thing got queerer every moment.

He crossed the room and stood by the window looking out. What he saw told him very little—a narrow strip of garden, a few bare trees, and a grey sky over all; other trees to right and left, other town gardens.

He was in a town. What town? And how long had he been here? How long was it since he had been hit? It was the fifteenth of November when they had gone up—a topping morning before they ran into the fog. He looked again at the trees in the narrow garden. To the eye of a boy brought up in the country, they did not look like November trees. Bare, yes—and brown; but the buds were swelling on them, and the brown had the warm, purplish tinge that comes with the rising sap.

He turned abruptly, and looked about the room. There was a wash-stand, dressing-table, chest of drawers—all the usual furniture of a comfortable bedroom. A couple of steps took him to the dressing-table. He tilted the glass and, as he did so, saw his own image in it flicker and blur. He gripped the table so hard that the edge came near to cutting his hands. The glass, tipped back, showed him, not himself, but a figure unfamiliar and repulsive, heavy-shouldered, with a forward stoop of the head, shaggy-haired, and bearded almost to the eyes. The bandage that crossed the forehead alone told him that what he saw was himself. Months—it must have been months since he was wounded; a beard like that takes months to grow. He stepped back and took another look about him.

There were two doors to the room. He thought he would go and prospect a bit. The need to know where he was and what had been happening took possession of him to the exclusion of everything else. With a glance at his bare legs, he pulled the coverlet off the bed and wrapped it about him. Then he turned the handle of the nearest door, opened it, and found himself looking through into another room.

It was a dining-room this time. There was a red carpet on the floor and red curtains at the windows. A bowl of snowdrops stood on a bare, polished table.

The man who had been Anton Blum nodded. Snowdrops—"I thought those trees looked like spring all right." December—January—February—it must be at least February; and that meant that he had been knocked out for three months. He frowned again, spread out his hands, and looked at them. They were not the hands of a man who had been three months on the sick list. They were not his own hands as he remembered them. They were broad, blackened, horny; and every nail was broken, worn to the quick, and thickened at the edge; the palms were ridged with callosities. The muscles of his fore-arms stood out like cords.

He looked again about the quiet, empty room. There was a writing-table in the window, and a magazine thrown down carelessly on a chair beside it. He picked the paper up and turned the leaves. A page of pictures caught his eye—a young man; a smiling girl; and underneath: "The Duke and Duchess of York en route for—" The Duchess of York! There wasn't any Duchess of York. What on earth were they gassing about? He looked up impatiently to the top of the page and saw the name of the paper, the *Weekly Whisper*, and the date, March the seventh, 1925.

March? So it was March. 1925? That was a misprint of course; it was 1915—November the fifteenth, 1915 was the last date he remembered. He stood there with his head bent forward over the paper, his mind fumbling with the figures. They came and went. November the fifteenth—March the seventh—1915—1925. It was as if he was leaning against a closed door. On the other side of the door things were happening; people were talking. He pushed against the door, and felt it give. In a moment it would open and he would see and hear. November—March—fifteen—twenty-five.

He gripped the paper in his hands, and a leaf fell over. Evelyn's face looked at him, and he saw Evelyn's name: "We all know Mrs Jim Laydon." He read the paragraph right through; and then, with the ground slipping beneath his feet and a roaring noise in his ears, he began to read it again: "We all know Mrs Jim Laydon. Some of us remember her pretty, tragic wedding ten years ago."

Evelyn! Time went by him. The roaring in his ears stopped; the floor was steady under his feet; the room was as still as a grave! Ten years! He had been dead ten years!

Ten years. Time and space were gone; all landmarks were gone. The shock was like the shock of some huge, shattering wave whose resistless force submerged and swept him into the unknown. After a timeless agony he felt the wave recede; and as it receded, it drew him with it, dragging him towards the abyss from which it had come. He began to resist, at first in a blind, confused flurry, then with increasing strength and clearing vision. The confusion began to pass; the sense of being drawn down into madness and chaos passed. He was left battered, but himself. As he lifted his head from that victory, he heard footsteps and voices that seemed to sound from a long way off. They came nearer. The door opened. He saw a face most blessedly familiar—Manning—it was Manning—good old Monkey Manning!

Chapter Seven

FOR THE BRIEFEST moment he looked at Manning and felt that astonishing relief. Then, as Manning exclaimed, Anna Blum passed him quickly and stood a yard inside the room, with her hands out, and a cry of "Anton!"

To the man who had been Anton Blum, that was in some way the most dreadful moment of this whole dreadful hour. He had fought with all his strength to hold on to himself; and in the very moment of victory he felt himself betrayed, felt sanity slip and his hard-won footing fail beneath his feet. This woman belonged to the senseless, interminable dream which had no relation to reality. She stood there between himself and Manning, a broad figure with an anxious, comely face. He knew her face, every line of it; he knew the battered felt hat, the faded cape with straps that crossed the ample bosom; he knew the voice that said "Anton!" It was Tante Anna—and she belonged to a horrible, formless dream.

Manning looked over Anna's shoulder and saw the man he had left sleeping stand ghastly between the windows, O'Neill's bandage about his head and a crumpled paper at his feet. The long folds of the white coverlet gave him a strange, fantastic height. But before the terror in the man's eyes all other strangeness died.

Manning came into the room, shutting the door behind him, and the man called out hoarsely:

"Monkey! For God's sake, Monkey!"

"Anton!" said Anna Blum again. She came towards him. But Manning was before her.

"Who are you?" he said, quick and sharp.

The man took a blind step forward and caught at him with his great hands.

"Monkey! For God's sake—who's that?"

A shaking hand pointed at Anna, who stood grave-eyed and motionless, her hands locked together, her mouth twitching a little.

"Monkey, is there anyone there?—or am I mad? I tell you I can see her. She was in the dream; but I can see her just as plainly as I can see you. Monkey—" The voice broke, gasping. The whole great form shook as Manning tried to steady it.

"My dear chap, hold up. You're all right; you're not seeing things; you're as right as rain. This is Frau Blum, who—"

The man had his hands on Manning's shoulders; his face was convulsed; his teeth chattered.

"You—see—her—too?"

"Good Lord, yes—of course I do."

Nothing mattered except the torture of uncertainty in the eyes that searched his face. Manning saw the uncertainty break into bewilderment.

"You can see her? She's here?" The words were jerked out and, even so, hardly audible.

"Yes, yes—I say, hold up!"

For a moment the man's whole weight came on Manning. Then he reeled back, lurched to the table, caught at it, and came down heavily on a chair. Still gripping the table, he looked long and steadily at Anna Blum. Long and steadily Anna looked back at him. At last he turned his head, looked at Manning, and spoke as a man speaks when he has come to the last of his strength.

"Monkey—I must know—she knows—make her speak!" With the last word he put his arms on the table, and bending forward, laid his head upon them.

Manning's look of pity and concern passed into one of sharp inquiry as he swung round on Anna.

"Well, Frau Blum? What have you to say? You'll hardly stick to last night's story now, I imagine."

"No," said Anna. There was a great sadness in her voice, but no fear. She took a chair and sat down by the table. The bowl of snowdrops was between her and the man who had been as a son to her for ten years. She said, "No. I have understood." She took out a clean, folded handkerchief, shook it out, and wiped her brow. Then she undid her cape and pushed it back.

Manning, leaning over the high-backed chair at the end of the table, watched her closely. When she had wiped her brow a second time, she sighed and said,

"Yes, I will speak now, *Herr Major.*"

"You'd better," said Manning, and saw her head lift a little.

"I am not afraid. I have done no wrong. I will tell you everything now."

"Wait a minute," said Manning. He went over to the man, whose face was hidden, and touched him on the shoulder. Then he said in English:

"She'll speak. Can you follow the German?"

The man moved, raised his head a little, nodded, and resumed his former position. Manning went back to the head of the table.

"Now, Frau Blum."

Anna nodded.

"Yes, now I will speak." She paused for a moment as if considering. "I must begin at the beginning, or you will not understand." She frowned slightly, and began to speak slowly, with pauses here and there. Every now and then she looked over the table at the man, who lay half across it with his head on his arms. Then her eyes came back to Manning again—round, serious eyes, very clear and blue.

"When the war came we were living in the Schwarzwald. My man had inherited a little holding there, and we were just making a living, no more. Everything had been very much neglected. Then the war came and my husband was called up—not just at first, you understand, but after Christmas. He went to garrison duty, and then to the Russian front. And then I heard that he was killed. That was in April; and at the end of the month I had his nephew Anton, the real Anton Blum, on my hands. He had been wounded in the head, and they sent him to me from hospital because his mind was gone and he had no other relations. Well, *Herr Major*, that was a hard blow. I had no love for Anton, whom I had only seen once or twice, and who had always given himself airs towards us and behaved as if we were not as good as he. I had my hands full enough without him, I can tell you—two cows until the Government took them; pigs; geese; hens; and an acre of potatoes to plant. That, you may really say, was work enough for one woman's hands. With Anton, everything was at once a hundred times more. When the mood came on him he would be violent and dangerous; and when it passed he would do nothing except eat and sleep. Very soon no one would come near me, because they were afraid of Anton. So it went on all the summer.

"In July I had to take him to the hospital. They said he was no better, and never would be, but I must bring him again in six months' time. We went back. And in November everything happened. I remember that there was a very fine day, and then a fog such as one gets in November; and then, on the top of that, a three days' storm as wild as any I have seen. When the storm came on, Anton became very hard to manage. When he was in bed that night I took away his clothes and locked them up. It was the first quiet time I had had all day. I went into the kitchen and began to put things tidy. Then I went into my own room. But I was uneasy. After half an hour I went to look at Anton—and he was gone. *Ach, Herr Major*, think of it! It was a night like the night that you came for *him*." She put out her hand across the table and almost touched the man's bare arm. "Thunder and rain like the day of judgment; and Anton gone out into it in his shirt, not even a pair of shoes to his feet."

She drew back her hand and folded it with the other on her lap. Manning saw the fingers lock and the knuckles whiten. She went on:

"Though I had no love for him, he was in my charge. I dressed myself, and I was out for two hours calling to him. At the end of two hours I came back. My clothes were drenched. I made up the fire and set a light in the window to guide him home. I did not sleep.

And he did not come. As soon as it was light I went out again. It was still fearful weather. I went up through the forest calling. I thought I would go as far as the waterfall, because Anton used to like to watch the water come down with such a roar on to the rocks in the pool below. I could not see why he should go there on such a night of storm; but—it is the truth—I did not know where to go. The wind blew so that I could hardly keep my feet, and the noise was terrible; but the rain had stopped. It was when I could already hear the sound of the fall that I smelt something burning. I came out between the bushes into a clearing. And there was an aeroplane fallen down and broken to pieces. I had never seen one so close before. It had been burning, and the bits of it still smoked. I looked all round, and I saw a man sitting on a fallen tree a dozen yards away. He had his head in his hands and the blood was running down between his fingers.

"I knew at once that it was an English officer—I have seen many of them, because, when I was sixteen, I went to England for three years to be under-nurse in an officer's family. The lady's mother was German from near my home, and she engaged me to go to her daughter; and I was happy, and I learned to speak English. There was a little boy whose name was Hugh—girls too and a baby. But it was the little Hugh whom I loved most. Often after the war came I wondered where he was fighting, and I said many prayers for him. Well, when I saw that English officer, I thought of my little Hugh. I knew that it could not be he; but I thought of him. Then I went up to the man, and put my hand on his shoulder, and spoke to him in English. He did not seem to hear. I sat down beside him and wiped away the blood from his wound; and I tore a strip from my petticoat and bound it round his head. He kept saying one word over and over, 'Fog—fog—fog,' just like that. And then he groaned. I could not make him understand anything. But in the end I got him on to his feet and put my arm round him, and he came with me, leaning on my shoulder. Fortunately I am very strong.

"I got him home, and took his clothes off, and put him into Anton's bed. Everything that he had on was soaked. I gave him a night-shirt of my husband's; and I fed him, and he went to sleep in

Anton's bed. When he was asleep I locked all the doors and went out again to look for Anton." She paused, took up her handkerchief, and wiped her forehead. "Well, *Herr Major*, I found him. First I found his shirt, which he had taken off and folded up. It was lying by the stream at the head of the waterfall. God knows whether he meant to bathe, or what he meant to do, but Anton himself I found in the pool below. He had fallen on the rocks, and I do not think that his own mother would have known him. I took his shirt and I went back. Later I meant to go and get help. But when I got home I found the Englishman so ill that I could not leave him. I stayed with him all that day and all the night, only leaving him to see to the animals.

"*Herr Major*, he was only a lad, and in his illness he was like a child. He would hold my hand tight, tight, and look at me with eyes that were always asking something. But after I brought him home he never spoke more than two or three words. When the morning came he slept, and I sat down and thought what I must do. To go down into the village and say 'My nephew Anton is drowned, and there is an English officer in my house—come and help me'—that would be one way. I thought of doing that, because, after all, I am a God-fearing, law-abiding German woman. But all the time I thought of it a voice said to me, '*Jawohl, Anna*, but if you do that, the Englishman will die—they will take him away, perhaps not very gently, and he will die.' I thought again. I thought about my little Hugh. I thought about Anton in the pool under the waterfall. And a plan came to me."

Anna looked again across the bowl of snowdrops at the bowed head with the bandage about it. This time, as she looked, the head was lifted, and for a moment the man looked back at her. She said quickly, "*Ja, ja, mein bester*, it was like that," and he caught his breath and let his head fall again upon his arms. Anna's eyes dwelt on him sadly. Then she turned back to Manning.

"The plan came to me. At first I thought to myself, 'One cannot do such a thing—but in such and such a way it *might* be done.' I went on thinking about it as if it were a story in a book. I did not mean to do it; but in the end I did it because there did not seem to be anything else to do. I could not let him die."

"What did you do?" said Manning harshly. He leaned nearer, his arms upon the table, the lines in his face cut deep.

"I went back to the waterfall," said Anna Blum. "I took with me the English officer's clothes and his identity disc. I laid them down in the place where I had found Anton's shirt. Then I went home again and waited. It was in my mind that perhaps the Englishman would die. But he did not die. Then I thought, 'If he recovers, what shall I do?' And I thought, 'Perhaps when he is well I can give him up.' Well, I waited, and after a time he stopped being ill, his strength came back; but he remembered nothing, and he was dumb. When I saw this I knew that the way was easy and I need not give him up. It was a fortnight after the storm that they found the aeroplane and Anton's body. No one had any thought but that it was the Englishman. They believed that he had gone in to bathe and been carried over the fall. There was a lot of talk about it, but no one had any other thought—how should they? Presently they stopped talking. I gave out that Anton had fallen in one of his fits and that his wound had broken out again. When the Englishman began to go out he had a bandage round his head, and I had let his hair and beard grow. He was of the same age as Anton, and about the same height; also his hair and eyes were the right colour. There was no one who really knew Anton, because all had been frightened of him and had kept away. It was quite easy. And he was easy to manage too; he was like a child, good and obedient, never violent as Anton had been. I taught him as one teaches a child. It needed great patience, but he got to understand what I said to him. And I taught him to dig and plough, and to do all the heavy work. By the time the spring came I was thanking God every day that I had him to help me."

"No one suspected?" said Manning. His clenched fist struck the table as he spoke.

"No one, *Herr Major*. The worst time was when I had to take him to the hospital."

"You took him?" Manning stood amazed at the woman's courage.

"*Jawohl*—and all went well. I was very much afraid, but all went well. The journey frightened and confused him, and when we came to where the doctors were, he knew nothing and could understand nothing. They were not the same doctors as before, and there were many, many for them to see; they made haste, or they would never have been done. They told me that his mind was gone, and that he would have his discharge. And we came home again. That is all, *Herr Major*."

"Not quite," said Manning sharply. "When the war was over, when the Armistice came—why didn't you speak then? Did you never think of his people?"

Anna returned his look with one of reproach.

"*Ja gewiss*, I thought of them. And I thought 'If he has parents, what can I do? Can I give them back their son? They have wept for him—and they have stopped weeping. Can I give him back to them? He will not even know who they are. For them it would be a new and heavier sorrow; and for him—*Ach, mein Gott!* What would it be for him? They would put him in a hospital, perhaps in an asylum. God forbid! They would take him away from me!' No, *Herr Major*, I could not do it. With me he was safe—yes, and happy. He had grown broad and strong—stronger than other men—and he was proud of his strength. He loved to work hard and to be in the open air. I could not send him away. Presently my brother, Josef Müller, wrote to me from here that his wife was dead, and that he could not manage his daughter. He asked me to come and keep house for him. I told him that I must bring Anton with me; and he said 'Bring him.' So we came. Now that is all."

"You should have spoken," said Manning.

Anna lifted her head.

"Do you think it would have been easy for me to speak?"

With no more than a little click the door opened, and Lacy Manning came in. She was warm and flushed from sleep, and drowsy eyed. Her left hand held about her a pale pink *négligé* trimmed with fur; a little lace cap with a pink satin rose on one side rested on her dark curls. She gave a startled cry at the sight of Manning's guests— the broad German woman, and the sprawling, half-dressed man.

The man lifted his head, looked at her, and saw an image out of that past which filled his mind. He saw an eighteen-year-old bridesmaid in a pink frock and a little lace cap. He said "Lacy!" just above his breath, and Lacy Manning screamed and went back against the door.

Manning came quickly round the table and caught at the arm in the blue checked sleeve.

"Who are you? For God's sake, who are you?"

The man was staring at the door.

"It's Lacy Prothero!" he said. "I tell you, it's Lacy!"

Manning's grasp tightened.

"It's Lacy Manning. We've been married nine years. Who *are* you?"

The man sat back in his chair, his head against the high, carved rail.

"Monkey, don't you know me?"

Manning looked long, and saw the bandage, the ragged hair, eyes full of a questioning agony that was no less agony because it was now controlled. He shook his head.

"My dear chap, I don't—"

"And Lacy doesn't either." The eyes were turned for an instant to where she leaned against the door, one hand at her breast, her face white, her voice for once struck silent. "No, Lacy doesn't either." With something that was almost a smile he faced round on Manning. "I'm Laydon," he said, and waited.

Manning felt the room heave. He gave back a step, and heard his own voice say hoarsely,

"Laydon?" Then very slowly, "There were two of the Laydons. There was Jack Laydon, and Jim; and they were both missing the same day. Which are you?" The words came jerkily. The tension was extreme.

Manning looked into the eyes that had questioned him, and found them steady now, and calm. They were looking behind him, where a crumpled paper lay between the windows.

"I don't know," said the man.

Lacy Manning fainted.

Chapter Eight

"IT'S A MOST extraordinary case," said Major O'Neill. "I don't think I ever heard of anything in the least like it. It seems incredible that he should know his name is Laydon, and not know whether he's Jim Laydon or Jack."

The crimson curtains were drawn across the dining-room windows. There was a pendent light in the middle of the room, and a reading-lamp with a green shade on the writing-table at which Manning was sitting. O'Neill was in a big armchair, and had the air of a man who was comfortably intrigued by a problem that did not touch him personally.

"What's the good of saying incredible?" snapped Manning over his shoulder. He folded the letter he had been writing, put it in an envelope, addressed it rapidly, and tossed it on to the dining-table. Then he swung round and said,

"I'm putting in for leave on urgent private affairs. The Colonel's promised to push it through."

"It's a most extraordinary case; I can't understand it. You say you don't recognize him at all?"

"No," said Manning, "and that's a fact. The Laydon boys were nice-looking lads of two and twenty, the spit and image of dozens of English boys of their class—grey eyes, brown hair, fresh skin—you know the sort of thing; England's chock a-block with them. This poor chap in there"—he flung out a hand in the direction of the bedroom door—"he weighs another three and a half stone, to start off with; and you can't really see him for hair."

"Were the cousins alike?"

"So so—same height and general type, with a family likeness on the top of that."

"Most extraordinary!" repeated O'Neill. "But his people'll be bound to recognize him; there's sure to be something they can go by. By the way though, who are his people? Any parents?"

"H'm—no," said Manning. "There's a grandfather, old Sir Cotterell Laydon. He lost both his sons in the Boer war. Jim's mother was already dead. And as for Mrs Jack, well, the less said about her the better. The family was immensely relieved when she married again and went out to Australia. I don't think they've ever heard from her since. The old man had both his grandsons at Laydon Manor—brought them up in fact. My people live quite near, you know; and my wife's mother was a Laydon—half-sister of the old man's, and about thirty years younger. The families are all mixed up because the girl Jim Laydon married was a Prothero too—a cousin of Lacy's."

O'Neill exclaimed, and sat up. "Married? Good heavens! You don't tell me one of them was married?"

Manning, who had been pacing up and down, came to a standstill a yard away.

"Yes, Jim Laydon was married. It's a bit of a complication, isn't it? He married Lacy's cousin, Evelyn Prothero. I was at the wedding. Lacy was bridesmaid."

"Good heavens!" said O'Neill again. "But she'll know—if one of them was married, the wife'll know—bound to."

"I don't know. She might, or she mightn't. It's not an ordinary case, because they never lived together. Both the Laydons were recalled on the wedding day, and something between a week and ten days later they were both missing. They were in the same squadron in the Flying Corps. They both went out on the same raid, and never came back. This chap says he remembers running into fog and being fired at. Lord knows how he landed up in the Schwarzwald. But I've driven a car myself when I've been asleep or next thing to it, and it's my belief he just went on flying his machine mechanically after he was hit."

"Very likely. But look here, Monkey, has he spoken about the girl at all? If he were the married one, he'd surely remember something. Hasn't he asked any question?"

"No, he hasn't. As a matter of fact, he hasn't had much chance. I told you Lacy fainted. And then I had to take Anna Blum home. I rather thought it was up to me, because—well"—Manning grimaced—"I was pretty short with her while she was telling her story. And, after all, if he's one of the Laydons, the family owes her a good deal, for it's pretty certain she saved his life, and dead certain that she risked a firing party every hour of the three years before the Armistice. Honestly, O'Neill, the woman's courage staggers me. They'd have shot her as soon as look at her if they'd found out. When we were going along I asked her if she knew it; and all she had to say was *'Ja gewiss, Herr Major.'* Astonishing creatures, women." He broke off and crossed to the writing-table again. "As soon as I know I've got my leave, I shall wire to my father-in-law, Sir Henry Prothero. And then someone will have to tell Sir Cotterell. He was most frightfully broke about the two boys, and it'll want careful doing."

"I suppose," said O'Neill slowly, "that whichever of them it is is the heir?"

"Yes." Manning gave a short laugh. "There's one man who won't be overjoyed, and that's Cotterell Abbott, the nephew who's had Laydon Manor in his pocket for the last nine years. I loathe the man myself, but I must say I think it's hard lines on him—and you can bet he'll think so too."

"By the way," said O'Neill, "were the Laydons regular soldiers?"

Manning shook his head. He was writing, and spoke frowning at the paper:

"No, they weren't. As a matter of fact they had both just come down from Cambridge. Jim was going to study scientific farming and do agent to his grandfather, and Jack meant to have a shot at Indian Civil. Of course they both joined up at once."

O'Neill got out of his chair and stretched himself.

"Well, that'll probably save complications. I must be going along. I'll go round and see Hooker, and borrow some clothes—he's the only person I can think of large enough. Yours, of course, were no earthly. And when you've got him dressed like a Christian and shaved, you'll probably be able to place him. He won't want the bandage after to-day—the cut was nothing but a scratch."

When the door had shut behind him, Manning finished his letter. It was to Evelyn Laydon, and it was very short. It ran:

"DEAR EVELYN,

I'm coming over at once. Will you be at your flat? If you're away, I must ask you to come back, because I want to see you very urgently.

Yours,

MONKEY."

He addressed the envelope to "Mrs Jim Laydon, 9, Halliday Mansions, Chelsea," and threw it down on the table beside the bowl of snowdrops. As he did so, the bedroom door opened, and Laydon came into the room. He wore Manning's dressing-gown instead of the coverlet, and looked, in consequence, several degrees less striking. He came across to the table, and even in that short distance it was noticeable that he did not walk as Anton Blum had walked, nor hold himself as Anton had held himself. Anton had shuffled with his feet and walked with a forward slouch of his big shoulders: this man held his head up and lifted his feet. He came to the table, stood there, and looked down at the letters which lay upon it. If his face changed, it was not noticeable. After a moment he frowned and said,

"I thought that man O'Neill was never going. And—look here, Monkey—" He paused, walked to the window, and stood there with his back to Manning. "Ten years is the deuce of a long time. Is my grandfather alive?"

"Yes, he's alive and well. He was most frightfully broke. But you know his pluck. He said he wasn't going to let Cotty Abbott in an hour before he could help it."

"Poor old Cotty! He's going strong, I suppose—same fussy old hen, nosing round and picking up scraps." He gave quite an amused laugh, and then broke in on a new note with a "Hullo! Why of course this'll be no end of a knock for him. Poor old Cotty!"

"He won't be pleased," said Manning drily.

There was a pause. Manning struggled with a sense of embarrassment. Evelyn—which of them was going to mention Evelyn? Someone must. The man went on looking out of the window.

"Lacy hasn't changed a bit," he said.

"Er—no," said Manning.

There was another pause, a longer one this time. Then the man spoke again, his voice quite cool and steady:

"I'd like to hear about Evelyn. How is she?"

"She's quite well." Manning said these words because he had to say something; but he really had no idea what to say.

"I saw your letter on the table. She hasn't—married?"

"No."

"Or thought of it?"

A flare of temper came to Manning's assistance.

"You'd better ask her that yourself!" he said with some heat.

"Thanks—I will."

Manning found words suddenly.

"Look here," he said, "d'you mean to tell me that you remember Evelyn, that you remember Lacy being bridesmaid to Evelyn, and that you don't know whether you're Evelyn's husband? It's not possible!"

The man stood by the window and drummed on it.

"Whether you're Jack, or whether you're Jim, you were at that wedding—you remember that?"

"Yes, I remember that."

Manning came up, caught him by the arm, and pulled him round.

"You remember being at the wedding! Good Lord, man, tell me exactly what you do remember."

The man looked down at him.

"Well, d'you know, Monkey, I think I won't. It's a bit too confused to be of much use."

"You remember Lacy?"

"Lacy—and the other girl—what's her name?—the cousin they didn't like much—Mary Prothero. Yes, they had pink frocks and caps like the thing Lacy had on when she came in just now. I thought—" He fell silent and moved away from Manning.

Both men were remembering Evelyn Prothero in her wedding-dress—lilies and orange-blossoms, and Evelyn's golden hair in the dark church. Manning looked the question which he could not force to his lips, but there was no answer to it. After a moment:

"You must know!" said Manning, sharply, and then—"Look here, I don't even know what to call you. What are any of us to call you?"

"Embarrassing, isn't it?" There was a hint of sarcasm in the voice. "I know I ought to apologize. Well, for the present, I think, we'll have to compromise. I won't ask you to commit yourselves until I can remember."

"Laydon!" Beneath the sarcasm there was something that jabbed at Manning and caught him on the raw.

"No—I've been thinking—better stave off the Christian name for the present. I've got to get my bearings all round. I've been Anton Blum for the best part of ten years, and I think I'd better be Anthony Laydon until I know—until I *know*." His voice was quite cool until the last word, when it broke suddenly in a sound that was like a sob, but rougher and harder. For a moment he stood where he was, his hands clenching and unclenching; then he sat down in the big arm-chair and covered his face.

"Put out those infernal lights, can't you?" he said.

Chapter Nine

SIR HENRY PROTHERO was a distinguished exception to the rule that a prophet has no honour among his own people. He had had a brilliant career in India. He had governed a province with great wisdom and tact. And he was now, in retirement, the recognized repository for all family secrets, and the accepted stand-by in family quarrels, alliances, or disasters. He had rooms in St James' Street and a cottage at Laydon Sudbury. His tastes were music, golf, and Indian history. He was a widower of many years' standing, and Lacy was his only child.

His large, clean-shaven face was grave as he talked with his son-in-law in a comfortable, shabby room which had a great many books in it. The roar of the traffic sounded faintly here at the back of the house. There was a fire in the grate. Outside a dense fog pressed against the windows and made the fire a very pleasant thing.

Sir Henry Prothero sat forward in a big leather arm-chair, elbow on knee and chin in hand. Manning, on the arm of the other chair, swung a restless foot.

"Of course," Sir Henry said meditatively, "as far as the personal factor goes, I stand right outside the problem. I think the Laydon boys were about twelve when I saw them last, and I've no real recollection of what they looked like. It's just as well—yes, it's just as well. You say you and Lacy can't find anything to take hold of?"

Manning struck his knee; the swinging foot shot out.

"He has me beat," he said. "I don't mind saying so. Honestly, sir, he makes my head go round. It's always 'We did this,' and 'We did that.' Then if you press him, he'll say 'Jack Laydon did so and so,' or 'Jim Laydon went somewhere else.' You can't get past it. One minute he's talking as if he were both of 'em, and the next as if they were two separate people—pals of his. He's so infernally cool and detached. Lacy now"—Manning chuckled—"she was absolutely certain she was going to recognize him as soon as he'd been shaved and tidied up a bit. She said a lovely piece all about woman's intuition and childhood's memories, and as good as told me that, as a mere man, I was naturally no use when it came to the finer shades of intelligence." He laughed again. "Well, he came in in Hooker's clothes; and she had a good look at him, and hadn't a word to say—Lacy without a word to say is really a most edifying sight. She swears now that he isn't either Jack or Jim. So that's that!" He broke off, and Sir Henry said quickly:

"I don't value Lacy's opinion—she'll probably have a different one every time she sees him; I want yours. Do you see a likeness?"

"Nothing to speak of."

"What do you mean by that?"

"Well—I mean—no." He shook his head, frowning. "It's jolly difficult to say. When I look at him, he's a stranger. When he's talking, he's Laydon all right; but I couldn't, for the life of me, tell you which Laydon. He's got something that neither Jim nor Jack had; and that's what puzzles me all the time. They were just boys—awful nice boys too—, and he's a grown man. And whichever one he was, he's something different now. We may be able to identify him, but we can't turn him back into one of those jolly youngsters again. He's different; he's new; he's himself; and, by Jove, he's a cool hand."

"Yes?"

"I went with him to the War Office this morning. They put him through his paces pretty sharply, and he didn't turn a hair. It seems four of them went up that day—the two Laydons, Jim Field, and a man called Thursley. Thursley was the only one who came back. Well, they got Thursley on the 'phone—he's at Farnborough—, and he came up. They didn't tell Laydon of course—sent us to wait in another room. After an abominably long time they had us in—room full of people, bad light, beastly fog. Well, Laydon took a good look round; then he walked across the room, clapped Thursley on the shoulder, and said—'Hullo! Hullo! Where did you spring from, Jobbles?' Sensation in court; the blushing Thursley explaining to a lot of brass hats that Jobbles was a nickname of his unregenerate youth. He didn't like it a bit. After that they wanted to know whether he recognized Laydon as either Jack or Jim." Manning shrugged his shoulders. "He got rattled, and hedged for all he was worth—said it might be Jack, three stone heavier; and then again it might just as easily be Jim, only his voice was different. When they wanted to know how it was different, he said he didn't know, and got frightfully tied up—a perfectly hopeless witness. Laydon never turned a hair the whole time. Mind you, sir, it's like seeing a fellow riding a horse on the curb; there's something about it that makes you feel sick. I believe he's having a perfect hell of a time." Manning jumped down from the arm of his chair, went to the fire, and pushed the embers with his foot. After a moment he turned round again. "We put in Anna Blum's statement and came away. You've got your copy?"

Sir Henry nodded.

"Is there anything that strikes you specially?"

Sir Henry took out a sheaf of typewritten pages, turned the leaves, and put a large, white forefinger down in the middle of a line.

"Yes," he said, "the identity disc. She mentions it specially, I see—says she put it with his clothes at the edge of the stream above the fall. What happened to it?"

"She doesn't know. I thought we ought to send someone down to make inquiries on the spot."

"Yes," said Sir Henry, "certainly." The large finger jabbed the page again; the rather colourless eyes looked mildly at Manning. "Yes, certainly. But hasn't it occurred to you, my boy, that this Anna Blum must have seen the name on the disc? She took it off him, handled it—she *must* have seen the name."

"She says she didn't. I put the point to her when we had her over to get her statement properly taken down; it occurred to me at once, and I rather urged it. She only said the light was bad, and she hadn't thought of reading the name. When I pressed her she shrugged her shoulders and came out with '*Na, Herr Major*, do you not think I had enough on my mind without prying into matters that did not concern me? Why should I care what his name was? For all I knew, he was going to die. And whether he lived or died, it was likely enough to be a stone wall and some German bullets for me, as you yourself have said. It seemed to me that already I knew too much.' And when you come to think of it, sir, she wasn't far wrong."

Sir Henry turned the pages on his knee, nodded, and folded the papers again.

"Well," he said, "we've been talking about everyone except the one person who matters most. We've got to consider Evelyn's position, you know, Monkey. What exactly have you done about Evelyn?"

"I wrote from Cologne—said I was coming over and wanted to see her—, and I've had a wire to say she is getting back to her flat to-night. I've written and told her what's happened; and I enclosed a copy of Anna Blum's statement."

"You've *written*?" There was a shade of surprise in Sir Henry's voice.

Manning pulled viciously at his moustache.

"Yes," he said. "Evelyn'll get it first thing to-morrow. I wrote because I thought she wouldn't want anyone there for a bit—not at the first go off, you know. I thought, better give her time to pull herself together, and then either you or I could go round and talk it over."

Sir Henry was sensible, not for the first time, of the fact that his son-in-law was possessed of unexpected delicacies and those intuitions asserted by Lacy to be the special gift of Woman with a capital W.

"Yes," he said. "Yes, I think you're right. Then if you will go and see Evelyn, I'll go down to Laydon Manor and tell Cotterell."

Manning made a most hideous face.

"Don't you think you'd better see Evelyn?" He didn't look at Sir Henry, but pushed the fire again and scowled at the falling embers.

"I don't think so," said Sir Henry, leaning back. "For one thing, you're nearer Evelyn's age. I don't mean to say that the actual years count for anything. But you talk the same language—play the game of life, in fact, by the same rules. It's all a convention of course; and the strange part is that it is just in moments of catastrophe that these conventions count for most. I know it's not the commonly accepted idea; but it's a fact for all that. I've seen lives ruined because, in a moment of great emotion, the people concerned were unable to understand each other's conventions. If novelists are to be believed, the early Victorian woman played a swoon where the modern girl plays a piece of neo-Georgian slang. I don't suppose their feelings differ at all; but the swoon convention and the slang convention won't mix. No, my boy, you shall see Evelyn, and I'll tell Cotterell. By the way, Monkey, someone ought to let Cotty Abbott know; he's very directly concerned."

"Poor old Cotty! I should think he was. Yes, he ought to be told. But I think old Gregory might do that."

"Yes, he offered to when I saw him this morning. I thought he ought to see the statement, and also I wanted to get clear as to the legal position. I had, I may say, horrifying visions of a *cause célèbre*. Mercifully, we're saved from any danger of that by the fact that neither the estate nor the personal property involved is entailed. As Gregory pointed out, if Sir Cotterell Laydon accepts this man as his grandson, he has only to alter his will in order to leave him anything he chooses. And I must say it was an enormous relief to me to hear it. Oh, whilst we're on the subject of Gregory,—he laid tremendous stress on our preventing Evelyn from committing herself in any way. I agree with him, though I rather suspect you'll have your work cut out to make her see it."

"What do you mean by 'Evelyn committing herself'?"

"Well, Gregory proposes what, in fact, amounts to a family council. He thinks he ought to be there as legal adviser to the family, and he says Cotty Abbott should be invited. Laydon would meet the whole family, and they could talk things over and see whether they couldn't come to some conclusion. And what Gregory lays great stress on is that Evelyn shouldn't compromise herself or the family by seeing him alone first."

Manning swung round with a jerk.

"Oh, I say, sir!"

"He laid great stress on it. You see, Evelyn might be as undecided as you are yourself. But on the other hand,"—he raised a large, white finger—"she'll naturally be in a state of very considerable emotional disturbance; and we don't want her emotions to hurry her into a recognition which couldn't afterwards be substantiated."

"Yes, I see the point," said Manning angrily. "But it's pretty cold-blooded to expect her to meet him under Cotty Abbott's eye, for instance."

"I don't think either Gregory or myself would insist on Cotty Abbott," said Sir Henry. His lips relaxed a little, and a faint twinkle appeared momentarily. "No, I don't think we need insist on Cotty Abbott. But I thought, and Gregory thought, that Sir Cotterell and myself should be present."

"Evelyn," said Manning, "will kick."

"Evelyn is the most reasonable woman I know," said Sir Henry.

"No woman is really reasonable," said Manning in tones of profoundest gloom.

Chapter Ten

CHRIS ELLERSLIE once said of Evelyn Laydon that it would be impossible for her to be unhappily married. She had, he explained, the opposite of Circe's gift. Instead of being a fatal enchantress who roused and inflamed warring and discordant qualities she had the home genius, the one gift which puts a more than ordinary happiness within a woman's grasp. One could not imagine her experiencing a *grande passion*, but one discerned the capacity for a great love, something as high as the stars and as useful as bread. But then Chris Ellerslie was a poet in spite of being addicted to *vers libre*; also he was as much in love with Evelyn as a calm and self-centred nature permitted.

There was a letter from Mr Ellerslie on the top of a small pile that was waiting for Evelyn at breakfast on the day after Manning's conversation with Sir Henry Prothero. Evelyn looked at it with just the very faintest contraction of the golden-brown eyebrows, which were a shade deeper than her gold-brown hair. She was of the fair type which expresses a warm and generous nature. She brought warmth, light, and colour into any room she entered. Her skin had a golden fairness; her eyes were the dark grey-blue which can deepen until they are almost black, or brighten until they look like sunny water; her lips were very firm and red.

She took up Chris Ellerslie's letter, opened it, and read:

"MY DEAR EVELYN,

I bow to your decision, and will not even say that I regret it, inasmuch as I would a hundred times rather possess the free gift of your friendship than be placed in the intolerable position of demanding what you were not willing to give.

My own feelings have remained unaltered for the last ten years. I do not imagine that the future is very likely to modify them. I am therefore always, and in every sense of the word,

Yours,

C. E."

Evelyn finished the letter with a look of relief. Then she frowned again and immediately broke into a little laugh. Chris was so reasonable. He expressed himself so beautifully. Perhaps that was why she was still Evelyn Laydon.

She turned back to her letters and saw a long envelope addressed in Manning's hand. It looked as if it might contain legal documents. As she picked it up, she wondered what on earth Monkey had sent her, and why he had dragged her back to town to meet him. Then she opened the envelope.

It was half an hour later that the telephone bell rang. It rang a second time before Evelyn Laydon heard it. She got up from the chair in which she had been sitting, rising with a strange, jerky movement and walking stiffly. As she got up, Manning's letter, the long envelope, and the typed sheets of Anna Blum's statement fell unheeded on the floor.

Manning, at the other end of the line, said "Hullo!", and did not recognize the voice that answered him.

"I want to speak to Mrs Laydon."

"I am—Mrs Laydon."

"Oh, Evelyn? It's Monkey speaking. You—I—I say, my dear girl, have you had my letter?"

"Yes," said Evelyn. She was finding it quite difficult to speak.

"I thought you'd better have the letter first. And then I thought I'd like to come round and see you. I mean I don't want to butt in.

But I thought we might talk it over—and there might be things you wanted to ask."

"Yes."

"Shall I come round then?"

"Yes."

"At once?"

"Yes."

Evelyn felt that she was quite incapable of more than that one word. She hung up the receiver and, turning, picked up all the fallen papers. Then she went into the drawing-room of the little flat and sat down to wait. It was a very charming room, with the effect of being sunny in the dullest London weather. Shades of gold and apricot, warm Persian rugs with prevailing tones of orange and brown made up the background of this effect. But the greater part of it came from Evelyn herself; it was her own sunny atmosphere which filled and brightened the foreground.

At this moment it was as if that sunny atmosphere was torn and convulsed by storm. A rushing wind drove in upon it, and brought with it a sense of panic fear and blind confusion. Evelyn felt herself driven as the wind drove, back through the years from a hard-won calm to the passionate place where she had broken her heart. From that place she had climbed slowly and with bleeding feet—and now the wind drove her back to it.

Manning came into the room unheard, and saw her sitting in a low brown chair, her head a little thrown back, her eyes fixed. She wore a dress of honey-coloured wool, long in the sleeve and high in the neck. Her face showed white above the high collar and against the dull brown of the chair; only her hair was warm and bright. Her hands were folded in her lap; bare, beautiful hands, the right one lying uppermost and clasping the other so that the wedding ring was hidden.

Manning looked at her with concern for a moment. Then he crossed the room, drew up a chair, and sitting down, slipped a hand inside her arm. He said, "Evelyn—old girl—" And she gave a little shiver, turning slowly round towards him. Manning withdrew his hand after giving her arm a friendly squeeze.

"You read my letter—and the statement—" He broke off. "My dear girl, are you all right?"

Evelyn smiled with stiff lips.

"I shan't do a faint, Monkey, if that's what you mean. I—I'm just a bit knocked out of time."

"You would be. I know what I felt like myself; I know I wondered whether I'd gone off my rocker. You know, there are some things that make one feel like that. You just can't believe 'em; it don't seem possible that they can be true. And when you find that they are true, it just knocks you out—makes you feel sort of thin and unsubstantial, as if you couldn't be real yourself."

He was talking to give her time; and as he talked, his kindness, the warm brotherly affection that lay behind every word, was thawing out the frozen stiffness which had fallen on Evelyn. When Manning stopped speaking she said with a little catch in her breath,

"Monkey, where is he?"

"He came over with me," said Manning.

She caught her breath again, more sharply this time.

"Is he well?"

"Fit as a fiddle."

"Is he—" She stopped, throwing out her hands as if she were pushing something away. "Monkey, which *is* he?"

Manning caught the hands in his own and held them tightly.

"My dear girl, if I knew, wouldn't I have told you straight away?"

She seemed to be searching his face.

"They weren't so much—so very much alike," she said in a piteous whisper. "They weren't, Monkey, they weren't."

"No, I know. But, my dear, he isn't—" He bit off the end of the sentence, frowned horribly, and made a new start. "He's not like either of them, and that's a fact."

Evelyn pulled her hands from his and sprang up.

"What do you mean? You said—what do you *mean*?"

"No, no, not that." Manning got up too. "He's one of them all right, but he's not like either of the boys that we remember. You see, for one thing, he's spent ten years doing very hard field work, with his mind more or less asleep all the time. He's put on at least three stone and terrific muscle, and his face has got full and rather heavy. It's beginning to fine down a bit; I notice a distinct difference already. But you mustn't expect to see anyone who looks like either Jim or Jack used to. I want you to realize that, or you'll get the most frightful shock."

Evelyn went to the window and stood there looking out. She saw, not the grey stone of the house over the way, but a very young, gallant, boyish figure with a world of boyish adoration in the eager grey eyes. She heard the voice that had said "Evelyn!"—with a difference. Without turning round she put another question:

"What about his voice, Monkey?"

"Not like either," said Manning; "deeper, you know—fuller."

"I must see him," said Evelyn. "You can't really tell me anything. But if I see him myself—Will you go and fetch him, please."

Manning began to blench at the task before him.

"Sir Henry thought that you—er, well, they thought you oughtn't to see him alone."

Evelyn half turned, her hand on the heavy curtain of gold and apricot.

"Not see him alone? What do you mean? How else does anyone expect me to see him?"

"They said—" began Manning. "I say, my dear girl, don't look at me like that. I knew you wouldn't like it—I told them you wouldn't like it. But they seemed to think it's desperately important. I did my best, but they stuck to their point—and of course I can see the force of it. You see, the succession to Laydon Manor is involved, and Cotty Abbott's position, and—er, several other things. And they've got it all fixed up. Sir Henry's gone down to Laydon Manor to tell Sir Cotterell. And to-morrow they want the family to meet there. I'm to bring Laydon down; and they thought you'd go down either to-night or to-morrow morning and see him quietly before the others come—just your uncle and Sir Cotterell there, you know. And—they've got it all fixed up."

Evelyn turned back to the window blindly. She had a passionate longing for darkness. To be looked at, to be watched, with every feeling stripped and quivering; to meet the man who might, or might not be her husband under keenly watching eyes—Her pride rose at the thing, and then suddenly broke. In a moment the tears were running down her face and burning as they ran. Manning, behind her, put his hands heavily on her shoulders.

"God knows, women can be brave," he said. "I believe you're as brave as any woman living. Stick it, Evelyn!"

Chapter Eleven

It was on a bleak and bitter day of wind and rain that Anthony Laydon came to Laydon Manor. He and Manning walked from the station, tramping silently through soggy lanes between bare hedges. Once a patch of blackthorn broke from the dark hedgerow like a splash of snow. Laydon stopped and stood looking at it for a minute, then tramped on again in silence.

When the big gate came into view he stopped again, looked at the stone pillars, and spoke for the first time:

"Let's go round by the door in the wall, Monkey."

"It won't be open; it's always kept locked."

"Yes—I forgot. I used to have a key of course. I'd forgotten."

They went on up the drive, with its over-arching trees all leafless in the rain. At his first sight of the house Laydon drew a long breath.

"Thank the Lord, there's something that hasn't changed!" he said at last.

Then they went up to the big oak door which stood open, and came through the hall to the door of Sir Cotterell's study without seeing anyone.

Inside the study Sir Henry Prothero stood with his back to the fire. He looked very large, very wise, and rather sad. Between the window and the fire was a long, narrow table of polished walnut. It carried, as a rule, newspapers, magazines and periodicals arranged in orderly rows; but for today's occasion it had been cleared and was empty, except that at the window end a sheet of blotting paper had been laid upon it, flanked by a silver presentation ink-stand and two or three pens. The chair at this end of the table was empty too, Mr. Gregory having not yet arrived. But at the other end, half turned from his brother-in-law and the fire, Sir Cotterell Laydon sat stiffly upright, his eyes on the door, his right hand stretched out upon his knee, where it beat time mechanically to some tune in his brain. He had pushed his chair back from the table, and had the air of a man who is listening intently. When the door opened his fingers stopped beating time, his hand clenched on itself, and he rose to his feet with a jerk.

Standing there, leaning with his left hand on the table, he was very noticeably a Laydon, true to the type which had furnished the half-dozen portraits on the panelled walls. It was a straight, slim, soldierly type, of notably upright carriage and proud bearing—not very tall, not very strongly built, with a straight nose, an obstinately moulded chin, clear-cut lips, and fine, well kept hands. In Sir Cotterell the brown hair of the last two portraits was as white as that of the powdered great-grandfather who hung between the windows.

Anthony Laydon came into the room with Manning behind him. He walked straight across the floor, and came to a standstill in front of Sir Cotterell with his hand out and a quick:

"Grandfather!"

Sir Cotterell kept his left hand on the table; but his right hand went up, shaking a little, and caught at Laydon's arm.

"You!" he said. "You!" and his voice was thinly incredulous.

"I've changed," said Laydon. "I was afraid it would come as a shock."

"Changed?" said Sir Cotterell. He took his hand away, stepped back, and sat down again rather heavily. "Changed?" he repeated; and then, "There's nothing left—there's nothing left at all!"

Laydon drew out a chair, and came and sat down knee to knee with him, leaning across the corner of the table.

"I was afraid you'd feel like that. But it's only on the surface really. Do you remember giving us our first ponies, and making us ride bare-back in the parson's meadow?"

"Eh!" Sir Cotterell looked up. "So you remember that? Do you remember what you called the ponies?"

"Nick and Dick," said Laydon at once.

"And which belonged to which?" Sir Cotterell's blue eyes—they were very blue—were looking out keenly now from under his pepper-and-salt eyebrows.

"Nick was Jack's, and Dick was Jim's," said Laydon.

Sir Cotterell's hand shot out and caught him by the wrist.

"And which was yours, eh? Which was yours?"

"I can't say, sir." The grey eyes met the blue ones quite steadily.

"Can't say! But you *must* know, my boy—you *must* know!"

"It's like this, sir. I remember all the things that we both did, but I can't say which of us did them."

Sir Cotterell took his hand off Laydon's wrist and looked down at the great fingers, the enlarged knuckles, the blackened, broken nails. He bit his lip sharply and looked again at Laydon's face.

The thick beard had been removed, and the unkempt hair trimmed to a normal length. Where the beard had been, the skin had an unnatural pallor; but forehead, nose, and the upper part of the cheeks were burnt to a deep and ingrained tan. The effect was very curious—almost that of a man with his face lathered for shaving, and very perplexing to eyes that were searching for a likeness. The right side of the forehead bore the mark of an old, puckered scar that ran up into the hair and was lost there; and this old scar was crossed by the stain of a yellowing bruise and the red line of a cut that had drawn blood.

Sir Cotterell dropped his eyes again with a sort of groan.

"I can't understand it," he muttered. "Not a trace of my boys—not a trace."

There was a short, painful silence. Then Laydon said in a curiously gentle voice,

"And you've hardly changed at all, sir." He paused. "Will you tell me about the people in the village? Are the Gaunts still at the Vicarage?"

Sir Cotterell nodded without looking up. His right hand tapped his knee again.

"What's Allan Gaunt doing?"

"Gone," said Sir Cotterell—"Loos or Messines—I forget which."

"Cotty Abbott's married, I hear."

This time he got a sharp look.

"Who told you that, eh? Manning, I suppose. Yes, he's married—and she's a deuced unpleasant woman—deuced unpleasant—can't stand the sight of either of 'em for the matter of that. Cotty Abbott always did stick in my throat, and his wife don't make him any easier to swallow. He'll be here directly. You know that?" Laydon nodded. "He rang me up this morning. He means to fight your claim."

"I'm hardly making a claim," said Laydon quickly.

"You're not? What are you doing if you're not making a claim? You say your name's Laydon. You say you're my grandson—you do say that, eh?" The blue eyes were fixed suddenly, piercingly on Laydon's face. But Laydon made no sign.

"Yes, I certainly say that."

"Then, for the Lord's sake prove it, my boy, prove it! Both of you gone the same day, and no one left but Cotty Abbott—it nearly broke me. It'd have broken me outright if I hadn't known that that's what Cotty was waiting for. And if one of you's come back, you must prove it—you must be able to prove it. The thought of Cotty Abbott here when I'm gone is gall and wormwood to me. But I'm a just man—I've tried to be a just man all my life—and I won't leave the place away from the natural heir because I've a personal dislike for him. He's my next of kin, and he's got a son to come after him, and I won't leave the place away from him on the grounds of personal dislike. I pushed Jim's marriage on so as to be safe from Cotty. And if there'd been a little more time, if Evelyn had had a boy—" All the time he was speaking he used a low, rapid undertone and watched Laydon's face with great intentness.

The low-spoken words hardly reached Manning where he stood by the window and watched the rain come down upon the budding daffodils in the Dutch garden. The grey stones streamed under the downpour, but the daffodil leaves stood up like straight, green spears round buds already streaked with gold.

"If Evelyn had had a boy—" Sir Cotterell repeated the words with a sort of angry regret, and saw the colour come suddenly into Laydon's face and change it. Behind the colour, emotion deep and transforming.

For a moment the self-control which had troubled Manning slipped. It was only for a moment; but in that moment Sir Cotterell saw two boys fighting, two faces flushed with anger. The picture came up out of the dark places of memory—the boys swaying, straining, with flushed cheeks and angry eyes. It came, and was gone. Laydon's change of countenance was gone too. But, for the first time, Sir Cotterell felt that here, in this changed figure, was one of those boys. The impression had been as brief as a lightning flash, and as startling. It was not exactly recognition; it was—he could not say what it was, but when the colour rushed into the face he was scanning, when the eyes blazed, he had seen his boys, seen them for a moment plainly, as he had not seen them through all the years of loss. He turned in his chair with a muttered "Henry!" And Sir Henry moved for the first time and came nearer.

"What is it?"

Sir Cotterell looked at him with a shaken air.

"I thought—No, it's gone again—it's gone." He turned back.

"You've got to prove it," he said. "Cotty'll have his microscope out, but—don't you let him rattle you. He'll be here in a moment, and he'll ask you this, that and the other, and try to trip you. But I want you to remember this. You haven't got to satisfy Cotty or a court of law: you've only got to satisfy me. If you can prove to me that you're my grandson, I'll alter my will to-day." He laughed grimly, "By Gad, I'll make Cotty Abbott witness it too! But you've *got* to prove it— you've *got* to satisfy me. Once you've done that, Cotty can go hang. But I'll not go past him for any except my own flesh and blood."

Laydon lifted his elbow from the table and leaned back, his face heavy, his look remote.

"How am I going to prove it?" he said.

"You've got to. There are plenty of ways. If you're Jim, now—" He paused, dropped his voice, and sat forward. "If you're Jim, there's a proof you could give me now. Jim and I had a talk together here, in this very room, on the night before his wedding—the night before he went back to France. If you're Jim, you'll know what passed between us."

Sir Cotterell put his hand on the table as he spoke. It shook a little; his voice shook with the eagerness that possessed him. In his own mind he saw himself and the Jim of ten years ago and listened to their talk. It came back to him word for word. He saw himself rise and unlock the safe behind his father's portrait. He saw the diamonds that his mother had worn, that his wife had worn, lie shining on the table where his hand lay now, his trembling hand. He heard himself say, "They're pretty things, eh, Jim? Evelyn'll look well in 'em. They're for her, but I'll keep 'em here till this damned war is over." Impossible that Jim should have forgotten—if this were Jim. Behind him the locked safe was hidden by the portrait—and Evelyn had never worn the jewels.

He repeated his question urgently:

"If you're Jim, you can tell me what we talked about. That's a proof that would satisfy me. Can you give it me?"

"No, sir, I can't."

Chapter Twelve

EVELYN LAYDON's little car drew up at the big open door and Evelyn ran quickly up the steps and into the hall. She stripped off a dripping raincoat, and appeared in a dark grey tweed coat and skirt. She had moved to one of the old wall-mirrors, and was pulling off a wet felt hat, when she saw in the glass the hovering form of Lake, the butler. Without turning round she asked:

"Where is Sir Cotterell? Is he alone?"

Lake moistened his lips and rubbed his hands together. He was a passionately nervous little man, with a worried eye and a hereditary devotion to the Laydons. For at least three generations a Laydon had sworn at and generally bullied a Lake.

"Sir Cotterell's in his study, ma'am—with Sir Henry, ma'am."

"Alone?" The question was quite steady. As she put it, Evelyn slipped out of her coat and turned towards him, bare-headed, in a white polo jumper and short skirt.

"Yes, they're quite alone, ma'am. There's no one else come yet." Evelyn nodded.

"Thanks, Lake—I'll just go in then." For the life of her she could not keep the relief out of her voice.

She went to the study door, opened it, and was fairly in the room before she saw that there were four people there already. She shut the door sharply, and for a moment gripped the handle with fingers which did not seem able to let it go. Then she lifted her head and came quietly forward as Sir Cotterell rose to meet her—Sir Cotterell and the man whose back had been turned when she came in.

An absolute silence seemed to have fallen on the room—one of those silences in which time and breath are suspended. It seemed as if it would never end.

Anthony Laydon stood with the table at his back and looked down the room. He saw Evelyn. Everything stopped there. It was Evelyn. She had worn white ten years ago, and she had come up the dark aisle of an old church like a white and golden glory, with lilies in her hands. That was on the far side of the lost, blind years. But he saw Evelyn now—Evelyn in a white sweater like a man's, and her face dead white above it—Evelyn unalterably beautiful, unalterably beloved.

He stood there and waited, whilst time stood waiting too. As she came up to him, Sir Henry Prothero made a step forward. Manning over by the window bit deep into his lip. He would have looked away; but he could not look away; not one of them could look away. But after all, Evelyn was as unconscious of the watching eyes as if she and Laydon had been alone in space. They were alone. Never in all her life had she felt such an isolation. Everyone in the world was gone, and everything in the world was blotted out except herself and this man with the unfamiliar face. She looked at him as the others had looked—Manning, Sir Cotterell—, and saw what they had seen. And then she ceased to see that at all.

Manning, watching, saw her lift her hand and put it to her throat. For an unendurable moment her eyes met Laydon's full. Then the colour came to her face suddenly, brilliantly. She drew a very long breath, turned away, and walking deliberately to the far end of the table, pulled out a chair and sat down. No one would have guessed that the room swam before her eyes, or that she was saying over and over to herself, "I mustn't faint—I mustn't, mustn't faint!"

From the time she had entered the room not a single word had been spoken. Evelyn rested her head on her hand, looked down into the polished surface of the walnut table, and saw her own reflection there, vague and misty. She went on saying to herself, "I mustn't faint—I mustn't, mustn't faint!" And still no one spoke.

Laydon stood just where he was, but turned a little so that he could see Evelyn's bent head with the golden hair cut short at the back, showing a beautiful curving line.

It was Sir Henry Prothero who broke the silence. He left the fire, took a seat opposite Evelyn, and stretching across the table, touched her lightly on the wrist.

"My dear," he said—"Evelyn, my dear."

It was just then that Lake opened the door. He stood, surprised and nervous, on the threshold—"struck all of a heap," as he afterwards explained to the housekeeper. "And they must have come in like ghosts, him and the Major, or I'd have heard them for certain." He stood there, and Anthony Laydon gave himself a sort of shake and came forward with his hand out:

"Hullo, Lake! How are you? Going strong?"

Lake took the hand in silence; his own was shaking very much. He looked at Laydon in dazed bewilderment, and murmured unintelligibly. Sir Cotterell called to him sharply, "Lake, what is it man?"

Lake pulled himself together with a great effort.

"Mr and Mrs Abbott have arrived, sir—in the morning-room, sir. And Mr Gregory has arrived, sir."

Immediately on the words, Mr Gregory was in the room.

"May I come in?" And then, without waiting for an answer, he advanced, greeted everyone, and took the chair with its back to the window, pushing the blotting paper a little farther off and adjusting the inkstand conveniently. He talked all the time in cheerful commonplaces—about the weather, the lateness of the spring. But when he was seated with his papers before him he fell silent, leaned back in his chair with his hands along the arms of it, and took a grave survey of the room and its six other occupants.

He bore a certain resemblance to the portraits of Sir Walter Scott, on the strength of which he collected first editions of the Waverley Novels. Looking now between short sandy eyelashes, his small grey eyes were shrewd and kind. They rested with undisguised curiosity on Anthony Laydon. Then he nodded and turned to Sir Cotterell.

"The Abbotts are here. I think better have them in—that is if you're ready."

"Yes. Show Mr and Mrs Abbott in, Lake." Under his breath Sir Cotterell added: "I didn't bargain for Mrs Cotty—no, I'm hanged if I did!"

There was silence until the door opened again. Laydon had come back to a lounging pose against the table. Evelyn sat without stirring, her forehead resting on her hand, her eyes veiled. She sat next to Mr Gregory, Sir Henry Prothero opposite with Manning leaning on the back of his chair.

The Abbotts came in, bringing with them, as they always did, an air of bustle and aggression. Mrs Abbott was a plump, colourless person with white lashes and pale, prominent eyes. As she walked, she chinked and rustled—one suspected bangles and a stiff silk petticoat. Her light, fuzzy hair was carefully controlled by a net. Neither she nor Cotty ever forgot for an instant that she had been a Mendip-ffollinton. Cotty, behind her, was Sir Cotterell in caricature—much smaller, much stiffer, with every trait exaggerated; the whole enveloped in a preposterous air of self-importance.

As they came up, Laydon passed to the other side of the table, leaving to the Abbotts the two places between Evelyn and Sir Cotterell. A sardonic humour rose in him as he listened to Cotty being very stiff and non-committal while Mrs Cotty exhibited the Mendip-ffollinton manner in one of its most irritating phases. She gave her staring bow to everyone in the circle except Laydon, and then sat down beside Evelyn, fixing her with inquisitive eyes.

Laydon's humour passed into savage anger as he watched Evelyn control a quiver of sensitive lips and for a moment raise her head with gentle dignity.

"Of course, I don't know how far these proceedings have gone." This was Cotty Abbott, bolt upright and speaking with some asperity.

Sir Cotterell beside him made the noise which is usually written "Tchah," and drummed on the table. He also cleared his throat and blew his nose.

Cotty Abbott produced a sheet of foolscap neatly typed, and took a fountain-pen out of his waistcoat pocket.

"I would like to begin by asking just how far this—this—claim has proceeded," he said. "And at the same time I wish to enter my protest, in Mr Gregory's presence, against this—er—highly irregular manner of dealing with such a claim."

"Irregular?" said Mr Gregory. He pounced on the word, and it at once gave up the ghost. With a lenient smile he appeared to display its corpse. "Irregular? Let us say informal, Mr Abbott—that, I think, is the right word."

Cotty Abbott pinched in his nostrils and tightened his lips. His voice when he spoke was thin and acid.

"I should be glad to know how far this—er—claim has proceeded. Have you, for instance, recognized this person, Uncle Cotterell?"

He ignored Mr Gregory, but it was Mr. Gregory who answered him.

"No formal recognition has, I believe, taken place as yet. I would suggest that you put any questions you wish to Mr Laydon, who has signified his willingness to answer such of them as he can. From these questions and his answers, and perhaps by one or two other simple tests, it will, I hope, be possible to arrive at a conclusion—a perfectly definite and friendly conclusion."

"You say, no *formal* recognition," Cotty Abbott's voice was high and unpleasant. "May I ask if anyone here pretends to recognize James or John Laydon in this—gentleman?"

Sir Cotterell swung round in his chair, glaring. Mr Gregory interposed:

"I have said, Mr Abbott, that no recognition has taken place. I think you would do well to ask your questions. And, in your own interests, I would beg you to remember that this is a friendly meeting."

Evelyn was looking down again at the polished table. It was like looking into still, brown water. She saw her own reflection very dimly, and the men's voices seemed to come from a long way off. She began to get a grip of herself, to hold on to her vaguely flowing thoughts and order them. The misty sense of isolation began to pass; she found herself an integral part of this family circle, listening and intent. Cotty was asking his questions, and Laydon had given the names of his head-master, his house-master, and of half a dozen boys who had been in the same house. Now it was:

"Your birthday?" very quick and sharp.

And Laydon's drawled answer:

"Afraid that's one of the things I can't give you, Cotty."

"Jim Laydon's birthday then?"

"May the fifteenth."

"And Jack's?"

"The twenty-second."

The questions went on. Evelyn heard Laydon give his grandmother's maiden name, the names of the servants at Laydon Manor in 1914, the names of the village carpenter and the man who kept the general shop in Laydon Sudbury. There Cotty Abbott paused.

"These, of course, are just the questions which anyone would expect," he said—"anyone who was making a claim of this sort."

Anthony Laydon smiled pleasantly.

"That's because I knew the answers. It's quite easy, of course, if you do. Why don't you go on and ask some more?"

As he spoke, Manning looked at him sharply, opened his mouth as if to speak, and then appeared to think better of it.

Evelyn sat back in her chair and let her eyes travel slowly down the table. The faces were faces now, not whiter blurs in the general mist. She could even be stirred to faint, inward laughter at Monkey's bitten lip and really terrifying scowl. She found herself looking at Laydon quite steadily. There was a little smile on his lips, but his eyes were angry, with a cold, still anger that frightened her. He was looking across at Cotty and saying:

"Anything else you'd like to ask me?"

"I'd like you to sign your name," said Cotty Abbott in the stiff voice of a man who thinks he is being laughed at.

Laydon's smile became a little more pronounced.

"And what name do you suggest that I should sign?"

"I should like you to sign 'J. Laydon.'"

Sir Henry Prothero nodded.

"A handwriting test, Cotty?—is that what you're thinking of? If so—" He paused, looking at Gregory, and Laydon broke in:

"I'll write anything you like. But I'd like just to point out that neither Jack nor Jim ever signed 'emselves 'J. Laydon' in their lives."

"Yes, that's true, that's perfectly true," said Sir Cotterell.

Laydon took the pen that was passed to him. He held it clumsily, fidgeting with it. Then he dipped it much too deeply, made a heavy blot, smudged it, and wrote 'J. Laydon.'

Cotty surveyed the large, awkward characters with an air of importance.

"Now write 'Jim Laydon,' and under that 'Jack Laydon,'" he commanded—and again the pen travelled laboriously.

Cotty stretched across the table and picked up the sheet of paper with the three signatures.

"Not much like anything I remember," he said, and passed the paper up the table to Gregory.

Evelyn kept it for a moment before she passed it on. Sophy Abbott, at her elbow, craned forward, darting sharp glances, first at Evelyn's face, then at the paper, and then back again at Evelyn.

"Well?" she said. "What do you make of it? Do you recognize the writing?"

All at once Evelyn became aware that Laydon was watching her too—they were all watching her. She became aware also that what she did or said just now would matter immensely. She steadied that something in her which quivered and shrank under all those eyes; and she said in a low, natural voice,

"No—not exactly. It's—well, it's like both of them in a way. But it's bigger."

Gregory leaned towards her, looking over the paper.

"Could you show us what you mean, Mrs Laydon? I have both their signatures here on separate letters." He laid them on the table as he spoke.

"Don't you see?" said Evelyn quickly. "The 'J'—that's like Jack's writing—the long tail. But the 'L' isn't like Jack's. And neither of them made a 'd' quite like that."

"Yes, I see. Well, we'll get an expert opinion about it—that'll be best."

"No!" said Sir Cotterell. He struck the table with his fist and spoke with a good deal of violence. "None of your experts for me, Gregory! Swear themselves black in the face, they will, and give each other the lie direct in court. The fellow that said there were three degrees in lying—lies, damned lies, and statistics, might just as well have left statistics out of it and put in expert evidence instead. I've always said so, and I'll go on saying so. And I'm hanged if I'll have any of 'em mixed up in my private family affairs. I'm the person who has to be convinced one way or another; and that's not the sort of thing that's going to help me to make up my mind.

There's a photograph album behind you there, Manning. Will you give it to me."

When he had it in front of him he went through it slowly, pausing at every page, and looking first at this or that faded group or blurred snapshot, and then at the man beside him.

And now it was Sir Cotterell whom everybody watched. There was something tragic and piteous in the tremor with which he passed from page to page. Evelyn saw that momentarily he was losing hope; and she saw a gleam of pity and comprehension change the set lines of Laydon's face. The Abbotts wore an air of triumph when the book was shut and pushed away with a groan.

It was Laydon who broke the silence.

"I'm afraid I'm not like any of those old photos now."

"No," said Sir Cotterell; the word was another groan. "No, that doesn't help—that doesn't help at all."

"Perhaps someone else," said Cotty—he made a gesture that took in the whole circle, one of those exaggerated gestures that went so oddly with his stiff carriage—"Perhaps someone else would like to ask some questions—you, Manning, for instance."

"No, thanks, Cotty."

"Sir Henry then?"

Sir Henry smoothed his chin.

"Well, I don't know that I can be very helpful. No, I don't think that I could ask anything that would clear matters up at all. But— well, let me see." He turned to Laydon and smiled a little, his mind chiefly occupied with the desire to ease the sense of strain that had fallen upon all except the Abbotts. "Let me see—I wonder if you can tell me when and where I saw you last. I'm afraid my own recollection is rather hazy; but it might clear up if you could remind me."

Quite visibly Laydon relaxed.

"That sounds a bit like the blind leading the blind, sir," he said. "But as a matter of fact I remember quite well. You were just going off to India, and you came out of this room with my grandfather into the garden out there. I can't remember how old I was—about twelve I think; but I remember you tipped us, and we started our stamp collections on the strength of it."

Sir Cotterell looked up sharply.

"Eh?" he said. "Eh? If that's so—by Jove, if that's so—Henry!"

"*If*," said Cotty Abbott. "It's for Sir Henry to say whether all this is within his recollection." His little bleak eyes dwelt on Sir Henry's puzzled frown. "Do you remember all this, Sir Henry? Could you swear to it?"

There was a pause. Sir Henry, still frowning, shook his head.

"I'm not clear," he said.

Cotty Abbott gave a short laugh.

"Perhaps there's something else you could ask. Or perhaps Mr. Gregory would like to put some questions."

"Or Evelyn," said Sophy Abbott. She sat forward, clinking and rustling, then turned so that she could look at Evelyn full. "After all, my dear Evelyn, you are really more concerned than anyone, and the questions you could ask if you *chose* would naturally be most valuable. Of course, if you'd rather *not*—"

The slight sneer in the Mendip-ffollinton voice, the inquisitive bulge of the Mendip-ffollinton eyes, produced an unexpected reaction in Evelyn. Faintness was gone. The feeling of being a pinned specimen under the microscope was gone. The desperate, wounded quiver at her heart was gone. The colour came into her face until her cheeks were like burning roses. But inwardly she was cool and balanced, very well able to hold her own with Sophy Abbott; able even to meet Laydon's eyes and be pleased because they were hot with anger.

"That's very kind of you, Sophy. But I don't mind at all— why should I?" She smiled, let the smile flash across the table to Laydon, and went on, her voice on its own pretty level. "Here's my question—and I think it's quite a good one. Uncle Henry wanted to know when you saw him last. Well, perhaps you can tell us when you saw me first."

The anger went out of Laydon's eyes. Something else took its place—admiration—relief—no one who watched him could be sure. He looked back at Evelyn, laughing, and said,

"You were up a tree." There was no pause between question and answer.

Sir Cotterell stared; Manning broke into a sudden laugh; and the Abbotts stiffened as Mr Gregory inquired blandly:

"Is that so, Mrs Laydon?"

Evelyn found it a relief to turn to him.

"Yes, I was up a tree, Mr Gregory—I really was. I think I was fourteen. I was staying with Lacy for the holidays."

"Yes?" said Gregory.

Sir Cotterell got up, leaning on the table.

"Evelyn!" Then as she looked round at him: "Evelyn—Evelyn, my dear."

"What is it?" There was a tinge of distress in her tone.

"My dear, if you remember this—this incident, you must know which—which—" His voice failed. He stood there, all his weight on his hands.

"Oh, Sir Cotterell, I'm so sorry! It—it doesn't help that way, I'm afraid, for the boys were together, all three of them; and they all helped me down."

"Three?" said Sir Henry Prothero. "Who was the third?"

"Jim Field—Jack and Jim Laydon, and Jim Field. I met them all together. Jim Field was always about with them that year and the next."

"Then I don't think that Evelyn's question has thrown very much light on things—does anyone?" Mrs Cotty sneered a little more openly this time, and more openly still as she added, "Can't you think of anything better than that, Evelyn dear?"

Sir Cotterell took his hands from the table and stood erect.

"I want a proof," he said. "I want a proof."

Laydon stood up too.

"I think—I believe I can give you one."

Cotty Abbott, who had been whispering to his wife, swung about. Everyone turned. Laydon looked only at Sir Cotterell, and spoke in a voice pitched for Sir Cotterell's ear:

"You asked me just now whether I remembered having a conversation with you in this room the night before—I went back to France; and I told you that I couldn't say at all what had passed at that particular interview. But I do remember another conversation—"

"What conversation?"

"It was in 1914. We had our last leave before going over to France—I think it was November. You called us in here, and we sat round the fire. You talked to us both very seriously about getting married. You said you had a very special reason for wishing to see the succession secured. I remember you told us what that reason was. You said we were both very young—too young in the ordinary way, but the war made all the difference. And you asked whether either of us had an attachment. I remember that Jack said 'Yes,' and Jim—"

Sir Cotterell had a hand on his arm, gripping him hard.

"And Jim?"

"And Jim said nothing."

"And then?"

"I'm afraid my recollection stops there."

"It can't! You must go on!"

Laydon shook his head, falling back a pace, and Cotty Abbott broke in:

"You said my uncle gave a special reason for pressing marriage on two boys of twenty-one. But you didn't tell us what it was. Is that another of the things you've forgotten?"

Laydon laughed.

"Oh, no. I could give you the reason, but I think I won't. I don't mind writing it down though, for Mr Gregory and my grandfather to see. Can anyone let me have a pencil and paper?"

Manning picked a sheet of paper off the table, and handed it across behind Sir Henry Prothero together with a pencil fished out of his trouser pocket. Laydon said "Thanks, Monkey," bent over the table and wrote, still standing. He folded the paper and passed it to Mr Gregory. As Gregory opened it, Sir Cotterell came round the table and stood behind him.

There was only one word, scrawled boldly across the sheet—"Cotty."

Sir Cotterell slapped his thigh and broke into unsteady laughter.

"Yes, by gum!" he said. "Reason? You don't want a better reason than that, eh, Gregory? Reason enough and to spare! Eh, Gregory, eh?"

There was something painful in this laughter, and no one joined in it. Mr Gregory raised his eyebrows very slightly and appeared to be about to address Laydon, when all at once a complete change came over him. The words he had been about to speak were not spoken. Instead, he pushed back his chair, sprang up, and taking Sir Cotterell by the arm, he bent close and spoke quickly with dropped voice:

"Look, Sir Cotterell! Look! Mr Laydon—your father's portrait! Look!"

"Eh?" said Sir Cotterell with a catch in his breath. "Eh?"

Mr Gregory's grip tightened.

"Look!" he said.

And in a moment everyone was looking.

Laydon stood as he had been standing ever since he had passed the folded paper to Gregory; his right hand and part of the arm rested on the tall back of the chair in which he had been sitting. He was leaning forward a little, his eyes turned on Sir Cotterell, his face heavy, controlled and stern. Behind him on the dark panelling hung the portrait which masked the safe—the portrait of Sir James Laydon, eighth baronet, standing against a black curtain, his arm across the back of a tall carved chair, his head slightly bent, his expression stern and gloomy. The face was heavier than Laydon faces were wont to be, and set in rigid lines. The grey light from the window behind Gregory fell directly on the portrait and on the man who stood below it. The likeness between the living face and the painted one was startling in the extreme—the same pose; the same dark look; the same control.

Sir Cotterell pulled himself away from Gregory's hold and squared his shoulders. His excitement was gone; he spoke in a quiet, level voice.

"Yes—there's my proof. That's good enough for me."

As the words left his lips, the likeness was gone, broken by a look of astonishment. Cotty Abbott said,

"What do you mean?"

"I mean," said Sir Cotterell—he broke off, came round the table, and put a steady hand on Laydon's shoulder—"I mean that this is my grandson, one of my boys come back. And I say 'Thank God for it.'" His voice changed sharply. "Gregory, I take you to witness—I take you all to witness—that I am satisfied that this is one of my grandsons."

Chapter Thirteen

EVELYN HAD no very clear idea of how she came into the hall. Her one overwhelming desire was to get away. She had neither part nor lot in what was happening in the library now. Neither the Abbotts' indignant protests nor Sir Cotterell's triumphant relief concerned her at all. She wanted to get away.

Manning found her already in her rain-coat, cramming on a damp black felt hat with shaking hands. He said, "Hullo, old girl— you off?"

She nodded, biting her lip.

"Well, will you give me a lift? He'll stay here now; but I must get back to town."

"I must get away—I'm through," said Evelyn in a dry whisper.

Manning gave her a little push towards the door.

"Got your car there? All right, go and get in. I won't be a moment."

She turned, catching at him.

"You won't let anyone come. I can't—"

"Good Lord, no. What do you take me for? You go and get in. I must just let them know I'm off—that's all."

Evelyn went out to the car and put the hood down. She wanted to feel the rain and the wind. She had just buckled the last strap, when Manning ran down the steps.

"Shall I drive?" he said, coming round to her. "My dear girl, we'll get sopped."

"I don't mind. Yes, you can drive."

"I simply hate getting wet," said Monkey. He made his crossest face and took the wheel.

The car was started. He took a look at Evelyn.

"Want to talk?"

"No."

After that they drove for thirty miles in a blessed silence whilst Evelyn let the tears come as they would and felt the rain drive cold against her burning face.

The rain had thinned to a drizzle and the grey day was dimming into dusk, when Manning said suddenly and cheerfully:

"There's a clean handkerchief in my coat pocket on your side if you'd like it."

He heard Evelyn's shaky laugh:

"Monkey, you *are* an angel!"

"Yes, I know I am."

"You really are."

"My dear, Lacy has me trained. If there's a man in Europe, Asia, Africa, or America who knows the exact moment when a woman wants a clean pocket handkerchief better than I do, just you point him out, and I'll assassinate him quietly. As a matter of fact, I'm frightfully glad you didn't bottle up and do the hard, stony woman all the way back to town."

"It's such a lovely large handkerchief," said Evelyn. "I've got one—in fact two, but—"

"No woman's handkerchief will stay the course of a real good cry. They're all right just to dab your eyes with when you want to look pretty and pathetic, but when it comes to business they're absolutely no earthly."

"Monkey, when do you go back?" said Evelyn presently.

"To-morrow, I expect; but I'm not absolutely sure. Fact is—this is confidential, please—they're offering me a job at the War Office. It's not fixed up; but I'm going round there to-morrow, and then I'll be able to let you know for certain. I don't really expect I'll get away till next day."

For the rest of the way they talked of Don, of Lacy, of the chances of getting an unfurnished flat—in fact, of everything except Laydon. When they stopped in the quiet square, where two or three of the pleasant old houses had been modernized and turned into flats, Evelyn got out:

"Will you take her round? Same garage, just round the corner. Thanks awfully."

She came round the car and stopped, standing silent for a while. Then she said,

"Monkey, who do you think he is?"

His brow wrinkled sharply as he threw her a quick, upward glance.

"Did you mean who, or which?"

It was too dark for him to see her face, but her voice thrilled with impatience.

"Monkey, don't fence! Tell me!"

"I'm not fencing; I'm being cautious."

"Don't be cautious. I want the truth—what you really think."

"I think—" He paused for so long that her foot tapped on the pavement. "My dear girl, it's no good doing that. I think—well, what is there to think?"

"Do you think he's Jack, or Jim?"

"I think he's one of them. And if you don't know which one, well, how in heaven's name do you expect me to?"

"That's what you really think?"

"That's what I really think."

Evelyn turned, went up the steps, and let herself into the house.

It was about an hour later that the telephone bell rang. Evelyn went into the dining-room, shut the door, took up the receiver, and said,

"Hullo!"

"Can I speak to Mrs Laydon?" The voice was a man's voice, and Evelyn recognized it instantly. It was the voice which she had listened to in the library at Laydon Manor only that afternoon. It had sounded strangely to her there, without one kind, familiar tone; but now some trick of the wires altered it, raising the pitch and bringing out a quality which set memory quivering.

"Mrs Laydon speaking. Who is it?" She spoke with her hand pressed close against her cheek.

There was a noticeable pause. Then the voice, the familiar voice, answering her question with a single word:

"Laydon."

Evelyn's hand pressed closer. Laydon—yes, that's what he was, just a surname, just—Laydon. A grandson for Sir Cotterell, and an heir for Laydon Manor—but for her, what? Husband—lover—friend—or nothing but an empty name? She held the receiver to her ear and would not speak. What had she got to say to a name? If there was anything behind the name, anyone with a need that she could meet, the next move did not lie with her. She heard Laydon say anxiously "Are you there?" and she heard herself say "Yes" with a sort of mechanical ease.

Then Laydon:

"I want to come and see you."

She said "Yes" again.

"I must see you. You'll let me? You went away so quickly."

"Yes."

"When may I come?"

"I don't know."

She heard the voice rise a little, eagerly.

"It's too late to-night, I suppose?"

"Yes."

"You're sure?"

"Yes."

"To-morrow then?"

"Yes."

A note of concern crossed the eagerness.

"You're all right?"

"Oh, yes."

"It was *beastly* for you this afternoon." Tone as well as words were boyish.

Evelyn hung up the receiver with a quick jerk. She could bear no more. The voice did not belong to Laydon; it belonged to her memories, and it played on them, calling up the hopes and joys and tender anticipations of ten years ago. They were gone; they were dead and buried, and the past had closed down on them. It hurt most terribly to have them called into a mocking semblance of life again.

When Laydon came into the flat next morning it seemed to him that he had stepped out of winter into spring. He shut the door on greyness and a tearing north-east wind, and stood looking into a room which suggested sunshine even when the sun was hidden.

A small table had been pulled out into the middle of the floor, and standing on it was a large wooden tray covered with bunches of spring flowers—wood-violets, primroses, Lent lilies and bright blue squills. Evelyn stood just behind the table. She wore a green dress, and her hands were full of primroses.

As Laydon came forward, she let the flowers fall, and gave him a pale smile and a cold, wet hand. It was rather chilling—to look like spring and be so wintry cold to touch.

"You must have had an icy drive," said Evelyn. "Aren't these lovely?" She took up the primroses again and bent her face to them. "Jessica sent me a great box of them this morning."

Laydon took the obvious opening:

"Who is Jessica?"

"Jessica Sunning. We share this flat. She's an artist; she has a studio just round the corner. We've been here six—no, seven years. I think you'd like Jessica. She's visiting her people in Devonshire just now; and when she's there she always sends me heavenly flowers."

Evelyn turned from him as she spoke, and went to the hearth. On the white mantel-shelf were half a dozen delicate china cups— turquoise blue, apple green, rose pink, primrose, blood red, and lilac. She put primroses into the lilac, and violets into the turquoise cup. Then she came back to the table for more flowers.

Laydon's eyes followed her. She picked up a bunch of squills, talking all the time:

"Jessica has one real virtue—she always ties up flowers as she picks them. I've cried over the flowers some people send one, all mashed up and huddled together. Now Jessica never does that."

She put the squills into the apple green cup and heard Laydon move behind her.

"Won't you come and sit down?" he said. "I want to talk to you."

Evelyn settled the little blue flowers before she turned. She came slowly back to the table and stood there, looking down at the Lent lilies, but not touching them.

"Won't you sit down?" said Laydon again. "I want to talk to you—I think we must talk."

Something in his voice came through Evelyn's guard and pricked her to a change of mood. She stopped being afraid, and became very much mistress of herself and of the situation. They were set down to a strange game, she and Laydon and Sir Cotterell and the Abbotts; and she meant to pick up her hand and play it gallantly without counting the cost.

She sat down on the arm of a big chair, leaned one elbow on the back, and smiled, really smiled at Laydon for the first time.

"All right," she said,—"talk."

"I don't know where to begin," said Laydon, "except that I wanted to say how frightfully sorry I was about yesterday." He came and sat down on the arm of the other big chair, quite close to her. "My hat! What a show! It was bad enough for me, but it must have been perfectly beastly for you."

With the most extraordinary suddenness the relationship between them had changed. Constraint had gone. The need to save the situation was gone. Evelyn nodded and said,

"Thank goodness it's over!"

"That's one thing—however beastly things are, you don't have to go through them twice. I expect we were all glad when yesterday was over Evelyn—"

Evelyn stopped him with a quick gesture, the colour bright in her face.

"Yes, I'm Evelyn—but what are you? I mean, what am I to call you? That's the first thing we have to settle. What *am* I to call you?"

"I thought"—his voice was eager and confidential—"I thought perhaps you'd call me Anthony. You see, that's what I'm calling myself."

Evelyn said "Anthony" once or twice, frowning a little over it and hesitating, as if she did not find it easy to say.

"Why Anthony?"

Laydon did not answer for a moment.

"You've talked to Monkey—I don't quite know how much you know." He threw her a look that searched her face, and found it grave.

"I've read Anna Blum's statement."

He looked away from her, down at the brown and orange of the carpet. It was like fallen leaves, like a drift of fallen leaves. He saw the bare trees of a wintry forest, and the leaves that lay in drifts below.

"Amazing, isn't it?" he said.

He had forgotten that they were talking about his name, but she recalled him to it.

"You were called Anton Blum. Is that why? Anton is Anthony of course. I should have thought—"

"What?"

"Well, I shouldn't think you would want to be reminded—but I don't know."

"I don't feel like that. There's no other name I can call myself, and somehow I seem used to it. After all, if you've been called by a name for ten years, I suppose you do get used to it."

Evelyn leaned a little nearer and said rather breathlessly,

"But do you remember it all? Don't talk about it if you'd rather not. Perhaps you'd better not talk about it."

"No, I don't mind. I think I'd like to—if you'll let me—if it doesn't bore you."

Evelyn shook her head.

"No, it doesn't bore me," she said in an odd, still voice. Then she smiled rather beautifully, and Laydon's heart cried out in him.

"I remember like one remembers a dream"—he wasn't looking at her now—"You know how it is. You have a dream, and then you wake up and it's gone. You see all the everyday things, and you get up, and there's a frightful lot to do. And you don't think about the dream until something reminds you. Perhaps it's some rotten little thing, and you don't know why it reminds you; but it does, and all of a sudden you can look into your own mind and see the dream there, frightfully clear and distinct." His right hand opened and shut twice, sharply. "I'm making a most awful bungle of it; but I can't put it any better."

"You mean when you first woke up—came to yourself—out there in Cologne, you didn't remember much about all the time you were Anton Blum; but now you do remember—is that what you mean?"

"Yes, something like that. Not all the time, you know, but by fits and starts—if anything reminds me. Just now, for instance—" He paused, hesitated, and let the words come with a rush—"Just now I remembered the forest frightfully plainly. It was like seeing it—the leaves, you know,—rather a jolly colour—" He broke off and looked at her. "You don't think it sounds—mad?"

Her eyes were very kind.

"I think it sounds as if your memory was coming back and—and steadying down. It will come back."

"I wonder," said Anthony Laydon.

The big chair slid back on its castors as he jumped up and went over to the window. He had known that it would be hard; but it was being harder than he had reckoned. It was bad enough to play the stranger, to watch her, pale and controlled, with a sheet of ice between them; but with the ice gone, and Evelyn just Evelyn, looking at him with lovely kindness, it was unbearable. Thought, will, and resolution melted in him and flowed out towards her.

He stood at the window, holding back a rush of words. If he could no longer hold his thought, he could at least forbid it utterance. Only a fool would hazard everything now. Wait—wait as he had planned to wait. Give her time—give her time, you fool! Don't rush her. You've got ten years to bridge somehow.

He heard Evelyn's voice:

"What is Anna Blum like? I wondered so much when I read her statement; and I thought perhaps you could tell me. You remember her, I suppose?"

He turned, leaning against the window frame.

"Anna—yes, I remember, of course." He frowned. "It's pretty well all Anna, you know—just a long dream going on, and on; and Tante Anna always there. She was *frightfully* good to me. That's a thing I've got to see about, you know. I've asked Monkey to find out. I mean, what she did for me must have leaked out by now, and I've got to make sure that she's not suffering for it in any way. Monkey can find out quietly. She—it rather appals me to feel under such a terrific obligation. I don't quite know what to do."

"You'll find a way."

"Yes, I must."

There was a pause. Laydon didn't want a pause; the moment there was silence, all those things he must not say clamoured in him again. He spoke quickly, brusquely:

"Don't you want to know what happened after you went away yesterday?"

"Yes, of course. I *had* to go." Her voice dropped a little, and her colour changed. "What did happen?"

"Oh, a scene with the Abbotts. My grandfather didn't let 'em down any too gently, I'm afraid; and after all I bar Cotty, but my coming back like this is a bit rough on him, I must say. I think my grandfather'll have to do something about it—and I think he will too. But just at present"—he laughed—"just at present, I'm not at all sure that the feeling that he's scored off Cotty isn't stronger than the feeling that he's got one of us back."

"I can't *stand* the Abbotts," said Evelyn, frankly. "But I'm sorry for them. If Sophy wasn't a cat, I'd be sorrier still."

"I thought she was an absolutely poisonous female. Where did Cotty pick her up?"

Evelyn broke into a gurgle of laughter.

"She was a Mendip-ffollinton."

"What's that?"

Her eyes danced; there was a dimple in her cheek. All the ice was gone.

"If she and Cotty could only hear you! She's a Mendip-ffollinton. They spell it with two little 'f's'—and there's never, never, *never* been a title in the family."

Laydon laughed too—laughed with his eyes as well as with his lips.

"Are they proud of that?"

"*Frightfully.* Dukes are dirt, and Marquises are mud compared with the Mendip-ffollintons. Some day, if you and Sophy are ever on speaking terms, she'll explain to you just how vulgar it is to be a baronet. I'm beyond the pale altogether because I wear short skirts and shingle my hair. *She* wears a net. All the female Mendip-ffollintons wear nets, and little waists, and bushy skirts—it's part of the family tradition."

Laydon had stopped laughing. His eyebrows drew together, and he said abruptly:

"Why did you cut your hair?"

His eyes accused her, and she met them with a challenging spark in her own.

"Why, because I'm not a Mendip-ffollinton. We don't have hair now, you know—except in front." She put up a hand and touched the thick waves above her brow and the little curls that hid her ears. "It's simply not done. You've no idea how comfortable it is. If we ever go back to hair, we shall be fools."

As she talked, she felt a dangerous moment pass. Laydon came forward.

"Aren't you going to put the rest of your flowers in water?" he asked in the restrained voice which she had heard in the library at Laydon Manor.

They put the Lent lilies into a copper lustre jug, and he told her that Sir Cotterell had already altered his will:

"He insisted on doing it then and there, though Gregory tried to make him wait."

"I don't see why he should wait. I think he was quite right to do it at once." She put the jug on the top of the piano, and turning, leaned on the key-board.

"He's been awfully generous in every way. I thought I'd like to tell you. He's opening an account for me under my present name, and—in fact he's being so generous that I rather wish he wouldn't."

Evelyn looked at him gravely and directly.

"What are you going to do?" she asked.

If he hesitated, it was only for a moment.

"I had a long talk with him and Uncle Henry last night. I want to study up-to-date farming and estate management. Jim was going to, you know; and I'm quite sure it's the only way to keep things going. Uncle Henry is awfully keen about it, but my grandfather—well, you know what he is—what most of the men of his generation are. There's a good deal of the 'What was good enough for me and my father and all my great-grandfathers ought to be good enough for this generation. Then they get a bit off their chests about Socialism and the country going to the dogs. We talked him round, and he doesn't really mind. I thought I'd take a fortnight or so to look round, and then start in. I'm most horribly at sea, you know, about everything. I've got ten years to fill in." He gave a short laugh. "Talk about being knocked out of time! I've been knocked out of ten years of it—clean out." His tone was so harshly bitter that Evelyn's heart contracted. And then, all at once, he was saying lightly—"Have you got a tape-map? There's an address I want to look out—someone I've got to go and see."

When she had brought him the map, he spread it on the floor, shifted the table, and bent over it, saying the two numbers over once or twice just under his breath, Evelyn watched the rough, clumsy hands with the broken nails. As she watched them, her heart full of pity and trouble, he looked up unexpectedly and broke into a schoolboy grin:

"Beastly, aren't they?" he said cheerfully. Then he folded up the map and stood up, "Thanks awfully—and thanks for letting me come. I must get along now."

Evelyn put her hand in his, and felt a dreadfully strong grip which suddenly relaxed. As he went out of the door, she spoke to his back:

"Good-bye—Tony. I've decided to call you Tony."

Chapter Fourteen

WHEN THE DOOR had shut behind Laydon, Evelyn turned thoughtfully back into the room. She went first to the window, and stood there looking out. Grey houses; a stretch of grey, wet pavement; and a patch of wet, grey sky.

She saw Laydon come into view, walking with a quick, swinging step. When he had passed out of sight, she took away the tray that had held the flowers, and set the little table back against the wall. Then she took up the tape-indicator map to put it away. And as she did so, a scrap of paper dropped from it and fell to the floor. She picked it up, and saw a name and an address scrawled big across it:

PEARL PALLISER, 391 Morningdale Road.

She looked at it for a long time. Then she put the map away in a drawer, and sat down in the big arm-chair by the hearth, still holding the paper tightly.

There was a fire burning in the grate, a small, bright fire that sent out a pleasant warmth. Evelyn was quite horribly cold. After about five minutes she leaned forward and dropped the paper into the fire. For a moment it lay on the red embers, whilst a faint brown stain crept across white surface and pencilled scrawl. Then, with a little puff of flame, it was gone, leaving a thin, trembling sheet of black ash which suddenly fell away into nothingness.

Evelyn was cold because she had had a shock. If the red embers into which she stared had reproduced first the black ash, then the scorching sheet, and finally the white paper which she had thrown on them, she would hardly have been more startled. It was just over ten years since she had seen that address at the head of a letter and read Pearl Palliser's name signed at the foot of it.

She went down on her knees and spread her hands to the fire. It was all over long ago. But it had hurt so dreadfully at the time. Jack Laydon and she just three days engaged, and Lacy their only confidante. She had been so frightfully happy, so frightfully excited when the post came in and brought her his first letter. Phrases from it came back to her now: "I've never cared for anyone before. I never thought I could care for anyone like this"; and then lower down, "I've had a ripping letter from Lacy which I'm sending for you to see."

Evelyn had read her love-letter twice before she picked up and unfolded the enclosure, which was not from Lacy. It was headed 391 Morningdale Road. And it was signed "Pearl Palliser." Between heading and signature an extraordinary medley of abuse, appeal, and slang. Odd scraps of it rose up in Evelyn's mind: "Of course, if you've got off with an heiress—Jacky, you swore you loved me"; and at the end, "You needn't think I care, or that I can't get a dozen as good as you and better."

Evelyn drew her hands back sharply, because they were scorching. If Jack hadn't been the careless creature that he was, she would have married him, not Jim—married him in the spring of 1915.

The front door bell rang. When the maid showed Sir Henry Prothero in, Evelyn was standing looking down into the fire, a little pale, but ready to return an affectionate greeting and an affectionate kiss.

"What a nice surprise!"

"A surprise is it? I drove Laydon up, and told him to tell you I was coming round. I suppose he forgot."

"I suppose he did."

Sir Henry plunged straight into the middle of what he had come to say:

"Fact is, my dear, I was particularly anxious to see you. I couldn't catch you yesterday."

"I ran away," said Evelyn. "It's better to funk than to make a fool of yourself; and I couldn't stand another minute of it. Monkey was an angel; he drove me back to town, and let me cry all the way."

Sir Henry leaned forward and patted her shoulder. "Much the best thing you could do, my dear. And that brings me to what I was going to say. You went away so suddenly that no one had any opportunity of asking what you thought about it all."

Evelyn was silent.

"Did you, my dear, for instance, come to any—conclusion?"

She looked at him then, her blue eyes bright and dark.

"You mean, did I recognize him?"

"Well, I don't know that I meant quite so much as that. I think I meant just what I said—did you come to any conclusion?"

She did not answer, but, after looking at him for a little longer, turned away with an impatient movement.

"Why—I don't know what you mean."

"You see," said Sir Henry very gently, "as far as Sir Cotterell and the estate are concerned, the matter is really settled. But as regards yourself—well, it's all quite in the air."

A little flicker of colour showed in Evelyn's cheeks.

"If I don't know already just how delicate my position is, it isn't for want of telling. No, that's beastly of me, because you're a lamb, and you do really want to help. But, darling, have you any idea of how exasperating it is to be in a delicate position, and have everybody in the family telling you so and watching you through microscopes and telescopes and periscopes? It makes my blood boil, and it makes me want to go and do something frightfully compromising. So if you hear I've eloped, don't be surprised."

Sir Henry laughed.

"Where are you going to elope to?"

"Cologne, I think,—with Monkey. But don't tell anyone, please."

He looked surprised, then nodded.

"Lacy'll do the telling."

"Let her. It won't matter by then."

"Well, well," he said. "Now look here, my dear. I come into this matter from outside as it were, because I never saw the Laydon boys after they grew up, and even as boys I never really knew them. But you knew them intimately for years before you married Jim. And you haven't answered what I came here to ask you. There must be things that strike you one way or another, quite apart from features and what is ordinarily called a likeness—the little unconscious or half-conscious things, like the way a man gets up, comes into a room, shakes hands; and the things that spring out of character and temperament. Those are the things I want to know about."

"I can't help you," said Evelyn. "He's different—he isn't like either of them."

"H'm. Well, there's another thing—and you'll just have to forgive me for speaking about it. Laydon has the most extraordinary self-control, but when you came into the room yesterday he wanted every bit of it. Now, my dear, you have just to consider what that points to."

"It doesn't point to anything, I'm afraid."

"Why doesn't it?"

"Because they both—they both—cared."

"I didn't know that."

Evelyn looked up defiantly. There was a little moisture on her lashes.

"Lacy knew. She doesn't tell *everything*, you see, darling."

"H'm! Well, you've taken away my best clue. You're not very communicative, you know, Evelyn. And yet—" He passed his hand slowly over his chin and asked, "Which was the untidy one?"

"Jack," said Evelyn before she knew that she was going to answer him.

"He was? A bit careless too?"

"Yes."

Yes, Jack was careless enough, or she would never have seen that letter from "Pearl Palliser." Now Jim could no more have enclosed the wrong letter—Jim—With startling distinctness she saw the scrap of paper with the address on it, left carelessly between the folds of her map. She spoke suddenly, eagerly:

"Uncle Henry, darling, what's the good of all this? It's like trying to dig up things that are dead and buried. He isn't Jack, and he isn't Jim; he's someone who's lived ten years away from us in a dream and come back different. We can't dig things up and put them together again, and it's no use trying. If we could do it, I shouldn't want to do it. I don't want the past—it's gone, it's dead, I want to let it go. I want the present, and the future. And I want time—time for both of us. Don't you see, we've got to find our feet, and find out where we are and *what* we want?"

She came up close to him, looking extraordinarily beautiful, with the tears in her eyes and the colour in her cheeks.

"Don't let them rush us! That's the thing I'm most afraid of— being rushed before we know—before we know. Make them keep quiet! Make them leave us alone. You can if you will—but will you?"

Sir Henry put a large hand on her shoulder.

"My dear child," he said. "My dear child."

"Will you? Will you?" Her eyes were as insistent as her voice, insistent and yet soft.

"I'll do my best. And mind you, I think you're right, my dear—right, and wise. But, you know, it's all easier said than done. Families aren't so easily kept quiet."

"Darling, you're so frightfully clever. You can do it if you like. And if you think I'm right, you'll like doing it, and everything will be quite all right."

Evelyn said "Darling" in rather a charming way; there was just a little emphasis on the last syllable, a little inflection of the voice that took it right out of a form and made it very personal. Sir Henry was not unaffected by this charm. He patted his niece's shoulder and observed:

"Manning won't bother you. And I can manage Cotterell—I think I may say that I can manage Cotterell—for a time, you know. But I can't undertake to keep Cotty Abbott off the war-path."

Evelyn broke into a ripple of laughter. "I just saw Cotty with feathers in his hair and a tomahawk. And oh, wouldn't Sophy make a lovely squaw!" Then, suddenly grave and low-voiced: "Is Cotty on the war-path?"

"I'm afraid he is," said Sir Henry.

When Sir Henry Prothero had gone, Evelyn rang Manning up. She smiled when she heard his rather cross "Hullo!"

"It's me, Monkey—Evelyn. Do a nicer voice, please."

"My voice is my misfortune, not my fault."—It was still rather cross.

"Pouf!" said Evelyn. "That's a kiss I'm blowing you. Feel any better?"

"H'm. What do you want?"

"How dreadfully suspicious, Monkey!"

"It's not suspicion; it's certainty. It is the old married man who speaks. Lacy always wants something when she coos. What is it?"

"I think you're nearly too clever to live, Monkey—not quite, but nearly."

"Woman, *what* do you want?"

"I want to come to Cologne with you."

"An elopement?"

"With Lacy at the other end—yes."

"My good girl, why?"

Her voice dropped half a tone.

"I want to see Anna Blum."

She heard Manning whistle. Then he said:

"The deuce you do! Well, I'm off to-morrow. What about a passport?"

"Oh, Pat Winter'll manage that for me. I'll ring him up. What about your job—have you got it?"

"Yes, worse luck." He sounded very cross indeed. "Lacy'll like it; but I shan't—regular office-stool, nose-in-the-ledger stunt."

"Lacy'll love it," said Evelyn with conviction.

Chapter Fifteen

LACY MANNING sat curled up in a big arm-chair one foot dangling, the other tucked beneath her. The electric lamp on the table behind her diffused a becomingly shaded light over the slim, rose-coloured figure. Lacy was sewing, and as her hand moved to and fro, her rings caught the light and sent it back in sparkles of blue, and red, and green. The dangling foot wore a golden shoe.

"You know, Evelyn," said Lacy, "you know Monkey was simply *fiendish* to me about the whole thing. Now I'm sure he told you a whole lot of nonsense about my being quite muddled— I'm *sure* he did." She took little, vicious stitches that stabbed the fine white stuff on which she was sewing.

Evelyn, in the opposite chair, laughed a little. She was leaning back, her arms along the arms of the chair, her head tilted against a brilliant emerald cushion. This vivid green and the golden lights in her hair alone broke from the shadow which covered half the room.

Lacy, frowning and looking across at her cousin, could not really see whether Evelyn smiled or not.

"Didn't he?" she repeated. "I *know* he did, because I know what a fiend Monkey can be."

Evelyn laughed again.

"And weren't you muddled, Lacy?"

Lacy stopped sewing.

"No, of course not—not *really*. Of course, just at first—just for the minute, you know,—well, it was really *too* bewildering. What would anyone feel like if they opened their own dining-room door and saw a perfectly strange person about eight feet high, in a counterpane and a *beard*, calling them 'Lacy.'"

"Poor old Lacy!"

"I fainted," said Lacy with modest pride—"*naturally*. And afterwards—well, of course it *was* most dreadfully agitating. I mean, when I really did see him—next day, you know—I kept thinking of you, darling; and of course I couldn't help feeling upset and confused. But afterwards—*afterwards*, when I thought it all over, I wasn't a bit confused; and I made up my mind then—I don't care what Monkey says—I made it up *then* and *there*."

"Did you?"

"Yes, I *did*. You know, Evelyn, Monkey doesn't believe a bit in woman's intuition. And *I* believe in it *most firmly*. Don't you?"

"Depends, my child."

"What do you mean?"

"Well, supposing your woman's intuition said one thing, and mine said another?"

"You're laughing at me. I didn't think you'd *laugh* about a thing like this."

Evelyn's left hand just rose and fell again. There was a dark gleam from the one ring she wore above her wedding-ring, a dark emerald gleam.

"If I couldn't laugh—"

"Well, *I* couldn't. I think you're frightfully hard to understand, Evelyn."

Evelyn laughed quite naturally.

"I know—'Life is real, life is earnest.' "Well what did your woman's intuition say?"

Lacy pressed her lips together. Her eyebrows rose, making perfect arches over dark, reproachful eyes.

"You know you mean to tell me, so you'd better out with it."

Evelyn's voice was lazily teasing, but her hands tightened a little on the chintz-covered arms of her chair.

"I tell you because I think you ought to be told, and because— Evelyn, when I went over it all in my own mind afterwards, I was sure, *quite* sure, which one of them it *was.*"

"Were you?"

"Yes, I was."

"And which was it?"

"Oh, I'm sure that he's *Jack*," said Lacy in her high, sweet voice. She dropped her work and gazed in Evelyn's direction, wishing with all her heart that she could see her cousin's face, and not just golden hair against a green cushion. All the light seemed drawn to a focus about her own rose-coloured figure. The other side of the room was deeply washed with shadow; the chair in which Evelyn sat looked black and formless. Evelyn in her dark dress was just a shadow in the shadow; her hands, on the arms of the chair, showed pale against the dusk background; her face was a pale oval whose features could hardly be discerned.

"Jack?" said Evelyn. Her voice was quite toneless.

"Yes, I'm sure he's Jack—I'm quite *sure*, Evelyn."

"Why—Jack?"

"That's what I want to tell you. I've had plenty of time to think about it, you know, with Monkey away; and the more I think about it, the more *certain* I am."

"But why?"

Lacy leaned forward, needle in hand, her colour bright and clear.

"I'll tell you. I think you *ought* to know. You know that horrid paragraph in the *Weekly Whisper*?"

"Yes."

"Well, I brought the paper over with me to show Monkey; and he was so *furious* that he just pitched it into a corner of the room."

"But I don't see what that's got to do—"

"*Wait!* I'm telling you. Monkey pitched it on to a chair. Well, when I came in—it all happened in the dining-room, you know— when I came in and saw *him*, Jack,—only of course I never thought of it's being Jack till afterwards, what with the beard and the counterpane, and his saying 'Lacy,' and my fainting—"

"Yes—go on."

"I *am* going on, darling." Lacy's voice was reproachful. "I *am* telling you, and you *mustn't* interrupt. Well, when I went in and he said 'Lacy!', I saw that wretched paper all crumpled up on the floor; and it wasn't where Monkey had thrown it at all, but over by the window, right in front of the bureau."

"Oh!" It wasn't a word, but a sharply indrawn breath.

"I didn't think of it at the time because of it's all being so frightfully upsetting. But afterwards I thought of it a *lot*. And I'm sure, I'm *quite* sure that he'd picked it up and read the paragraph about you, and then he'd scrumpled it and thrown it down in a fury just like Monkey did." She drew a long complacent breath and leaned back. "So that's why I'm quite sure it's *Jack*."

"Oh," said Evelyn again; and then, "You know, you've left out a good deal. Suppose you fill in the gaps. I don't see why he should be Jack just because he read that disgusting paragraph—if he did read it."

"I'm *sure* he read it. Don't you see that it explains everything? He read the paragraph, and he realized that he'd been away for ten years." She shuddered lightly. "I think it's horribly creepy. That's the *first* thing he'd take in. And then he'd see from that paragraph that you weren't married yet, but that you—well, that you were thinking about it, or at any rate that people *thought* you were thinking about it. Oh, Evelyn, don't you *see*? He always *adored* you. Poor Jack! He *did*—you know he did. And I never could make out why you threw him over. Don't you see, all in the same moment it must have come home to him that he'd been away ten years, and that you were a widow, and that he'd got a chance again if only he could gain *time*?"

"Time!" said Evelyn. "Time!" There was a note of bitterness in the pretty, quiet voice. "After ten years—time, more time!"

"*Yes*," said Lacy, speaking eagerly. "You see, he'd want time more than anything. If he could only stop you getting engaged to anyone else, don't you *see*—and of course you couldn't get engaged to anyone else as long as you didn't know whether you were a widow or not—Evelyn, you *must* see."

As the disjointed sentences tumbled over one another, Evelyn sat up and leaned forward, her hands pressed together on her knees.

"Lacy, stop! You don't know what you're saying!"

"Yes, I do."

"You're talking as if he knew who he was all the time, and was just pretending not to know in order—"

"To gain time!" Lacy too leaned forward. "That's exactly what I *do* mean. Why, Evelyn, do you mean to tell me that you—*you* can believe for a single instant that he *doesn't* know who he is?" She gave a little, excited laugh. "Oh, my dear, you can't, you really can't believe it! Those stupid men can swallow it if they like. But don't tell me that *you* believe in it. If he'd just lost his memory, and didn't know who he was at all—that would be quite another pair of shoes. But to tell me that he's either Jack or Jim, and *doesn't know which*—no, I'd *never* be able to believe that, not if I lived to be three *hundred*. No, I'm sure, sure, *sure* that he's Jack. And oh, Evelyn, you will make him happy and not keep him waiting too long, won't you? You see,"—Lacy's torrent of words slowed down a little—"it's quite *simple*. And I can't see what you've got to wait for. If it's Jack, all you have to do is to marry him. And really, my dear, even if it was Jim, I should advise your having another wedding, just in *case*—"

"*Don't*, Lacy!" The words came with a gasp; and as they came, Evelyn was on her feet and half way towards the door.

Lacy stared after her, on the edge of offence. But when the door opened and shut again sharply, she smiled and nodded to herself.

"I believe she's *frightfully* in love with him," she said. "And of course it's Jack—it always *was*."

Manning, busy over his correspondence in the dining-room, looked up from a half-written letter with a scowl which was meant to discourage Lacy, in case she should be—as she usually was—in a conversational mood. Instead of Lacy he saw Evelyn. She had her hand on the door, and it was evident that something had shaken her. There was no colour in her face, and her breathing was quick and irregular.

Now what had Lacy been saying, was Manning's thought as he swung round in his chair with a "Well, what is it?"

Evelyn tried to force a smile, but her trembling lips betrayed her. She stood where she was, and said,

"Monkey!"

Manning came across to her.

"What's the matter, old girl?"

"Monkey, did he read it? Do you think he read it?"

"He?—oh, Laydon. Did he read what?"

"That horrible paper. Lacy says he did." There was just the faintest quiver in the low voice.

"What paper? I'm afraid I haven't got there."

Evelyn put one hand to her throat.

"The paper with that paragraph in it—about me. Lacy showed it to you. Monkey, do you think he read it? She seems to think he did."

Monkey gave a long whistle of dismay. Lacy deserved a spanking for this. Too bad of her—yes, really too bad!

"My dear girl, why should he have read it?"

"It was here? He might have read it?"

Manning screwed up his face.

"I suppose so. How on earth can I tell? My dear girl, what does it matter? Who's going to take any notice of what that sort of rag has got to say about anyone? It's all lies anyhow."

Evelyn lifted blank, pathetic eyes.

"Do you think he read it? Lacy's sure he read it. It—it wasn't just lies, you know, Monkey. If it was, I wouldn't mind. But it wasn't. I *was* thinking about Chris; and I had really made up my mind that I would marry him. I thought he wouldn't be like most men. I—I haven't got what most men want. But I'm fond of Chris, and I didn't think he'd be one of the demanding sort—" She broke off and put her hand on his arm.

"All right, old girl—steady!"

A very faint smile trembled on her lips for an instant.

"I want you to know"—the smile trembled away—"I've been so frightfully lonely—I didn't think I could go on. And Chris—it wouldn't have been fair with most men, you know,—taking a lot, and not giving very much isn't fair. But Chris"—she laughed very faintly—"he's so fond of himself that I didn't think he'd miss what I hadn't got to give. Only when it came to the point I couldn't do it. That's what I wanted you to know. I'd refused him before I got your letter—I really had."

She gave his arm a convulsive squeeze and ran out of the room without another word.

Chapter Sixteen

MANNING DROVE Evelyn out to the Königswald next day. She had not seen him alone since the evening before. As soon as they were clear of the traffic she turned to him and said,

"I made a fool of myself last night—I'm sorry."

"Nonsense!" said Manning.

Evelyn laughed.

"What a nice, polite host!"

Manning scowled.

"I'm not."

"You are. The perfect host, polite and polished. You do Lacy great credit, you know." Then her voice changed. "You hated it like poison—you know you did."

"Why dig it up?"

"Well, I just wanted to say—" She stopped, biting her lip; quite suddenly her smile came out—a delightful smile, as sunny as a spring day. "I *did* make a fool of myself, and I don't want you to have a wrong idea about what I said. I mean I don't want you to think I just go on being stupid and unhappy all the time. I don't, you know; I—I'm afraid I can't. Some people can, but I can't. I can't go *on* being unhappy. I can be as miserable as anyone for a bit, but I can't go on with it; I—I get bored."

He looked at her and saw her eyes full of tears, and behind the tears a twinkle. She nodded at him and winked away a very bright drop.

"I get spasms of being lonely—like toothache. And then it stops, and everything seems pretty good again—you know, nice people like you and Lacy, and one's bulbs coming up, and kittens, and babies, and things like that. I simply can't go on morbing. Is that dreadful?"

Manning glared at the radiator cap.

"For the Lord's sake, don't talk rot!" he said violently. "Thank heaven you're normal, and not one of those beastly, morbid people who spend their time with their heads screwed round backwards looking into the past. Women love doing it—simply love it, the same as they love making scenes."

"Monkey!"

"You do. All women love scenes, same as all men detest 'em. The proper place for Woman—Woman with a capital W, my dear— is melodrama. She loves every minute of it, because any proper melodrama is just a series of scenes one after the other, all deuced painful and harrowing, with the heroine bang in the lime-light."

"Monkey, you fiend!"

He gave her a malicious grin.

"You don't like it because it's true. Talking of melodrama, I saw a topping one once, where the villain kept on following the girl all round the stage; and every time she said 'Unhand me!' he came out with 'I will not tell herrr I have killed herrr fatherrr' in one of the best parade voices I've ever heard. He'd corpsed the old man a little earlier in the same scene, and he and the girl had to dodge Father's boots every time they crossed the stage."

He slowed down and pointed with his left hand.

"That's where the bank fell in."

Evelyn looked. Her mind filled with the picture of the pitch dark, rainy night. They drove on in silence. When the car stopped she got out without a word, took off her fur coat, and threw it down on the back seat.

"Sure you'd rather go alone?" said Manning.

"Yes, quite sure."

"Well, it's no distance—straight on up that path until you come to the clearing."

Evelyn walked slowly up the path. It was cold and damp among the trees—cold and damp and still. She wished that she had kept her coat. She wished that she were already face to face with Anna Blum. She wished that she had not come.

Anna Blum was washing up. When she heard the knock at the door she took her red hands out of the steaming water and called, *"Herein!"*

The door was pushed a little, timidly, and there was a second knock. Anna dried her hands and went to the door, wondering who might be there. Not someone from the village. No, certainly not someone from the village—and Mina would not knock. She saw Evelyn first as a slim, dark figure, then as a girl with a young, beautiful face and anxious eyes. The eyes looked at her, and a pretty voice said in halting German:

"Are you Frau Blum—Frau Anna Blum?"

"Certainly."

Anna still held the door in one moist, steaming hand.

"May I come in?"

"Certainly," said Anna again; and this time she let go of the door and stood back.

Evelyn took the chair which Anna set for her and there was a little silence. It was broken by Anna.

"You are English, Fräulein?"

"Yes," said Evelyn. Then she smiled. "My German is so bad; I have not spoken it since I was a child."

Anna nodded.

"Since you are English, it is because of Anton you are come. *Na?*"

"Yes."

Anna had remained standing by the table. Now she drew forward her usual chair, and sat down just where she had sat on the night of the storm while Manning questioned her. This girl too would ask questions no doubt. Perhaps she was a sister. Yes, she must be Anton's sister.

"If we are to talk, it will be better if we can understand one another," she said. "When I talk like this, can you understand me, Fräulein?"

"Yes, I can understand."

Anna picked up her knitting.

"That is famous. I will speak in German, and you can speak in English. Oh, yes, I understand English very well. I can even talk it—very much as you talk German, Fräulein. But each will be happier in her own language—*nicht wahr?*"

Evelyn said 'Yes,' and was increasingly aware of Anna's command of the situation. It was Anna, not she, who would conduct this interview; and what Anna desired to say would be said, no more and no less.

Evelyn had not felt so much at a loss for years. She sat with her hands in her lap, waiting. Anna finished a row, and began another before she spoke:

"You wished to see me, Fräulein—to talk?"

"Yes, Frau Blum."

"Tell me then what it is that you want?"

Evelyn felt her colour rise. A rush of emotion gave her words.

"You saved his life—you took care of him all those years—I wanted to see you."

Anna's face did not change. The needles clicked steadily.

"Is he well?" she asked.

"Yes."

"He wrote to me," said Anna with a tinge of pride in her voice. "He said that he was well, and that his grandfather had acknowledged him." She bent a sudden, direct look on Evelyn. "Of you, Fräulein, he said nothing. Are you his sister?"

Evelyn pulled off her left-hand glove and held out the hand with the wedding-ring upon it.

"I am married. I am Jim Laydon's wife."

"Jim." Anna repeated the word in a slow, meditative fashion.

"Frau Blum," said Evelyn, "I've come here to ask you a question. May I ask it? And before you answer it, will you think what the answer means to me? He says he doesn't know whether he is Jim Laydon or Jack Laydon. And I—I am Jim Laydon's wife. You can think what that means. He's come back like this; and I don't know whether I'm his wife, or whether I've been a widow for ten years."

Anna Blum went on knitting.

"*Herr Je!* You look so young!" she said.

Evelyn made an impatient gesture.

"I was eighteen when we were married. I'm twenty-eight now, Frau Blum."

"You look very young," said Anna placidly.

"Frau Blum, *please*."

"You have not asked me anything yet."

"No, but I'm going to. And you will—you will try and remember, won't you? It's so terribly important."

"I will do my best."

"The thing I want to ask is this. His identity disc"—she put her hand to her throat—"you know, the medal with the name. They all had it—your people too. What happened to it?"

Anna's gaze was candid.

"*Ach, ja*—that? It was in my statement; the *Herr Major* can show it to you. I took it from his neck and put it with his clothes at the top of the waterfall where my poor nephew was drowned."

"Yes, I know. But, Frau Blum—the name. If you took it from him, if you had it in your hand, there was the name on it. Didn't you—didn't you see the name?"

Anna shook her head.

"All was as I told the *Herr Major*. I took it from his neck, and I put it with the clothes by the waterfall. There is nothing else to say."

Evelyn was leaning forward, her hands stretched out, palm upwards.

"Frau Blum, you *must* have seen the name. Think what it means to me!"

"That is what you all say—must, must—I must have seen it—I must have read the name."

Evelyn felt that she was being spoken to as if she were a child; Anna's tone was so good-humoured and unhurried.

"*Na*, I will tell you just how it was, and you will see whether there was that *must*"—she used the English word—"I will tell you. And you have to think that there was a great storm, and that I was alone with him in a dark house, and nothing but one small light to see by. It is very easy to say *must*. But I was there with a wounded man, and all my work cut out to get the clothes off him and get him to bed. Then when I had done it, I remembered the medal, and I took it off his neck. There was just the one little light, and the draught blew it here and there. I took the medal in my hand, and I looked at it; and where the name was, blood had run down from his wound and dried. That's the truth. I didn't touch it or wash it off. I did not tell that to the *Herr Major*, because very certainly he would have said 'Why did you not wash it? Why did you not look?'" Anna nodded gently over the clicking needles. "Yes, he would have said that. Men do not understand these things; but you perhaps will understand. Quite suddenly it came to me that I did not want to touch it, or to know who he was. Perhaps there has been a time when you have felt like that or—perhaps not. But that is the truth, and if you like, I will put my hand on the Bible and swear that it is so."

"You didn't see anything at all?" Evelyn was a little breathless. She believed Anna. It was impossible to sit there looking at Anna, listening to Anna, without feeling convinced that every word was true. "Didn't you see anything at all?"

There was a quiet pause. The room felt still, unnaturally still. No room should feel like that in the day-time.

Anna had dropped her knitting on to her knee.

"Yes, one thing I saw." The words came with great deliberation.

"Please, Frau Blum, *please*."

Anna looked at her. Behind the quiet composure of this look she had her thoughts. She looked at Evelyn, and the thoughts clamoured in her; they were like creatures behind bars. Fortunately the bars were very strong. "You are beautiful, and you are young"— that's what the thoughts said—"Young and beautiful, and perhaps you think that you love him, that you know how to love him. *Mein Gott!* How should you know how to love him? Presently you will take happiness from him, and love from him; and because you are happy you will think that you know how to love him. I have taken nothing. And I am not young, and I am not beautiful. You will take; but you cannot give as I have given, because I have given everything—the love of my country and the love of my own folk, and the friendship of my neighbours, all given, all gone. And it will never come back. And he will never come back. So now I have nothing."

The thoughts did not pass into words in Anna's mind. They were present as feeling only, and this feeling had something high and proud that mixed with the pain and helped her to bear it.

"Please, *please*, Frau Blum," said Evelyn quivering. She felt that she could not support Anna's gaze for another instant—Anna's calm, serious gaze. "Oh, please," she whispered—"*please*."

Anna took up her knitting again.

"I saw one letter. It was a 'J.' That does not help you?"

Evelyn put her hands over her face. After a moment's silence she said,

"No, that doesn't help at all."

She felt the tears run down behind her hands—hot, burning tears. She did not cry easily; and yet, now she was crying, she could not have said why. She believed Anna, but she did not understand Anna. She had the feeling that in this room, just beyond her reach, there was something vital to her happiness, and that no effort of hers could bring it within her grasp. After a moment she dried her eyes.

"I am sorry," she said. "I hoped so much that you would know."

Anna said nothing.

"I hoped—" said Evelyn. Then her hand tightened on the wet, rolled-up handkerchief it held, and she stopped. When she could trust her voice, she leaned forward. "There was one other thing I wanted to ask you. Major Manning said you told him that once or twice in the years Anton was with you—you said—you told him, that he had talked—when he was ill. I wanted to ask you about that."

"*Ach, ja,*" said Anna. "That is true."

"Then will you tell me about it? If he talked and you heard what he said, it might be such a help. You see that, don't you?"

"Certainly. But what he said would not help you—no."

"If you would tell me! *Please* tell me."

"Certainly I will tell you." Always the calm friendly voice, the calm, assured manner. "I will tell you, but it will not help. There were three times that he spoke, as I told the *Herr Major*—once before we came here; and once after; and once at the very beginning of all. The two last times"—she shrugged her shoulders—"*Na,* it was nothing. Perhaps you have heard someone speak in their sleep, quick and indistinct, so that no one could tell what the words are—a sound of words, but not real words at all. Well, it was like that. I could not tell you whether the sound was like German or like English. I think he dreamt that he was talking, and made a sound. I do not think there were any words to hear."

"And the first time?" said Evelyn quickly. "Tell me about that."

Anna was silent for a moment; she did not know whether to speak or not. She knitted her row to the end, and considered the matter. After all, it was only a word or two; and perhaps if she spoke, this girl would go away satisfied. Anna wanted her to go before Josef came in. "Yes, the first time was different. But it will not help you."

"Please, *please* tell me."

"Yes, I will tell you. It was towards morning on the first night, the night of the storm. It was still dark, and he was tossing this way and that and very restless. I did not dare to leave him in case he should get up and wander out into the forest. He began to mutter to himself. And then, all at once, he said words that I could hear, the same words over and over. He went on saying them for a long time, perhaps for half an hour. And then he fell asleep. And after that he never spoke a word that anyone could understand."

"What did he say?"

"I will tell you, but it will not help you—you will see," Anna fixed her eyes on Evelyn's flushed and eager face. "He said, in English like this: 'Pearl—I must go—Pearl—I must go,' just like that, over and over."

"You are *sure*?" Evelyn's voice dried in her throat. The last word was hardly said.

Anna saw all the colour pass from her face.

"Yes, I am sure. I told you that it would not help. Over and over he said it, just like I have said: 'Pearl—I must go.' I told you it would not help."

Evelyn pressed a handkerchief to her lips. She got up slowly. The room was full of mist. It would be dreadful to faint here. The words she had just heard rang in her ears like bells: "I must go—I must go." She repeated them mechanically. And then Anna was opening the door. Evelyn crossed the threshold and came out into the cold, still air. She did not know whether she spoke again to Anna. She went down the path with one word ringing in her ears— Pearl—Pearl—Pearl....

Chapter Seventeen

EVELYN FOUND Jessica Sunning at the flat when she got back to town. She was very glad to see her. Jessica fussed over her tartly, asked a great many questions about things that did not matter in the least, and did not so much as mention Laydon's name. It was very restful to hear Jessica raging because there was a cobweb on her bedroom cornice, and to be brought hot soup, and to have her suit-case unpacked, and to be scolded vehemently for the way she had crushed a tea-gown.

Jessica did everything vehemently. She was a little, peaked creature with sharp, transparent features and short, tossed hair gone prematurely grey. She had scolded Evelyn incessantly for the past five years, and loved her with an intense devotion.

Evelyn fell asleep after her journey, feeling that it was pleasant to be at home again. In the morning, when breakfast had been disposed of, Jessica planted herself on the hearth-rug in a manly attitude, and said in her quick staccato:

"I suppose you know your beastly cousin, Cotty Abbott, has been here every single moment of the day and night, wanting to know when you were coming back."

"He's not my cousin, and how should I know?" said Evelyn. Then she added with a gurgle, "I wonder Sophy let him."

"Sophy's been round too. When it wasn't one, it was the other—sometimes both. *Now* when the bell rings, I just say 'Damn' and bolt,—it's certain to be one of them, and a little of your Cousin Cotty goes a long, long way."

Evelyn looked worried.

"I don't want to see Cotty. Why should I see Cotty? I *never* want to see Cotty."

"Cotty wants to see you," said Jessica grimly. "You're for it, my child. He's a sticker, Cotty is. Damn! What's the odds that's him now?"

The bell rang its peal to the end, and Jessica darted to the drawing-room door.

"Oh, Jess, *stay*!" wailed Evelyn.

"Not I!" Jessica whisked away as the maid came into the hall. A moment later Evelyn was having her hand pressed by Cotty Abbott, whose tight hand-shake was one of the things which endeared him to his relatives. "Beastly feeling having your hand held on to as if it was a bone and Cotty was a dog," Jack Laydon had said once long ago.

Evelyn detached her fingers, resisted the temptation to rub them, and sat down. Cotty sat down too, stiffly erect and rather on the edge of his chair. He was dressed with extreme correctness, and wore a ceremonial manner.

"I am very glad to find you here," he observed. Cotty didn't say things; he made observations and remarks. "Miss—er—Sunning will perhaps have told you that I've called here several times during your absence. She was rather—er—indefinite as to the probable date of your return."

"Yes, she didn't know. You wanted to see me?"

"Yes, I wanted to see you most particularly—er—most particularly."

Of all the unconscionable hours to want to see one *most particularly*! The sound of Ponson clearing breakfast could be heard from the next room, and the sound of Jessica clattering the fire-irons, a thing she was very prone to do when annoyed.

Cotty Abbott gazed at Evelyn solemnly, cleared his throat, and remarked,

"Your position, my dear Evelyn, is, if I may say so, one of great delicacy." He cleared his throat again. "As I said to Sophy only this morning, 'Evelyn's position in this matter is really one of extreme delicacy.'"

"And what did Sophy say?" Evelyn looked down to hide an exasperated twinkle.

"Sophy agreed with me—she agreed with me fully. She said that she really failed to recall a situation of similar delicacy in her—in fact, in all her wide social experience."

"Oh—" said Evelyn. Cotty made her want to scream. And the worst of being properly brought up is that you can't scream when you want to.

"As Sophy said to me from the very beginning: 'It is your undoubted duty to speak to Evelyn.' 'My unpleasant duty,' I said. And Sophy thereupon reminded me that it was not my habit to shirk any duty merely because it was unpleasant. All the Mendip-ffollintons hold very strong views indeed on points like these—er—very strong views indeed."

"What did you want to say to me?"

Cotty drew himself a trifle more erect.

"My dear Evelyn, it's not what I want to say, but what I feel it my duty to say. As I pointed out to the children at a local gathering in the school-house the other day—a festive occasion, in fact a treat very generously given by Sir John Tipton, but I was asked to say a few words, to—er—in point of fact, address them—as I said to the children: 'Duty—er—is—er—at once the mainstay and the—er—sheet anchor of the British character. In—er—duty our national institutions have their roots, their growth, their—er—foliage,—and their fruitage.' Sophy considered that I had put it very happily."

Evelyn felt a little bewildered—one did with Cotty; he digressed so much that one did not always know whether one was listening to quotations from Sophy, or from a speech, or to something which Cotty really wanted to say to you.

"Which bit of that was what you wanted to say to me, Cotty?" she asked with a charming smile.

Cotty pursued his way:

"No, as Sophy said, I am not the man to shirk an unpleasant duty. And as I said to Sophy, 'She ought to know—Evelyn certainly ought to know.' Tom Mendip-ffollinton thought so too."

"My dear Cotty, if you would tell me what it is that I ought to know."

"Tom Mendip-ffollinton was very strongly of the opinion that you should be fully informed—all the Mendip-ffollintons have very strong opinions. He added that he considered your position an extremely delicate one, and that you had his fullest sympathy."

Evelyn felt a strange ingratitude for Mr Thomas Mendip-ffollinton's sympathy. She felt her colour rise and her voice lift as she said:

"I do wish you'd tell me what you've come to say. If it's unpleasant, do let's get it over."

Mr Abbott looked reproachful. His little grey eyes and his tufted eyebrows registered a considerable degree of reproach. What was the use of being delicate and making a tactful approach to an unpleasant subject? Tact and delicacy were entirely wasted on the modern young woman. Sophy had said as much only yesterday—

and Sophy was always right. Very well, he would throw tact aside and be brutally frank.

"I believe"—his voice was stiff—"that the—er—claimant paid you a visit here just before you went abroad?"

"The who?" said Evelyn. There was a sparkle of anger in her blue eyes.

"The—er—claimant."

"Do you mean Anthony Laydon?"

"I mean the—er—person who claims to be Jack or Jim Laydon. No, my dear Evelyn, your warmth does not offend me. But I would wish you to hear me before you indulge it. This—er—person—"

"No, Cotty!" said Evelyn. She sat bolt upright, her blue eyes blazing in what Cotty Abbott considered a most unsuitable manner. Blue eyes should be mild and gentle: Evelyn's were at the moment brilliant with anger. "No, Cotty!" she repeated. "It's no use. If you're going to talk of him in that ridiculous way, I shan't listen. You can call him Laydon, or Anthony, or Tony—I don't care which—, and I'll listen to anything you've got to say in reason. But I just can't do with 'claimants' and 'persons.'" She melted into a laugh and nodded at him. "So that's that, Cotty."

Cotty was considerably taken aback. After his forbearance and tact, to be treated like this! Modern manners, modern young women—Sophy had no opinion of them. He hemmed loudly and held up a protesting hand.

"Really, my dear Evelyn, really!"

"Yes, really, Cotty." Evelyn's anger had passed, and her smile was a disarming one. "Let's get on. You were saying that Anthony Laydon came here to see me. What about it?"

"I was not so much referring to his coming here; though, as Sophy says, in your position—"

Evelyn laughed.

"Yes, I know. But we'd really finished with my delicate position, hadn't we? Couldn't we go on to something else?"

"I was about to say that I was not so much concerned with—er—the visit to you as with the subsequent visits paid by Mr—er—Laydon."

"What on earth do you mean by subsequent visits? And how do you come to know anything about them?"

Cotty Abbott tapped his knee—Sir Cotterell's gesture, a little exaggerated.

"I would like to make it quite clear to you, Evelyn, that I do not accept Mr—er—Laydon as a member of the Laydon family. I do not believe him to be a Laydon at all, but a very different person. And this being my conviction, I conceive it no less than my duty to inform myself as fully as possible with regard to his movements."

"What do you mean?"

"I mean that I have placed the affair in the hands of thoroughly competent private investigators, with the result that I already feel abundantly justified in having taken these measures."

Whilst Cotty was speaking, Evelyn passed from anger to a sort of chill fear. What was coming next? She could not find any words to ask.

Cotty went on, well pleased with his own acumen.

"Abundantly justified," he repeated. "For where, I ask you, did this man proceed after leaving your flat?"

"My dear Cotty, why ask me?"

A look of annoyance crossed Cotty Abbott's face—rhetorical questions are not intended to be answered. He cleared his throat.

"Upon leaving this flat, he proceeded at once to the Upton Street registry office, where he inspected the records of marriages for the years 1913–14. From the registry office he proceeded to 391 Morningdale Road, where he inquired whether Miss Pearl Palliser still lodged there, adding that it was possible that she might be calling herself Mrs Field."

Evelyn bit her lip, but not quickly enough; a little sharp sound betrayed her surprise.

"Yes, Mrs Field—Miss Pearl Palliser or Mrs James Field—that was the form of his inquiry. It appeared that the lady had moved some years before, but the people of the house were on friendly terms with her and knew where she was staying. They furnished Mr—er—Laydon with the address, and he went straight on. On arrival he repeated his inquiries, was told that Miss Palliser was in, and went up to her room, where he remained for nearly half an hour. When he had gone, the detective went up and knocked at the door. He was, I believe, primed with some excuse, but he had no need to employ it. When Miss Palliser opened the door of her room it was evident that she had been weeping violently and was still in a good deal of distress. She used some very remarkable words. As I said to Sophy: 'Certainly remarkable, and probably conclusive,'" Cotty paused, savouring his triumph.

"What did she say?" Evelyn tried hard for a level voice, but it shook.

"She said, 'Oh, for the Lord's sake, go away! I've just seen a ghost.' And she banged the door in his face. Remarkable words, I think."

Evelyn said nothing.

"Certainly remarkable—and taken in conjunction with what follows, I think, conclusive. The detective"—Cotty was really enjoying himself a good deal—"returned to the Upton Street registry office, where he examined the register with this result—he found that on December the seventh, 1914, a marriage had taken place there between Pearl Harriet May Palliser and James Calthrop Field. As Sophy says, that is surely a remarkable piece of evidence."

Evelyn had the sensation of being in a very thick fog. It is no use hitting out at a fog; and it is no use to try and run away. What on earth was Cotty driving at? And what on earth did he think he was proving, with his detective, and his registry office, and all this rigmarole about poor Jim Field having married Pearl Palliser?

Later on Cotty confided to Sophy that he did not consider Evelyn Laydon at all an intelligent young woman: "She looked at me blankly, and seemed incapable of following what I really considered was a very lucid chain of reasoning."

At the moment, he remarked tartly, "Surely you see the inevitable conclusion to be drawn from these facts?"

"I'm afraid I don't."

For the second time Cotty determined to be brutally frank.

"My dear Evelyn, it is surely obvious—to Sophy and myself it appears quite obvious—that this man is neither Jack Laydon nor Jim Laydon, but simply Jim Field."

Evelyn sat up quite straight.

"Oh, no," she said.

"Ah, you say 'Oh, no' because you have not fully grasped what I have been endeavouring to convey."

"Jim Field? Nonsense!"

Cotty rapped his knee.

"Sophy and I have suspected as much from the beginning. It was Sophy who, whilst we were looking at some old groups and snapshots, pointed out to me that this man bore far more resemblance to Jim Field than to either of the Laydons. She spoke at first quite casually; we were looking at the photographs and she said, 'He is not like either of them. Now if he were claiming to be this young fellow, he would have more to go upon.' And then she asked, 'By the way, who is this? He seems to be in all the groups. Who is he?' And it was Jim Field. Tom Mendip-ffollinton was in the room, and he came and leaned over us and said, 'Remarkable, very—very remarkable.' This was the—er—germ of the idea, if I may so phrase it,—the—er—germ. As Sophy said, it came with a flash. We then proceeded to develop it and—er—examine it. It was, if I may say so, amazing that it had not struck us all before. As Sophy said to me: 'Nothing—nothing could be plainer.'"

"Nonsense!" said Evelyn again.

"You have not yet examined the facts, the—er—data. Jim Field, though a year older than the Laydons, was at school and college with them, and a most constant visitor at Laydon Manor. He was in the same squadron in the Flying Corps, and was one of the three who were missing on the fifteenth of November, 1915. The man who has been representing himself to be a Laydon had no proof to offer except the fact that he recognized various members of the family, and was familiar with a number of names and circumstances with which Jim Field would have been equally familiar. One of his first actions is to look up the entry of Jim Field's marriage to this Miss Palliser, whom I seem to remember by repute as a favourite of the music-hall stage a good many years ago. And he then proceeds to pay the lady a visit, asking for her in the name of Mrs Field. There, my dear Evelyn! You can, I think, no longer say 'Nonsense!' to all that."

Evelyn propped her chin in her hand and spoke quietly:

"I beg your pardon. You're making a mistake, of course. But I see how you got there. What you don't see is that there might be a perfectly natural explanation. Don't you see that if Jack or Jim knew that Jim Field was married, the first thing they would do would be to look up his widow?"

A small, superior smile appeared for a moment on Cotty Abbott's face.

"I'm afraid, my dear Evelyn, that you have overlooked Miss Palliser's very remarkable words. Whilst undoubtedly labouring under extremely strong emotion she—er—stated that she had just seen a ghost. As I said to Sophy, we cannot of course take such a statement literally. What she most undoubtedly meant was that she had just seen some person whom she had previously supposed to be dead. Certainly that was her meaning. As Tom Mendip-ffollinton observed—"

Evelyn's desire to avoid hearing this observation brought her to her feet.

"Cotty, do stop! You've got it all wrong." She walked to the fire, poked it, and turned round, her colour high and her eyes bright. "You've really got the whole thing topsy-turvy. I don't know whether Pearl Palliser knew Jim—I think she must have known him—met him anyhow—, but this I do know for certain—she and Jack Laydon knew each other very well, very well indeed."

Cotty got up too.

"I do not see that that affects the question at all."

"Go away and think it over," said Evelyn.

Cotty stared at her with an air of offence.

"Do I understand you to imply that you believe this man to be Jack Laydon?"

"I didn't say so." She turned round and put the poker down; it fell with a little crash.

"Let me understand your meaning: If not Jim Field or Jack Laydon, there remains only Jim Laydon. Are you prepared to state that you recognize him as Jim Laydon—as your husband?"

"He has not claimed to be my husband." Evelyn's voice was low and controlled. She was very pale.

"Then—"

"I don't want to talk about it any more. You go home and think it over. Get Sophy to help you, and—and Tom Mendip-ffollinton. I think you'll see that all the things you thought so conclusive aren't really so conclusive as you thought they were."

Cotty went away feeling rather cold.

Chapter Eighteen

JESSICA DARTED BACK into the room and banged the door. She found Evelyn with one arm on the mantelpiece and her face hidden against it.

"I'll kill that man if he comes here bothering you! I can't think why somebody *hasn't* killed him. Evelyn, what is it?"

Evelyn lifted her head.

"Nothing, Jess. I'll laugh in a minute. Cotty makes my head go round. I'm trying to sort out what he said from what Sophy said." She did laugh a little, but very faintly.

Jessica stamped her foot.

"Don't talk about him unless you want to. I'll say you've gone to Nova Zembla next time he comes."

Evelyn was gazing abstractedly into the fire. She heard Jessica flounce round, fluffing up cushions and straightening chairs. She looked at the bright flicker of a dozen little yellow flames, but her thoughts were a long way off. She turned presently with a long-drawn breath.

"I'm going to talk to Uncle Henry," she said, and went to the telephone.

Sir Henry Prothero had just finished breakfast when the bell rang. He was delighted to hear his niece Evelyn's voice, and said so:

"Very glad you're back, my dear. Yes, I'm in town. You want me to do something for you? My dear, you know very well that it won't be any trouble. What is it?" He thought Evelyn's voice sounded a little strained.

"Cotty's just been here."

"My unfortunate child! I thought you sounded depleted."

A very faint laugh.

"Cotty makes one feel like that, Uncle Henry."

"My dear."

"He's got hold of the most extraordinary mare's nest—only he called it a germ."

"A what?"

"A germ. And he, and Sophy and Tom Mendip-ffollinton have boiled it up and developed it."

"My dear, if I knew what you were talking about!"

"Uncle Henry, he thinks Tony is Jim Field."

"Tony! Oh—ah—is that what you call him?"

"Yes, darling. I must call him something."

"Certainly, my dear, certainly. So Cotty thinks he's Jim Field, does he? Why?"

Evelyn told him why.

"My dear, what a bewildering story!" he said when she had finished.

"Yes, it is, isn't it? And—and, Uncle Henry—"

"Yes? Look here, my dear, would you like me to come round and see you?"

"No, I've got to go out. But if you would do something."

"What do you want me to do?"

"I want you to go to the registry office place—Upton Street I think he said it was—and just have a look at the entry of that marriage. I think someone ought to verify it. After all, we don't know anything about Cotty's detective, and he may have made the whole thing up."

"He wouldn't do that. But of course I'll go. What was the date?"

Evelyn hesitated.

"December—yes, I think December the seventh; but I'm not sure of the year. He said something about '13 and '14, and I'm not sure—no, I can't be sure. Perhaps you wouldn't mind looking at '14 and '13."

"All right. And when shall I report? Will you be at home this afternoon?"

"Yes. But don't come then. We're having Jessica's adorable Lovey to tea—her sister's baby, you know—and we shouldn't be able to talk. Come to dinner. Jess is going to take the baby home and dine with her sister. Can you do that—eightish?"

Late that afternoon Evelyn's maid announced Mr Laydon; and Anthony Laydon came in upon what he thought was a very pretty scene. There was still some cold daylight outside, but Evelyn's apricot curtains were all drawn, and the room was full of firelight and a very soft, golden lamplight. Evelyn was on the hearth-rug, with a fat baby girl of three cuddled up on her lap. She put out a hand.

"Come in. I can't get up," she said. "This creature weighs tons and tons and tons."

The creature shrieked with laughter, beat at Evelyn with five spread-out pink fingers, and said *"Not!"* in a gurgling contralto.

"Yes, it does. Lovey, say 'How d'you do?' Say it nicely."

Lovey took a peep at the large, strange man. Her eyes reminded Laydon of the story about the dog with eyes like saucers; they were so very round, and so very, very blue. He came up close, and put out rather an awkward hand. Lovey went on staring.

"Do?" she said, gurgled, half turned to Evelyn, and then turned back, putting up a pursed, pink mouth to be kissed. Laydon kissed her solemnly, whereupon she said "Oo!" and flung herself with great suddenness upon Evelyn, catching her round the neck and going off into peals of laughter.

Laydon drew back and sat down in a low chair. He watched the little fat, laughing creature with rather an odd smile. The village children had always thrown stones at Anton Blum. He saw, with his outward vision, Evelyn rocking to and fro in the firelight, her bright hair tumbled by those fat, clutching hands; whilst, pressing upon his inward vision, came a picture of dark trees under snow, a child not much bigger than this child shrieking because he had looked at it; and behind it an older child with hand up-raised to throw, and a sharp-edged flint clutched in the bony fingers.

Evelyn's voice banished the picture.

"I'm so sorry, Tony. Lovey, be good. Jess is just getting ready to take her home. Oh, Lovey, you're choking me!"

Lovey bobbed up and down.

"Eve bad! Eve naughty! Lovey want Diggle!"

Evelyn buried her face for a moment in the baby's neck. Only two people in the world had ever called her Eve. One was this baby thing; and the other—she didn't know—oh God, she didn't know whether the other was here in the room with them now or not—not a yard away within reach and touch of her hand. She might guess— but she didn't know.

Lovey went on bobbing up and down. She patted Evelyn's hair, her cheek, her shoulder, with little cushiony pats.

"Want Diggle! Want Diggle! Eve bad! Man bad!"

Evelyn looked at Laydon in the fire-light.

"Isn't it a lamb?" Her voice melted on the last word. "Cosset lamb," she said, and kissed the dimpled neck.

The cosset lamb pushed her away with plump, deter- mined hands.

"Want *Diggle*! *Want* Cat and *Figgle*!"

"She wants me to sing," said Evelyn with a helpless ripple of laughter.

"Sing Diggle!" commanded Lovey.

"Only once then. And then you go home with Jess as good as good."

"'M," said the cosset lamb. She settled herself cross-legged in Evelyn's lap. "Sing Diggle!" she repeated.

Evelyn sang obediently.

"Hey Diggle, Diggle, the Cat and the Figgle—" She turned laughing eyes on Laydon, "She *will* have it that way—"

Lovey jogged impatiently and held out her hands.

"All right, Ducky." Evelyn took a pink right hand and pinched the thumb.

"This little Piggle went wiggle, wiggle, wiggle.
This little Piggle went squeak.
This little Piggle gave a wriggle and a giggle.
This little Piggle gave a shriek.
And *this* little Piggle went giggle, giggle, giggle,
All into Saturday week."

Each finger was pinched in turn, and the wiggles, wriggles, giggles, squeaks and shrieks were given in the most realistic manner. Lovey's shriek was one of pure ecstasy, and her giggle the most infectious thing imaginable. She and Evelyn were both at the end of their breath, when Jessica swooped in scolding.

"Lovey, you demon child, come home at once! Evelyn, you're worse than she is—much worse. Yes, quail, both of you! Nanna's in the hall and she'll say—well, you know the sort of things she'll say"—she snatched the reluctant Lovey—"hot—untidy—excited. Come along this minute, Villain!"

She whirled from the room, Lovey laughing all the time. The door banged.

Evelyn turned to Laydon with her hand at her dishevelled hair.

"Jessica's a whirlwind, but a perfect dear. It didn't seem quite the moment to introduce you, did it?"

"Not quite."

Silence fell between them, and a certain constraint. Evelyn leaned back against the big chair behind her. She felt that Laydon was looking at her. Then she heard him move, and risked a quick, upward glance. He was looking past her now into the fire.

His face was thinner than it had been; the heavy lines were fining down. Something in his expression gave Evelyn a sickening pang. She said, on a quick unguarded impulse:

"What is it?"

"I beg your pardon?" Voice and manner were those of a courteous stranger.

Evelyn leaned her elbow on the seat of the chair and shaded her eyes with her hand. The outside door had shut upon Jessica and Lovey; she and Tony were alone in this intimate fire-light. How could they be strangers? How could they not be strangers?

She said, "What is it?" And this time he answered her:

"I was remembering how the children threw stones at Anton Blum."

"Why?"

It was more like an indrawn breath of pain than a word.

His face kept its hard look.

"I don't know. I was different—I was dumb. A person who is different is probably dangerous."

A pause. Evelyn bit her lip hard. Laydon went on speaking:

"Curious how I'm remembering all that time. It gets a bit clearer every day."

"I wish you *didn't* remember. Don't think back, Tony,—why should you?"

"I don't do it purposely; it comes. I don't mind—in fact I'm glad. Being able to remember makes one feel more normal—safer. It would be beastly to have a ten years' hole in one's memory."

Evelyn made a quick half-turn and pulled down the cushion from the chair against which she was leaning. It was a violet-coloured cushion with gold tassels. She pushed it down behind her back, and leaning against it, said,

"I saw Anna Blum the other day. You know I've been over in Cologne?"

"Yes, I heard. I'm very glad you saw Anna, because I'm most awfully worried about her. I asked Monkey to find out how she was getting along. You see, the story was bound to leak out, and I was afraid she might be having a perfectly rotten time. Monkey wrote and said he was afraid the people round had rather sent her to Coventry. You know, the more I remember, the more I realize how extraordinarily good she was to me. So I wrote and asked her if she would come over here. My grandfather offered her the South Lodge."

"She wouldn't," said Evelyn quickly.

"No, I thought not too. But I had to do something. I got her answer this morning." He laughed a little grimly. "Just one line written very neatly: 'I stay with my own people.' Just like Anna!"

"I think she's an extraordinary person," said Evelyn. "She made me feel that I couldn't help believing every word she said. But she made me feel too that no one would ever get her to say a single word more than she meant to say. When I'd seen her, I could understand how she'd managed the whole thing—I couldn't before."

Laydon nodded without speaking. Silence again. This time it held no constraint. Laydon felt it invade his unquiet thoughts and touch them for the moment at least, into contentment. On the table at Evelyn's elbow there was a jade bowl full of violets. They brought a wild, sweet breath from the spring woods into the room. It was ten years since he had seen these little dark violets bloom in an English wood, ten years since he had sat with Evelyn in the fire-light. Just for a space the intimate moment held him—a golden moment in a golden room—Evelyn in that familiar attitude, her arm propped by the violet cushion, the folds of her dull blue dress against the dim mosaic of the Persian carpet. He had a sense of homecoming, a sense of what home might be. If things had gone differently with him and Evelyn, this might have been his home, and the little laughing creature who had kissed him his child and hers. A chill came over his mood, blowing in on the enchanted moment like a cold east wind. He frowned, and said in a rough, impatient voice:

"How am I to talk to you? I can't talk to you as if you were a stranger—and yet how else am I to talk?"

Evelyn started. It was the echo of her own thought, but it was strange that he should give it words. She looked down at her folded hands, and said quietly,

"Of course I know what you mean. But can't we just be natural? I'm sure it's the best way. I mean if there's anything you want to say, say it. I shan't mind." With the last word she looked up, met an intensely frowning gaze, and smiled suddenly and sweetly. "I'm not a frightfully terrifying person after all, Tony."

"No," said Laydon. "But you see—Evelyn, can you see how—how stranded I am? I'm remembering my own ten years—it comes a bit clearer every day; but I can't remember yours. You have put in ten years that I don't know anything at all about—everyone has. It gives one the most extraordinary, disconnected feeling, just as if something had come unhooked in the middle. No, that sounds—I can't get it right."

"Oh, but I know, I do know. Tony, won't you let me help you? I could, you know."

"Could you?" The inflexion of his voice pulled Evelyn up short. He looked past her, and stared at the bowl of violets. After a moment he said, "What do you do with yourself? What have you done with yourself all this time? Do you mind my asking?"

"No. Why should I mind? I haven't any dark secrets." She laughed a little; but his face did not relax. "It's a very simple history really. I was in Gertrude Hinton's hospital as long as the war lasted; in fact I didn't get away until the middle of '19. And then I took a holiday—a good, long one. Then Monkey was ordered to Egypt, and Lacy wanted to go too, so I took Don. He was such a darling; I did love having him. I got this flat, and Jessica joined me. The family were perfectly happy as soon as they saw that her hair was grey." Evelyn gurgled. "It's frightfully comic when you know Jessica. She doesn't even see conventions as a rule, or know that they exist; but if by any chance one is, as it were, forced upon her, she just naturally yearns to smash it to atoms and sing *The Red Flag* among the ruins.

However, as the family didn't know that, it was perfectly happy. Aunt Clorinda—do you remember Aunt Clorinda?—absolutely purred over Jessica; and you know what a dragon she was."

"Do dragons purr?" said Laydon in an odd voice.

The tears rushed scalding to Evelyn's eyes. He had said it just without thinking—playing up to her nonsense. It was almost the old voice, the old teasing way; only at the end he should have turned smiling, teasing eyes on hers and caught at her with teasing hands. He neither smiled nor looked at her. The tears burned, and dried.

Laydon was conscious of something that he could hardly control. So many years in a hospital, so many years of looking after Lacy's child—so much anyone could have told him. It was like looking from the street at the outside of a house where every window is tightly shuttered. He wanted to say to Evelyn, "Tell me about you, the real you. How many men have loved you? How many men have wanted to marry you in those ten years? Why didn't you care for any of them? Why didn't you marry?" That was the question he wanted to ask and couldn't ask. "Why didn't you marry, Evelyn? Why didn't you marry?" The paragraph that he had read in Manning's dining-room at Cologne came up before him, word for odious word.

Chapter Nineteen

THE TELEPHONE BELL rang in the dining-room. Evelyn pulled herself up by the arm of the chair against which she was leaning and ran out of the room. She left the door open, and Laydon could hear every word of the one-sided conversation which followed.

"Oh, Chris, is that you?"

Who was Chris? Someone had mentioned a Chris Ellerslie, and had then changed the subject abruptly.

"No, I can't to-night. How eleventh-hourish of you! Uncle Henry's coming to me. Tomorrow? Yes, I think I can—yes, I'd like to most awfully. What time? My *dear* Chris, how frivolous that sounds! Shall we be awfully late?"

He heard her laugh and say au revoir. Then she came back into the room smiling, and picked up the violet cushion. She set it decorously back into its place on the big chair, and in some indefinable way Laydon felt that it was time for him to go. He made no move to go however, but stood looking down into the fire.

Who was Chris Ellerslie that Evelyn should look like that for him? Why had Monkey changed the subject when somebody mentioned the fellow's name? He tried to steady himself against the black gusts of angry jealousy which beat upon his self-control. If he had come home to find Evelyn lost to him, it would have been as bitter as death; but to come home, to find her free, and to see her go to another man before his eyes—this was unimaginable torment. He thrust himself against it with bitter determination. Still looking down into the flames, he said, in a voice as casual as he could make it,

"By the bye, I meant to ask you—will you dine with me to-morrow?"

Evelyn's half-laughing "Oh, I can't" came from nearer than he had expected. He swung round to find her not a yard away, and seeing her like that, he received a strange, vivid impression of colour, bloom, and gaiety.

"Oh, I can't. You're just too late. I've promised Chris Ellerslie." Her eyes held a dancing, challenging sparkle; they laughed at him and said quite plainly, "You heard me—you must have heard me."

"Who is Chris Ellerslie?" His voice was as rough as the question.

Evelyn's colour rose ever so little; her dimple showed.

"He's a very old friend. We're going to be terribly frivolous and dine and dance and sup together. I haven't danced for—oh, about three weeks."

Under his look she turned suddenly nervous. The room seemed full of queer, unexplained waves of emotion; his eyes had a dark look—a dark, smouldering look. She stepped back and picked up the jade bowl full of violets. For a moment she bent her face to them; then she came back and held the bowl up to Laydon, laughing to hide the flutter in her voice.

"Smell them. Aren't they good? They're from the Laydon woods; old Mrs Brown sent them."

Laydon's self-control gave way momentarily. His hands closed hard on her wrists, and the flower-brimmed bowl shook between them.

"Evelyn!"

"Tony, you're hurting me!"

"Evelyn!"

"You'll—break—the bowl."

"Dine with me to-morrow."

She looked up. It was a look that he could not understand. The sparkle was still in her dark blue eyes; he thought it mocked him.

"Break an engagement, Tony? Oh, no. Ask me some other day."

His grasp tightened. His hands were very hard; she could not have moved; if she had tried with all her strength, she could not have moved.

"I want to-morrow."

"No," said Evelyn with a catch in her voice that was nearly a sob. She would not look away; but the dazzle of her own tears was all that she could see.

"That's plain enough. I've no right to ask."

"Tony, let me go!"

"I've no right to touch you."

"No," said Evelyn. It was such a fluttered breath of a word, a sigh almost. He did not know whether the little lift of the breath made a question of it or not.

He let go of her, turned jerkily, and went out of the room without a word and without looking back. The outer door shut heavily.

The jade bowl tilted more and more in Evelyn's shaking hands. When the door shut, it dropped and the violets were scattered. A silver stream of water began to wind slowly among the winding patterns of the Persian rug. The jade bowl lay on its side. The water made a dark pool and three little winding streams.

Evelyn stood and looked through her tears at the spilt violets.

Ten minutes later Sir Henry Prothero found her with the flowers in her hands, and the jade bowl, full of fresh water, in its place. There was still a damp patch on the floor.

Evelyn pushed all the violets into the bowl, and kissed him.

"Darling, are you early, or am I late?"

"Well, it's eight o'clock," said Sir Henry. "I think you said eight."

"Eightish. Sit down and be good. I won't take a minute to dress."

Sir Henry gazed at her benignly.

"My dear, are you *not* dressed?"

"Darling, of course not. This"—holding out a fold of blue marocain—"this is an afternoon garment." She came nearer and sunk her voice to a whisper. "If I were to dine in it, Ponson would leave me."

"Good gracious! As bad as all that? Now, to my unenlightened eyes afternoon dresses and evening dresses all look very much alike nowadays. They all have low necks, and—er—no sleeves, or next to no sleeves; and they come to an end with—er—most surprising suddenness. Run away and put on the evening frock, my dear; and then I'll tell you whether I can detect any difference or not."

After dinner, when Ponson had taken away the coffee cups and Sir Henry had settled himself really comfortably in the biggest armchair, Evelyn brought what she called a pouffe and sat at his knee. It was an orange pouffe with gold dragons at the corners, and it contrasted vividly with the brilliant emerald of her tea-gown.

"Now let's talk business," she said. "I do hate mixing it up with meals—don't you?"

Sir Henry looked gravely at the top of her head; it was just below the level of his eyes. He felt no enthusiasm at the prospect of talking business; he would certainly have avoided doing so had it been possible. As it was not possible, he made a plunge:

"My dear, the whole thing is very difficult."

"How do you mean difficult?"

"I mean complicated. It's very complicated."

Evelyn laughed lightly.

"It's not as complicated as Cotty thinks it is. Cotty'd make a nursery rhyme sound complicated. I can imagine his producing a version of Jack and Jill that would be as unintelligible as a Cubist picture."

Sir Henry did not smile.

"I'm afraid this business is quite complicated enough without Cotty."

Evelyn patted his knee.

"Don't worry, darling. We'll get it all straightened out. Tell me—you went to the Upton Street registry office?"

"Yes."

"And you looked up that entry? Jim Field's marriage—is it there? Or did Cotty's detective invent it to keep him happy?"

Sir Henry looked away from his niece and fixed his eyes on his own big hand, which lay idly on his knee.

"Got to tell her—got to tell her—better not make a song of it—better get it over quick," was his thought. But the silence grew, and he found it difficult to begin. Half a dozen ways of telling her presented themselves, only to be rejected. And then she was asking:

"Did you go? Did you find it?"

"Yes, my dear, I went," Extraordinarily difficult business this.

"And you found the entry?"

"Yes, I found it."

"Oh! Do you know, I really did hope it was a mare's nest. I should love to catch Cotty out."

"No, the entry's there. I made a copy of it. The date is December the seventh, 1914. There was certainly a marriage between James Calthrop Field, bachelor, and Pearl Harriet May Palliser, widow."

"Widow?"

"Yes, apparently. Why?"

"I didn't know she was a widow."

"Do you mean you know her?"

"N—no. I know of her."

"You say you know of her. Do you know—do you happen to know whether she and Jack Laydon were at all friendly?"

Evelyn did not start, but she drew back a little. It was as if a cold breath had passed between them; there was a little chill upon the easy friendliness of their relation.

She said, "Yes, they were friendly," in the same non-committal tone in which one says "It's a fine day."

An awkward business—a damned awkward business—must get on with it. Poor girl—poor Evelyn—afraid she did care for the fellow after all. Sir Henry lifted the big white hand on his knee.

"Evelyn, my dear, it's a much more complicated business than you imagine. I think I'd better tell you the whole thing from the beginning."

"Yes?" said Evelyn. She threw him rather a startled glance. "Yes? What is it?"

"Well, my dear, I found the entry, as I said. But I found another one first."

"Another one?"

"I was turning the pages—working back, you know—you said you weren't sure of the date—and I found—another entry."

"Uncle Henry!"

"Yes, my dear, another entry. It was the name that attracted my attention—the man's name. Evelyn, I'm afraid it'll be a shock—it was Jack Laydon's name."

There, the worst was over; he had got the name out.

"*Jack.*"

Evelyn was leaning forward, her hand on his knee, her eyes very wide, very dark.

"John Murray Laydon—that's right, isn't it? Wasn't his mother a Miss Murray?"

"Yes. But Jack—married—Uncle Henry, I can't—"

"I know. But there it is—John Murray Laydon, bachelor, to Harriet May Edwards, widow."

"Edwards—who is Harriet May Edwards?"

Sir Henry spoke slowly, letting each word drop separately into the silence, "Pearl—*Harriet—May*—Palliser."

"Oh!" said Evelyn. It was a very sharp cry of protest. She sprang up as she uttered it.

"Yes," said Sir Henry, "there's no doubt about it."

"Oh," said Evelyn again more gently. Then she moved to the hearth and stood there with her back to him. "Please go on. Please tell me everything."

Sir Henry looked at her with raised eyebrows for a moment. Lacy—yes, after all Lacy must have been right. One never expected Lacy to be right somehow; but in this case—

He gave her a moment, and then began to speak in his quiet, assured voice.

"Of course I didn't realize any of this at first. I was naturally very much taken aback. I made a copy of the entry with the date, and then I went on looking for the entry about Jim Field."

"What was the date?" said Evelyn quickly. She held back a fold of vivid emerald green, and pushed a log down into the fire with the point of a golden shoe; it was a hard, almost a savage little thrust. The log splintered and flared as Sir Henry said:

"The date? March the twenty-seventh, 1915."

Evelyn bent over the fire. March the twenty-seventh—that was just a week after she had broken her three days' engagement to Jack. *A week*.

Sir Henry went on after a short, uneasy pause:

"I went on looking for the other entry; and I found it, as I told you, on December the seventh, 1914. I was at once struck by the similarity, the odd similarity, of the bride's Christian names. If it had been Harriet by itself, or May by itself,—but Harriet May in conjunction—well, I could not fail to be struck by the singularity. Jim Field had married Pearl Harriet May Palliser in December, and Jack Laydon had married Harriet May Edwards in March. I had another look at the March entry, and the woman's handwriting settled the matter—large, emotional writing—letters about three quarters of an inch high—quite impossible to mistake. It left me without the slightest reasonable doubt that Harriet May Edwards and Pearl Harriet May Palliser were the same person."

There was a silence. Evelyn stood quite still, one hand hanging at her side, the other resting lightly on the mantelpiece.

"Why?" she said at last. She turned quickly and came back to her seat on the pouffe. "Uncle Henry, why?"

"My dear, how can I tell?"

Evelyn was composed and pale. She propped her chin on her hand and looked straight in front of her.

"It seems so senseless. I mean, if I were going to commit bigamy, I wouldn't go back to the same registry office only four months afterwards—would you?"

"I don't think I've ever considered the matter—er—seriously. But I see your point. As a matter of fact, it occurred to me almost immediately. I was inclined to think that the marriage with Jim Field might prove to have been invalid but on making some discreet inquiries at the Ministry of Pensions, I discovered that the lady enjoys a pension as the widow of Jim Field. Now if she married Jack Laydon, why in heaven's name didn't she take her pension as Mrs Jack Laydon?"

"That's what we've got to find out," said Evelyn slowly.

Chapter Twenty

EVELYN LAYDON stood on a dingy landing, and knocked for the third time on the door which faced her.

"All *right*," said a voice from within. There was the soft thudding of stockinged feet, and as the door opened, a lively smell of cheap scent rushed out and mingled with the smell of cooking on the stair; onions, patchouli, cabbage and Irish stew met in a horrible blend.

The open door disclosed Miss Palliser in what she called a *négligé*. It had been pink once. Its satin folds were unimaginably creased and faded, and the wisps of chiffon which clung to it here and there resembled, both in colour and limpness, the cobwebs which festoon a neglected room.

"Oh, come in. I can't see who you are, but come in just the same—I'm sure you're welcome."

Evelyn stepped into a room whose untidiness fairly took her breath away. An eiderdown, a pair of stays, and a hot water bottle were the first objects that met her eyes. They were all on the floor, whilst the rest of Miss Palliser's wardrobe appeared to be heaped upon the six chairs and the sofa-bed. The table held the remains of a meal, a pile of fashion papers, a comb, a pair of scissors, a very large powder puff, and a pot of rouge.

Miss Palliser whisked a pair of torn purple satin pyjamas off the nearest chair, and said,

"Do sit down, won't you? I'm all upside down. But what's the use of worrying? If you're caught in a mess, you're caught, and there's an end of it. Nobody's going to believe you if you swear yourself black in the face that you were as tidy as pie yesterday, and will be again to-morrow." She laughed a fat, jolly laugh, kicked the stays under the eiderdown with rather a deft twirl of the foot and subsided on to a chair which already supported a pair of flame-coloured tights and the remnants of an opera cloak.

Evelyn looked at her with intense interest. Ten years ago she must have been awfully pretty. The large dark eyes; the masses of curly dark hair; the white, even teeth—these were still beautiful. But Pearl Palliser was beautiful no longer; she was a very pink pearl indeed, and there was far, far too much of her. Stout, florid, untidy, and good-natured, she sat beaming at Evelyn and waiting to hear her business.

It was very difficult to begin.

"You must be wondering who I am," said Evelyn.

"Well," said Miss Palliser, "to be frank, I am wondering a bit. You see, dear, when I heard your knock I thought you were the wardrobe dealer that I was expecting—a new one that I haven't done business with before. But as soon as you came in out of that beastly, dark passage, I began to think I had made a mistake. You've not got the business look about you, so to speak."

"I'm Mrs Laydon," said Evelyn,—"Mrs Jim Laydon."

Miss Palliser regarded her with undisguised curiosity.

"Well, if that doesn't beat the band!" she said. "Mrs Jim Laydon, are you? Well, I did think there was something about your face that I ought to know. But after all, ten years is ten years, and I only saw you once; and when all's said and done, there's a lot of difference between what you've got on now and what you had on then. Orange blossoms and a white veil is one thing, and a plain black felt's another—well, *there*, isn't it?"

"When did you see me?" Evelyn felt rather bewildered.

"Oh, I saw you married—set my heart on it. I had reasons of my own, you see." She stopped short and threw a quick look at Evelyn.

Reasons of her own. Yes, if she had really married Jack Laydon, she might very well have had reasons of her own for wanting to see the girl whom—Jack—Evelyn's thought broke off. She hoped that her face had shown nothing.

"I stood in the crowd, and I saw you go in, and I saw you come out," said Miss Palliser. "I might have been in the church, and pretty high up too, but I was never one to push myself or to make unpleasantness. If I'm not wanted, I'm *not* wanted, and I stay away. I never think pushing's worth while—do you?"

Evelyn made an effort. If only there were not such a smell of scent in the room.

"Miss Palliser," she said, "why did you come to my wedding? Don't think me inquisitive; but I really came here to see if you could help me. I think you must guess what I mean, because didn't—didn't Mr Laydon come and see you the other day?"

"Ah!" said Miss Palliser. "Now we're getting there."

She leaned forward with her hands on her knees. On the third finger of her left hand there was a broad gold wedding-ring, so much too tight that it threatened to disappear from view. A passing wonder as to whose ring it was made Evelyn's lips twitch. She had a dreadful feeling that at any moment she might begin to laugh.

"Mr Laydon did come to see you, didn't he?"

Miss Palliser opened her mouth to speak, shut it again, stared hard at Evelyn, and inquired:

"What d'you want me to say?"

Evelyn did laugh at that; it was so unexpected. After a moment Miss Palliser laughed too.

"Well, you know what I mean, dear. It's all pretty queer, isn't it? I don't know when I got such a turn in my life; I give you my word, I don't—and I was in most of the air raids too. Talk about bombs dropping! I'd rather have a bomb than a ghost any day of the week. You don't catch me going to any of these mediums and people—not me. Leave well alone's my motto."

Evelyn touched the over plump hand with the wedding-ring.

"Do you mean that you recognized him?" Her voice was low, but very insistent.

"Well," said Pearl Palliser, "that'd be telling, wouldn't it?"

"Yes. But I want you to tell me."

"Well, it'd be easier if I knew what you wanted me to say. Now that chap that came bothering me yesterday—regular little Nosey Parker—he was keen as mustard for me to say that the first minute I laid eyes on him I knew him for Jim field, which would have been a good old lie—and so I told him. 'I don't care if you're Mr Cotterell Abbott a hundred times over'—that's what I said to him—'If you want me to tell lies to oblige you, you've got to show me the reason why.' Not a friend of yours, I hope, dear?"

Evelyn bit her lip, but it was no use. She laughed again. The vision of Cotty being asked to show good reason why Pearl should tell lies for him was too much for her.

"Well, I'm glad if he isn't."

Miss Palliser crossed her legs and leaned comfortably back in her chair. A length of silk stocking of a bright nude shade sprang into view. Several holes in the stocking disclosed the much lighter colour of Miss Palliser's leg.

"I give you my word he looked shocked," She drew her brows together, pulled in her cheeks, and mimicked Cotty's stiff drawl. "'I—er—really, Miss—er—Palliser, I merely inquired if you—er—recognized this—er—person.'" It was very well done.

"That is what I wanted to ask—*did* you recognize him?"

The dark eyes considered her. There was a pause.

"Oh, well, perhaps I did," said Miss Palliser easily. Then, as Evelyn's colour rose and Evelyn's lips parted, she laughed and added, "Perhaps I didn't."

"Oh," said Evelyn. It was rather a piteous little gasp.

"You see," said Miss Palliser, "there's a good deal mixed up with it that you don't know. And that's where my difficulty comes in. I'm sure I'm quite willing to oblige, and as I said to Nosey Parker—I'm glad he's not a friend of yours, dear for I don't know when I took such a dislike to anyone right at the very first go off— well, as I said to Nosey, I'm not at all sure it wouldn't suit me best to have him Jim Field—my own private reasons, you know, dear. Come to think of it, it *would* suit me better, because there's a gentleman that's a great friend of mine, and in a very good way of business, and nothing he'd like better than for me to say 'Yes,' and we'd be married in church and all, and a proper wedding-cake and a reception. I'm through with registry offices. They've got a bit common, don't you think, dear?"

Evelyn groped for a connecting thread.

Pearl Palliser had married Jim Field in December, 1914. Why would it suit her if Laydon should prove to be Jim Field? Or how would it enable her to get married in church to the gentleman friend in a good way of business?

She looked blankly at the large pink, powdered face.

"Weren't you—weren't you married to Jim Field?"

Miss Palliser was not in the least discomposed.

"December the seventh, 1914," she said. "At the Upton Road registry office. Nosey Parker'd been looking it up too. It was all right, I told him. And I get my widow's pension regularly, thank the Lord. I'm sure I don't know what I'd have done without it. You wouldn't believe how hard it is to get an engagement nowadays. Mind you, I'm not one of those to go round blaming everyone else when they can't get a shop. I'm past my best, and I know it. It's not so much *anno domini* as the extra three-stone-ten that's done it. I was all right as long; as the war lasted. But put me among the cakes, and I'm lost; I can't keep off 'em. But there, what's the good of worrying? It might have been drink or drugs—and then you go to bits. But taking it all round, it's time I left the stage and settled down."

Evelyn held on firmly to Jim Field.

"But if he's Jim Field—I mean if Mr Laydon is Jim Field—, you can't marry and settle down, because you'll still be married, won't you?"

Miss Palliser began to polish her finger nails absent-mindedly, using the left leg of the flame-coloured tights as a pad.

"Well, dear, you see," she said at last, "there's more in it than meets the eye; and the fact is I can't make up my mind whether to tell you the whole lot and get it off my chest or not. In a way it'd be a relief. But once the cat's out of the bag, you can't put it back—can you?"

Evelyn looked straight at her.

"I know you married Jack Laydon in March, 1915," she said.

Miss Palliser's mouth fell slowly open; she went on rubbing her finger nails mechanically. After about half a minute she gave a slow, deep chuckle.

"That's bright of you. But how did you find out?"

"It was accident, really. My uncle, Sir Henry Prothero, was looking for the other entry, and he stumbled on Jack Laydon's name."

"Oh," said Miss Palliser. She seemed quite composed and cheerful. "Well, that's that. Does Mr Nosey Abbott know?"

Evelyn shook her head.

"Only my uncle and me. He won't say anything if I ask him not to. Don't you think you'd better tell me the whole thing?"

"I dare say I had." She let the flame-coloured tights slide to the floor. "I wouldn't so much mind telling you, for I don't mind saying I've taken a liking to you. It's funny too, for I can remember the time when I hated you like poison. Jack and me'd been pretty good friends; and then all of a sudden he dropped off, and I heard he was going to marry a girl with a lot of money. Naturally I was wild. And if you can understand what I mean, what made me so wild was thinking about the money. If a boy likes a girl better, he likes her better. But if it's just for money,—well, I *was* hot about it."

"Miss Palliser!"

"Well, dear, I'd never seen you, so it was natural enough. After I'd seen you I thought different—I'm not a fool. And now, as I say, I've taken a liking to you, and I've a jolly good mind to tell you the whole thing from the beginning."

"I wish you would," said Evelyn. "I won't get you into trouble over it—I won't indeed."

"No, you're not that sort. As a matter of fact, I've not done anything to get into trouble over. Still it's just as well to be on the safe side, so I've kept my mouth shut."

"But you're going to tell me now?"

Pearl Palliser tipped her chair to and fro.

"All right, I will," she said. The front legs of the chair came down rather hard. "All right, I'll tell you the whole thing. It's a pretty fair old mix up one way and another." She paused, leaned towards Evelyn with her elbow on her knee, and said in a confidential voice, "Well, dear, it all began when I was seventeen, and I ran away from home to spite my step-mother and married Ted Edwards, that was about the biggest blackguard in London—though naturally I wasn't to know that. Well, it didn't take me long to find out—not just how bad he was, but quite enough. I got on at the halls through a friend of his; and I made a hit with a song that I dare say you never heard of—'Inky, Minky, Dinky Doo.' Very catchy chorus it had; they were humming it on buses in about a week."

She jumped up, struck an attitude, and gathering the once pink *négligé* well above the knee, she pirouetted with astonishing lightness and sang at the top of a loud, rollicking voice:

"Inky, Minky, Dinky Doo,
How I'd like to marry you.
Honey for me, and honey for you,
Inky, Minky, Dinky Doo."
She plumped, giggling, into her chair again.

"I'd a high kick at the end that brought the house down. You bet I had a good time, and you bet I didn't cry my eyes out when Ted Edwards got a five years' stretch for one of his nasty crooked games. He'd have spent all my money if he'd had a chance—spent it on other girls too and beaten me into the bargain. Honest, dear, he was the worst man I've ever met, and the only one I've ever been afraid of." She shivered, and a large tear rolled down her cheek, leaving a glistening track in the pink powder.

Evelyn spoke on a quick impulse:

"I'm so sorry."

"You needn't be." Miss Palliser swung round, snatched the powder-puff from the crowded table behind her, and rapidly dabbed her face with it. Then she resumed: "I did have a good time the next six years or so—lots of money, lots of good pals, lots of everything. I was a bit frightened when Ted's time was up; but he went off to Australia, and never came near me. I couldn't think why, till I found out quite by accident that there was something much worse against him, and he was afraid of it coming out." She put her face quite close to Evelyn's, dropped her voice, and whispered, *"Murder."*

"Oh!" Evelyn drew back.

"'M. That's the sort of man he was. Well, I went on having a good time. And when I hadn't heard anything of him for three or four years, I made up my mind he was dead, and I married a fellow I'd known before I ran away from home. Albert Laycock his name was, and I'd always had a bit of a fancy for him, if you can understand me. It was soft of me, because I could have done better ten times over. But I fancied Albert. And we got married, and I left the stage and went and lived at Tooting, where he'd a nice little hair-dressing business." Miss Palliser's large dark eyes took on a dreamy, sentimental look. "We were very happy," she said, and another large tear splashed down. She plied the powder-puff vigorously. "I don't say it'd have lasted—most likely it wouldn't. Anyhow, after eighteen months I heard a rumour about Ted being alive, and Albert said his conscience wouldn't let him live with me any longer, as his people were chapel, and he'd been very strictly brought up. That's what he *said*; but I've always thought he was getting a bit fed up. Anyhow he sold the business and went out to his brother in Ontario, that was always writing and asking him to come. And I went back to the halls. That was—let me see—somewhere about ought-five or ought-six. And I didn't marry anyone else till Jim Field came along. And when I married him, it was more than seven years since I'd had word of Ted Edwards—and that'd put me right in a court of law any day of the week. Well, dear, I married him on December seven, fourteen; and I used my stage name with my own Christian names stuck in between—Pearl Harriet May Palliser. And I put 'widow,' because I hoped I was a widow." She made a sound between a sob and a laugh. "Oh, Lord, dear, if you'd known Ted Edwards, you'd have hoped so too."

Evelyn began to see daylight.

"You poor thing," she said. "And afterwards you found out that your first husband was still alive? Was that it?"

Miss Palliser gulped down her emotion.

"Well, I don't know about poor thing," she said frankly. "I liked Jim Field all right, but I wasn't going to put up with any nonsense from him. And when I found he was going to turn nasty if I said howdydo to anyone else, we had words. So perhaps it was all for the best." She gave a retrospective sigh, paused, sighed again rather more voluminously, and added, "February it was when I got the letter from the parson in Australia to say that Ted was really dead at last—yes, the last week in February, because Jim had just had his leave and gone out again. The parson gave all particulars, and as luck would have it, it seems Ted died on December the eighth, just the day after I married Jim."

"Then it wasn't legal."

"No, dear, of course it wasn't. And by that time, I don't mind saying, it was a bit of a relief. And when Jack Laydon came along a month afterwards, and said, would I marry him, yes or no, I said yes. He didn't know about Jim of course, and Jim didn't know about him; and I wasn't taking any risks this time, so I married him in my proper, legal name as Harriet May Edwards, widow. Of course it was a bit careless to go back to the same registry; but there was such an awful lot of marrying going on, I didn't think anyone'd notice, what with the name being different and all."

"You say Jim Field didn't know," said Evelyn. "Do you mean he didn't know that you weren't legally married to him?"

Miss Palliser heaved an expansive sigh.

"Sounds deceitful, doesn't it? But it wasn't meant that way. What I thought was, why, either of 'em might be killed any day, and why not let the poor boys be happy? Jim'd have cut up awful rough if he'd known he'd lost me for good and all. So I thought I'd just wait. And I thought, if he wasn't killed, there was time enough to tell him, and if he was, I shouldn't have it on my conscience that I'd thrown him over."

Evelyn gasped.

"He never knew?"

"No, dear," said Miss Palliser, "he didn't. Well then, when he and Jack got killed the same day, of course I had to think about my pension. You see if I claimed as Mrs Jack Laydon, it might have been awkward. There were quite a few of my friends knew I'd married Jim Field, for one thing; and once you get started explaining things, there's a lot comes out that you'd just as soon *didn't* come out. Now, no one knew I'd married Jack Laydon, because we'd kept it precious dark; so I thought, least said, soonest mended, and I put in for my pension as Mrs Jim Field. See, dear?"

Evelyn saw. As stated by Miss Palliser, the transaction appeared quite simple. She struggled to emerge from this odd world in which one married, and un-married, and re-married with such engaging simplicity. That Pearl Palliser's story was true, she had no doubt. She sat for a while, looking down at her own folded hands and trying to see whether this astonishing story threw any light on the Laydon problem. At last she said, frowning a little,

"Miss Palliser, you haven't told me one thing—the most important thing of all; you haven't told me whether you recognized Mr Laydon when he came here the other day."

Pearl Palliser began to pleat the crumpled folds of pink satin that fell away at her knee.

"Oh, well," she said.

"You said you'd seen a ghost. Whose ghost did you think it was?"

"Oh, well," said Miss Palliser again. Then she gave a deep chuckle. "It wouldn't suit me to have Jack Laydon turn up, would it? I don't want him now any more than he'd want me. If it comes to that, I don't want Jim Field either. Why shouldn't it be the other one—the one you married? Come, that's an idea! Why shouldn't it be the other one?"

Evelyn stood up, her hand at her throat, her eyes dark in a white face. Something was shaking her—anger?—fear?—doubt? She tried to speak, and her voice failed.

Pearl Palliser got up too. Her laughter stopped.

"Well, what's the matter with it?" she said. "Don't you want him back either? Is that it? It's a funny world, isn't it, dear? I expect you cried your eyes out for him ten years ago. I know I did for Jack. And now—well, there it is, we don't want 'em."

"Oh," said Evelyn, "don't! How can you?"

"Well, there it *is*," said Miss Palliser composedly. "You can't get from it. Ten years ago I wanted a smart young chap to go about with; but nowadays I can't be bothered. I want someone like the gentleman I told you about—comfortable, you know, and glad to stay at home of an evening."

"Oh, stop!" said Evelyn desperately. She felt she had had as much as she could bear, but she steadied herself for another effort. "Miss Palliser, can't you tell me whether you recognized him? Don't you see it isn't a question of whether it suits you for him to be Jim Field or Jack Laydon? It's a question of fact. *Did* you recognize him? What did he say to you?"

"He said his name was Laydon. And he said Jim Field had told him he'd married me. And he said he'd promised to see after me if anything happened to Jim."

"Yes?" said Evelyn. "Yes?" The words came quickly, eagerly. "Please, please go on. Oh, please tell me, did you recognize him?"

"Well, I thought I did," said Pearl Palliser.

Chapter Twenty-One

WHEN EVELYN came out of the house where Miss Palliser lodged, she walked quickly to the end of the street, and then stood still for a moment drawing a long breath or two. It was a bitterly cold afternoon, dry now for a little space between showers of icy rain. The cold, cutting wind felt keen and fresh after the cabbage-haunted stair and Miss Palliser's violently scented room.

Evelyn walked on. She felt battered. She wanted to go home and go to bed; and she remembered with horror that she had promised to dine and dance with Chris Ellerslie. She didn't want to see Chris or any other human being she knew she wanted to go to bed and lie still in the dark; she wanted to be quiet. She certainly did not want to see Cotty Abbott or his wife; yet, as she turned her own corner, she almost ran into Sophy.

Sophy stopped. Evelyn could do no less.

"Ah!" said Sophy in a tone of satisfaction. "I thought I'd missed you. Now I can just turn and walk back with you. I mustn't stop of course, but I can just come in and have a quiet talk."

There was no escape. Sophy always began a visit by saying that she could not possibly stop for more than a moment. She would probably stay for an hour, and then go away offended because she had not been pressed to remain.

The curtains were drawn in Evelyn's room, and the tea-table stood ready. Sophy Abbott took a cup of tea under protest.

"I really cannot stop. And tea means nothing to me; I never have any appetite. Cotty often says he wonders how I exist. Only this morning at breakfast he said to me, 'My dear Sophy, you eat nothing, absolutely *nothing!*' Oh, no, not any cake, thank you. I never touch cake."

"Did you want to see me about something?" said Evelyn after a little pause.

"Well, yes, I was particularly anxious to see you. As I said to Cotty, 'Evelyn should be informed—Evelyn should certainly be informed.'" Here Sophy Abbott absent-mindedly reached out for the piece of cake she had refused, took a mouthful, swallowed it, and added, "At once—without delay."

"Yes?"

"Cotty agreed with me. And as he was going-down to Laydon to see his uncle, I put all my other engagements aside in order to come and have this talk with you. As Cotty said, neither of us are people who shrink from what they feel to be *right*."

Evelyn said, "Oh."

It was always so very difficult to make suitable responses to Cotty and Sophy. At regular intervals they would pause for a response, and Evelyn always had the feeling that her answers were weighed and found wanting.

"We felt that you should know without delay. My brother Tom thought so too."

Sophy finished her piece of cake and took a macaroon.

"Yes?" said Evelyn.

"Yesterday," said Sophy with an air of triumph, "Cotty made a very important discovery."

"But I saw him yesterday."

"He made the discovery later. He considered that the moment had come for him to take matters out of the detective's hands. As he said, 'These people are useful in the early stages of an affair; but when it comes to dealing with really important developments, a higher class of intellect is required.' My brother Tom agreed with him."

"Did he?"

"He did—and so did I. I said to him, 'If you want a thing well done, do it yourself.'"

"What did he do?—Will you have some more tea, Sophy?"

"Well, I oughtn't to—I don't usually—in fact I hardly ever touch tea." She handed her cup to be replenished and took another slice of cake. "All the Mendip-ffollintons have such very small appetites. I remember Sir Archibald Crosby telling my dear mother that he had never in all his long experience come across anyone with so small an appetite. And I remember my dear mother's answer, though I was only a child at the time. 'Indeed?' she said. 'Am I really so singular, Sir Archibald?' And Sir Archibald replied, 'Singular, my dear madam? You are a *marvel*.'"

Evelyn set down her cup.

"Were you going to tell me something, Sophy?"

Mrs Cotty's pale, bulging eyes took on a well-known expression. It indicated that the Mendip-ffollinton pride had been subtly offended. After a slight pause, during which she finished her piece of cake and took another macaroon, she said:

"Cotty made a most important discovery. He went himself to see this Palliser woman who was married to Jim Field."

"What did he discover?"

"Ah!" said Sophy. She held out her cup mechanically for more tea. "Two lumps of sugar, please, Evelyn, and rather less milk. He went himself to see Miss Palliser, and she convinced him beyond all doubt that this so-called Anthony Laydon is nothing in the world but her husband, Tim Field."

"Did she say he was Jim Field?"

"Not in so many words. As Cotty said, a woman of that sort will not readily commit herself to a direct statement. But her manner was, he said, very convincing."

"I don't think Cotty's account of her manner will do very much to convince Sir Cotterell," said Evelyn rather drily.

Sophy Abbott folded two pieces of bread and butter together, and took an offended bite. Then she emptied her cup, handed it to Evelyn, and said stiffly,

"Cotty was convinced. As he said to my brother Tom, 'I went there with a perfectly open mind, and I came away convinced.' My brother Tom told me afterwards that he thought there was no doubt at all that Anthony Laydon was Jim Field—No, only one lump this time, please; I don't touch sugar as a rule."

"Look here," said Evelyn, "what did Pearl Palliser say?"

Sophy sipped her tea.

"It was not so much what she actually said."

"Yes, but what *did* she say?"

Sophy stared at her.

"My dear Evelyn, I'm telling you. As I said to Cotty, 'What are words? They merely serve to conceal thought.' I forget where that quotation comes from, but it always strikes me as so true. Cotty agreed with me. As he said to Tom and myself, 'This Palliser woman *obviously* has something to conceal.'"

"Sophy, do try and tell me what she *said*."

"I am telling you. When Cotty asked her point blank 'Did you recognize him? Who is he?', she said—" Sophy reached for the last macaroon.

"What did she say?"

"She laughed, and said she hadn't made up her mind, but she supposed Jim Field was as good a name as another, and she wasn't sure it wouldn't suit her well enough too."

This at least was genuine Pearl Palliser.

Evelyn laughed.

"I don't think very much of that, Sophy."

"You haven't let me finish," said Sophy Abbott, putting down her cup. "She went on to say that if Cotty could show her good reasons for making a statement, she would be prepared to swear to his being Jim Field. There! What do you think of that?"

It was another half-hour before Sophy tore herself away, but the remainder of her conversation consisted of a repetition of what Cotty had said about Pearl, and what her brother Tom had said about what Cotty had said.

Jessica came in a little later, to find most of the brightly coloured cushions piled on the hearth-rug, and Evelyn in the midst of them looking limp.

"What have you been doing?" said Jessica severely. She flung her parcels into a chair as she spoke, and subsided cross-legged on a stray cushion at Evelyn's feet. "What *have* you been doing?"

"I never wish to see another relation so long as I live," said Evelyn, "or a relation's wife, or a relation's child. And if anyone mentions Tom Mendip-ffollinton's name to me, I shall scream."

Jessica plucked off a rather battered hat, flung it from her, ran her fingers through her wild grey hair, and said in briskly bitter tones,

"It's your own fault. Has Sophy been here?—or was it Cotty?"

"Sophy," said Evelyn with a groan. "Hours and hours and hours of Sophy. Why is it my fault?"

"I've told you a dozen times. You encourage them. You're the sort of person that relations absolutely cling to and cluster round. No one ever saw one clinging to me. But if you *will* have golden hair and blue eyes, and play up to your type—"

"I don't. Jess, what a pig you are!"

"You do. You gaze at them as if you adored them, and murmur at them sympathetically, and—"

Evelyn threw an orange cushion at her, and simultaneously Ponson opened the door and announced Sir Henry Prothero.

Jessica made a perfectly horrible face, jumped up, said "How do you do?", snatched her hat, and banged out of the room with astonishing rapidity Evelyn sat up and pointed to the nearest chair.

"I've got all the cushions, I'm afraid; but I'll spare you one." Then, as the door closed Ponson and Sir Henry made himself comfortable she added, "Oh, darling, I've had such a day! Sophy's been here, and Cotty's gone down to Laydon to worry Sir Cotterell, and I've been to see Pearl Palliser."

"Oh! You shouldn't have done that," said Sir Henry quickly.

"Don't be Victorian," said Evelyn, blowing him a kiss. "I'm frightfully glad I went, for—oh for lots of reasons, one of them being that I'm now in a position to check what Sophy says that Cotty says that Pearl said."

"Well, my dear, suppose you tell me about it. I came round because Cotterell rang me up from Laydon. He'd had Cotty there, and he was a good deal put out."

"I should think he was furious."

"Yes, he was angry—that goes without saying; but he was upset too. I think Cotty had shaken him more than he would admit. Did you know that Jim Field was a connection of the family?"

"No—yes—yes, I believe I did."

"'M. Well, it seems Cotterell stuck out about having been convinced by the likeness to his father's portrait, and when Cotty countered by reminding him that Sir James' sister was Jim Field's great-grandmother, he was rather knocked off his balance."

"Oh," said Evelyn. "Yes, I hadn't thought of that. I see. It's awkward." She looked at him frowning, then made a gesture as if she were pushing something away. "Now I'm going to tell you about Pearl Palliser."

"What is she like? I still think you oughtn't to have gone, my dear."

"Pouf! She's like nothing on earth; but a good sort, and she must have been most frightfully pretty; you can quite understand why they all married her."

"All?"

"Yes, darling, lots and lots of them." Evelyn sat bolt upright and waved her hands. "I think she just got married like getting a new hat. She said quite artlessly that she supposed it was a habit. 'Some do, and some don't,' she said."

"And she did?"

"Yes. Now, darling, just hold on to your head and attend. First she married Ted Edwards, who was a crook and beat her. And he went first to prison and then to Australia; and she thought he was dead." Evelyn ticked Ted Edwards off on her first finger. "Have you got him? And then she married Albert Laycock, who had a hairdresser's shop in Tooting. And he went off to Canada because he heard that Ted Edwards was still alive, and he'd been very strictly brought up, and he was getting tired of Pearl." She ticked Albert off on her second finger. "And then she didn't marry anyone for quite a time. I don't know why, and I don't think *she* does. On December the seventh, 1914, she married Jim Field; and in February she had a letter from Australia to say Ted Edwards only died on December the eighth. So she wasn't really married to Jim Field at all." She touched her third finger lightly: "Have you got that? And then in March, 1915, she married Jack Laydon."

"My dear!"

"What makes it so much more complicated is the fact that she never told Jim Field that their marriage wasn't legal; so he never knew about Jack, and Jack never knew about him."

"You shouldn't have gone to see her," said Sir Henry, frowning. "She must be a most infamous woman."

"No, she isn't. She's just casual, and—and frightfully good natured—anything to oblige. And I'm most awfully glad I went, because it's a check on Cotty."

"My dear, Cotty wouldn't—"

"Oh, I know he's honest. But he's so stupid. And Pearl Palliser— Uncle Henry, she'd say *anything* that anyone wanted her to as long as it didn't upset her own plans. She wants to get married again— yes, she does really. That makes five, and she was quite transparent about the whole thing. She thinks it would really suit her best to say that Tony is Jim Field, because her marriage with him wasn't legal. But she's quite willing to do me a good turn and say he's Jim—Jim Laydon, if—if I want her to." Evelyn turned very pale as she finished speaking, so pale that Sir Henry leaned forward and held out his hand.

"My dear—"

She bit her lip hard.

"You see it's a good thing I went. She'd say anything, and she'd swear anything. She doesn't like Cotty, and she rather likes me; so if I tell her to say that Tony is Jim Laydon, she'll say it. She won't say he's Jack of course, because then she couldn't marry her gentleman friend and settle down comfortably."

"I see," said Sir Henry.

There was a short silence during which Evelyn looked at the fire, and Sir Henry looked at her with a good deal of concern. Presently he said,

"She had really seen Laydon, then?"

Evelyn nodded.

"Do you think she recognized him?"

"I don't want to say," said Evelyn. "She's like water; her evidence goes for nothing."

"You don't want to say?"

"No. Don't—don't ask me."

"If I mustn't ask you that, I wonder whether I may ask you something else."

Evelyn looked at him with rather a tremulous smile.

"That depends," she said.

"Well, my dear, the fact is—" He hesitated and broke off. "Evelyn, my dear, forgive me—but I've sometimes wondered whether *you* had recognized him. May I ask you that?"

Evelyn went on looking at the fire. After a moment she said,

"Yes."

"I may ask?"

"Yes."

"Then I do ask. You recognize him?"

"Yes," said Evelyn again. She spoke in a quiet, low tone. Her hands were folded on her lap.

She remained quite still for a moment. Then, before Sir Henry could speak, she got up and went to the window. She pulled the curtain away and stood looking out into the darkness. Her flat was high up on the fourth floor of the house. She could see the black tops of trees just moving like shadows in the quiet square on her right. Below her street lamps like bright beads on a dark thread stretched away and away to the left. She threw the window open, and there came in a buffet of icy air and the distant sound of the great thoroughfare beyond.

She heard Sir Henry come up behind her, and felt his large, gentle hand on her shoulder.

"My dear, that's too cold. Shut it."

She gave a little broken laugh and pulled the window down; but she did not turn.

"Evelyn, my dear, am I not to ask you anything more?"

He felt her quiver under his hand.

"No—*please*."

There was a short pause; Sir Henry's hand fell to his side.

"My dear, do you think it is wise to withhold—"

Evelyn swung round.

"I'm not thinking about being wise," she said, "and I'm not thinking about Cotty, or the family, or even about you, darling; I'm—I'm only thinking about him."

She leaned against the dark pane and held the gold and apricot curtain in one tightly clenched hand.

"Evelyn!" Sir Henry was certainly startled, "Evelyn, what do you mean?"

Evelyn held her head high.

"I mean I won't rush him, and I won't help anyone else to rush him. When he wants to say who he is, he'll say."

"Do you think he knows? Evelyn—my *dear*."

Evelyn laughed.

"Oh, darling," she said, "of course he knows!"

Chapter Twenty-Two

ABOUT THE TIME that Mrs Cotty Abbott was having tea, Laydon was turning out of St. James' Street into Piccadilly. He was a good deal taken up with his thoughts—and Piccadilly is not really a very good place to think in. He bumped into someone, heard a voice that he knew say "Hullo!" in tones of protest, and found himself shoulder to shoulder with Major Thursley, the survivor of that party of four who had gone up on a November day ten years ago—Jim Field, the two Laydons, and Thursley, known familiarly as Jobbles.

Laydon laughed to himself at the recollection of how Thursley had looked when he trotted out the old nickname at the War Office the other day.

"Hullo, Jobbles!" he said. "How are you?"

Thursley responded without any marked enthusiasm. He had developed into one of those men to whom correctness is more than a religion, and he had no desire to be mixed up in what he feared might yet become "The Laydon Case." He was about to pass on, when the very pretty woman on his other side pinched his arm surreptitiously but severely. Next moment he was introducing Laydon to "my sister-in-law, Mrs Dick Thursley," and Mrs Dick was being, as the disgusted Thursley put it to her later, "all over the fellow." They had quite a brisk little quarrel about it.

"And why shouldn't I be all over him? I think he's frightfully attractive; and the whole story is simply just too romantic for *words*."

"You don't want to get mixed up in a *story* of any kind."

Mrs Dick laughed a light, silvery laugh.

"My blessed Jobbles,—wasn't that what he called you? I think it's simply the divinest name, and I'm never going to call you anything else—What was I saying? I mean what did you say? Oh, I know. You said that of course I wouldn't want to get mixed up with a romantic story. And I say that there's nothing in the world that I should more absolutely adore. *There*, Jobbles, dear."

"Don't call me Jobbles," said Thursley stiffly. "And look here, Elizabeth, even if you are all over the fellow, I think you might draw the line at asking a man you'd never set eyes on before to dine and dance to-night."

"Didums was?" said Mrs Dick. "If you're going to be cross, you can go home all the way back to Farnborough; and then I shall be a man short all over again; and my party'll be an absolute frost; and you won't care a bit; *and someone else will dance all the evening with Angela Meiklejohn.*"

Thursley permitted himself to thaw a little. He was a man of method, and fully intended that a carefully developed courtship should that evening culminate in a proposal. He could not, therefore, afford to quarrel with Elizabeth at this juncture. He reminded himself that she had her good points, that she was poor Dick's widow, and that he depended on her good offices with Angela.

He had reached this point, when Elizabeth gripped him by the arm.

"Oh, Lord, Jobbles, supposing he can't dance!"

"Nothing is more probable," said Thursley with some enjoyment.

Elizabeth groaned aloud in Bond Street.

"Tell me the worst at once. Did he—could he dance—a thousand years ago, before the war, I mean, when even you were a gay young thing—could he?"

"No one knows which he is."

"Could either of them? Jobbles, don't be a fiend. Put me out of my agony. Could they dance? *Did* they dance?"

"Oh, they danced."

"But how? How, Jobbles?"

"Elizabeth, I must really ask you—"

"HOW?" said Elizabeth firmly, and in large capitals.

"Oh, they were rather star performers, as a matter of fact." Thursley made the admission reluctantly.

"There!" said Elizabeth. "Doesn't that show how clever I am?"

Laydon would have been puzzled to explain exactly why he had accepted an invitation to dine at The Luxe and dance afterwards from such a complete stranger as Mrs Thursley. He was, in fact, more than a little surprised at himself, for he had the very clearest intention of avoiding social engagements of all kinds whilst his position was in doubt. He had the feeling that the people whom he would care about knowing would find him an embarrassment, whilst the people whom he did not want to know would jump at any opportunity of pushing themselves and him into the limelight. Why on earth then had he instantly accepted Elizabeth Thursley's invitation? Partly, no doubt, because it was quite obvious that Jobbles hoped he would refuse; partly because Mrs Thursley was a very pretty woman with an enchanting smile; and partly because Evelyn had refused to break her engagement to dine with Chris Ellerslie.

He found himself one of a party of eight when he arrived at The Luxe that evening. Everybody was very cheerful and frivolous except Thursley, who wore an air of high solemnity not particularly suited to a dinner party, but quite in keeping with the fact that he was about, with due ceremony, to propose marriage to Miss Angela Meiklejohn. Laydon, sitting between his hostess and a girl with cropped black hair and very bright blue eyes, listened to the flow of chaff and light talk. The black-haired girl was Marcia Lane, and the man at the end of the table was her brother, Tommy Lane. His hair was really a little longer than hers.

"That's because he composes," explained Elizabeth in a loud and piercing whisper. "Tommy, you're a genius, aren't you?" she continued in her ordinary voice. "I'm just going to tell Mr Laydon that you are, and I thought I'd better make sure first. Who should know if you don't yourself? You are, aren't you?"

Tommy showed his nice even teeth in a grin.

"Rather!" he said.

"I knew it," said Elizabeth, "because I do so hate your stuff—and I always hate works of genius. I like things with nice little simple tunes that you can sing in your bath, so I always know that any piece of music I admire must be 'the absolute dregs of vitiated taste.' That's a quotation."

Angela Meiklejohn allowed a slight frown to disturb her expression of placid enjoyment. She was a very tall, healthy-looking girl with red-brown hair, eyes exactly the same colour, and a really wonderful complexion. She was not clever. She looked seriously at Tommy Lane and asked:

"Couldn't you write some nice tunes if you tried, Tommy?"

Tommy's "I wouldn't be seen dead in a ditch with a nice tune" was lost in the general laughter.

It was at this moment that Laydon looked across the room and saw Evelyn. She was one of a party of four, and she was sitting half turned from him, talking to a tall, thin man on her left. Laydon could not really see her face, and he waited in an odd excitement for her to turn. The tall, thin man must be Chris Ellerslie—extraordinary small head the fellow had—straw-coloured hair—much too smooth and shiny—looked as if he had a pretty good opinion of himself—what on earth could Evelyn see in him? Suddenly he was aware of Elizabeth Thursley's pretty, light laugh.

"Mr Laydon, are you a medium? I mean, do you often go into trances like this?"

Laydon met the dark, smiling eyes. His own were hard and clear; only his lips smiled.

"I do it professionally on first and third Mondays; but this is a free, gratis exhibition. I'm really awfully sorry."

Mrs Thursley had her full share of curiosity.

"What on earth were you looking at?" Her eyes roved. "You looked absolutely spell-bound. Oh—"

Evelyn had turned and was facing them. She wore a gold dress that matched her hair. She wore the pearls which had been Jim Laydon's wedding gift. She smiled with her eyes, and just moved her head in recognition.

"Hullo!" said Marcia Lane. "Evelyn and Chris over there. Elizabeth, did you see them? Tommy, prepare to be blighted. Evelyn's over there with Chris. What's the betting you can't cut him out of a dance?"

Elizabeth's gay laugh rang out. Her colour had risen. "Tommy, you can rely on me. I'll make a dead set at Chris. He dances better than anyone else I know—yes, Tommy, he *does*. If he didn't, he'd find out that we all think him rather a bore. At present, I *know*, he thinks we love him for himself alone; and we don't—it's for his dancing. Some day I shall say to him 'Chris, darling'—that'll be to soften the blow—'Chris, *darling*, your dancing is a dream; but you, you, my poor Chris, are a washout.' Yes," she concluded meditatively, "I think washout is the right word, because he does so remind me of sketching."

"My good Elizabeth!" This was Tommy.

Elizabeth waved her hands.

"Well, you know, you make a sketch; and then you wash it; and you go on washing it until the edges have gone and everything is nice and woolly. That's what Chris reminds me of."

"By the way," said Marcia Lane in her abrupt way, "did I catch your name, or didn't I? Is it Laydon?"

"Yes, it's Laydon."

Her curiously bright blue eyes were rather difficult to meet.

"Then are you a relation of Evelyn's? I know her rather well, but I don't think she's ever mentioned you. Are you a cousin or something?"

Laydon laughed rather grimly.

"I'm something," he said, "Miss Lane. Ask Evelyn what the exact connection is next time you see her?"

Marcia Lane looked puzzled. She had been in Spain for the winter, and had only returned twenty-four hours before; no echo of the Laydon case had reached her. But the ground under her feet felt uncertain.

"Relationships are frightfully complicated things," she said, and turned her attention to Elizabeth.

Elizabeth was enjoying herself wickedly—Jobbles on her left pink with embarrassment; Giles Mostyn and his wife agog with curiosity; Marcia suspicious; and Laydon taking the situation ironically. She was thrilled, amused, and excited.

"I know," she said. "We'll get Chris and Evelyn to join us. That's Helen Temperley with them. And the back of the other man's head is quite a nice shape. Angela, darling, he shall dance with you."

Angela looked puzzled. Her attention was a good deal taken up with the *entrée*. An enthusiastic amateur cook, its composition intrigued her. She did not quite see how she was to dance with the back of anyone's head; and besides, she had promised all her dances to Major Thursley. She said so in her placid, even voice; and Jobbles became pinker than before.

Elizabeth scribbled rapidly on a menu, held up the next course whilst she explained to a waiter exactly which table she wished her message to be taken to, and then, as Tommy said, neglected her perfectly good food in order to indulge an indecent curiosity as to just how cross Chris would look when he got it.

"Fiend!" said Elizabeth. "Fiend in more or less human shape! He won't be cross at all; he'll love to dance with me. Anyone would— wouldn't they, Giles? There! He's got it. Now let's all watch!"

Chris Ellerslie took the menu card, turned it this way and that, frowned over it—"That," explained Elizabeth, "is because he's trying to disentangle my signature from the *pêches* Melba"—, and finally handed it to Evelyn. They saw his lips move, and the bend of Evelyn's head.

Presently the waiter returned with the menu. Chris Ellerslie had scrawled "Delighted" across it in letters about an inch high, and Elizabeth was duly triumphant.

Marcia Lane found herself wondering about the rather silent man at her side. She thought he was watching them all. He had a quality of aloof detachment which puzzled her. He was not shy—no, certainly he was not shy, neither was he bored. On the contrary, that there was something in the people or the situation which interested him to an uncommon extent, she felt convinced. She asked him if he was a keen dancer, and at once he countered with a request for the first two dances.

Marcia said, "All right;" and then, "You didn't answer my question."

"I was afraid you wouldn't dance with me if I told the truth."

Marcia's very blue eyes stared a little. When she looked like that they bore a certain resemblance to the round, blue, painted eyes of a cloth doll; her black cropped hair went oddly with them.

"What is the truth?"

"Promise you won't back out."

"I never back out."

"Well, then—I haven't danced for ten years."

Marcia gasped.

"Good Lord! Where *have* you been?"

Laydon's look was one of amusement. His voice had a tinge of irony.

"Farming," he said—"just farming."

And then Elizabeth broke in, talking to the whole table at once whilst her ice became syrup.

"It was an absolutely priceless book. I found it on an aunt's bookshelf. I believe it was called *The Art of Dress*. Perfectly and absolutely priceless, my children. No, listen,—it really was. Giles, tell your wife I'll never speak to her again if she interrupts. There was a woman in it who for thirty years had the reputation of being always well dressed. And how did she do it? Ah, you may well ask."

"We didn't ask," said Barbara Mostyn with her delicate drawl.

"Tommy asks—don't you, Tommy?—and all my really *nice* guests. She did it on three black velvet gowns. Yes, they were gowns—three in thirty years. After about ten years the original one descended to second best occasions like family gatherings and so on. The woman who wrote the book laid down the law like nothing you've ever read. You either wore black velvet, or else you had to match your hair in the day-time and your eyes at night. Think of me in black all day and changing into a nice dark brown for the evening! And oh! My angel children, what price Evelyn walking down Bond Street in a frock that matched her hair?"

"Ripping!" said Tommy Lane with conviction.

Chapter Twenty-Three

"Is IT REALLY ten years since you danced?"

Laydon looked down at Marcia Lane in her tight, short dress. The ball-room was filling rapidly. All the women wore dresses of the same scanty type; nearly all of them had short hair. Marcia's dress would, in colour, have satisfied the arbitrary lady quoted by Elizabeth, since it was a very bright cornflower blue, though nearly covered by a shawl of black net embroidered all over with brilliant silken flowers. In every other respect both Marcia and her dress would have shocked the poor Victorian lady past recovery. Laydon tried to remember how women were dressed in 1914. Not like this anyhow. He said,

"Yes, it's ten years."

"How *odd*!"

"Yes, isn't it? Shall we begin?"

"But look here, you won't know any of the dances. What *did* you dance?"

"Oh, one-steps, Bostons—"

"Oh, Lord!" said Marcia. "Well, if I'm for it, I'm for it. Come along."

Before they had gone the length of the room Marcia's spirits had risen. Modern dancing does not require much knowledge of steps, but makes unlimited demands on a sense of rhythm, poise, and balance. Laydon was holding her as only a good dancer holds his partner, with a firm lightness that promised well. When they were nearly round he said,

"This is quite easy. What do you call it?"

Marcia's suspicion flared.

"Look here, are you pulling my leg? Don't you really know a fox-trot?"

"No—I'm pure savage."

"Honest Injun?"

He nodded.

"Yes—really."

Chris Ellerslie's party was just coming in. As they passed the arch lined with mirrors, Evelyn stood there reflected, her dress a golden sheath, her neck and arms as white as pearls. Marcia threw her a nod.

"I'm back again. Yesterday."

Laydon did not speak. He saw Chris and Evelyn melt into the sliding crowd, and lost them there.

"Where was your farm?" asked Marcia abruptly.

"A little past the back of beyond, Miss Lane. I'm really not civilized at all. I didn't even see a newspaper or get a letter for ten years."

Marcia showed that she was startled, and he laughed a little.

"No, it wasn't penal servitude or a lunatic asylum; it really was a farm."

"And now you've come back? Doesn't it seem strange?"

"Yes, very strange."

"We must all seem queer to you—different to the people you remember. Is that why you watch us?"

"Do I watch you?"

"Yes. I noticed it at once, and I wondered why. Do we seem very queer?"

"You seem different of course—all this short hair, for instance. Why do women do it?"

"Because it's comfortable."

"Never!"—she thought his mocking glance attractive—"Even a savage can't believe that."

She laughed frankly.

"Perhaps because it's the fashion then. Is that better?"

"It sounds more probable."

"Well, as a matter of fact, and to be quite honest, I think people begin because it's the fashion; but they go on because it's comfortable. I wouldn't go back to hair for the world. But people did stare in Spain, I've just come back, you know." They were standing out for a moment, and she lifted a corner of her brilliant shawl. "I brought this with me. Isn't it lovely? I've got one for Evelyn when she really does make up her mind to have Chris. It's not given out yet, is it? We were expecting it every day before I went off, I can't think why she doesn't take him and have done with it. You know, Elizabeth wasn't a bit fair to Chris at dinner. Of course he *is* rather pleased with himself; but he's really brilliant in his own way."

"What way?"

"Well, his last book really did put him rather at the top of the tree. Of course Elizabeth doesn't care for that sort of thing."

"Doesn't she?" said Laydon. "Shall we dance?"

His next partner was Barbara Mostyn. She was so small that Laydon looked right down on to the top of a most exquisitely shingled head of dark red hair. But when they had begun to dance she tilted her face up to him, giving him a view of a little peaked oval, tinted to a greenish white. Her eyelashes were heavily darkened, her eyebrows plucked to a single line, and her small, close lips painted a brilliant orange. She appeared to be dressed in about half a yard of flesh coloured tulle and some beads. She felt as thin and light in his arms as a child of six. She danced exquisitely. During the whole time that the music lasted she did not say a single word; only every now and then the black lashes lifted a little, and a pair of grey-green eyes looked up disturbingly.

It was when they were sitting out that Mrs Mostyn made her first remark:

"You don't dance badly."

"Thank you."

"I very nearly didn't risk it." Here she paused, and the eyes came into play.

Laydon said nothing, and after a moment Barbara dropped her lashes and said, with her faint drawl,

"Have you forgotten how to flirt—or did you never know?"

Laydon looked at her with complete gravity.

"Which do you suppose? You are, I am sure, an expert."

She did not speak at once. Her words at all times were few, and she never hurried over an answer. She busied herself with a small gold vanity case, from which she produced a mirror powder-puff, and lipstick. When she had accentuated the orange curve of her lips, she opened them to say—

"Am I an expert?"

"I should imagine so."

She poised her powder-puff and murmured, "I think you could learn."

Laydon laughed and shook his head.

"I'm much too stupid," he declared.

Barbara Mostyn lit a cigarette, leaned back in her chair, blew a very perfect smoke ring, and said in slow languorous tones,

"Yes, you look stupid." She blew a second ring right at him, and added, *"Very"* after which she spoke no more.

It was with some relief that he claimed Elizabeth for the next dance. She began by telling him that he was really frightfully clever, and then immediately said,

"How did you get on with Barbara? She's the best dancer in the room, and Giles is about the worst, I always give him something at the very end, so that if he does stamp all over my feet, it doesn't so much matter. He's a frightfully good sort. He and Barbara have only been married a month—just back from their honeymoon."

Laydon felt a good deal of pity for Giles. Elizabeth's gay talk flowed on:

"I hope you liked Marcia. She's one of the very best. She's a friend of Evelyn's too. Oh, isn't this a ripping floor?"

Later on, when they were sitting out, she said quite suddenly,

"Do you know, I was at school with Evelyn."

Laydon was rather taken aback, a fact which obviously delighted her.

"I was. You needn't look so incredulous. We've only met about twice since, because I was out in Egypt during the war, and I've only just come back to town. Yes, we were at school together. And I was the Awful Warning and she was the Good Example. You know—just like a tract."

Laydon looked angry.

"I'm sure she wasn't a prig. She—"

"I never said she was."

"That's what you meant."

Elizabeth laughed.

"My Aunt Elizabeth, the one I'm called after, *always* said that the end of my tongue wanted snipping. I expect she was right. Do you really want me to talk discreetly about nothing at all? I will if you like."

"It might be dull."

"It *would* be dull—ditch-water dull. But I'll do it if you like. I *can* do it beautifully. Of course," she added, "I'd rather not. Indiscretion is really the only thing that's the least bit interesting—isn't it?"

Quite suddenly she allowed a softness to veil the lively mockery of her glance. Elizabeth pensive was really lovely enough to melt even the savage that Laydon had proclaimed himself.

"I'm going to be indiscreet," she said. "Why do you just stand and look on?"

"Do I?"

"You know you do. Why do you do it? Don't you just plunge in and let yourself go?"

There was a long pause. Then he said,

"I'm sorry I seem to—watch."

Elizabeth's colour rose brightly.

"But I didn't mean that at all. No, I didn't—*really*. I—my tongue does want snipping, you know. I only meant—" She tripped over her own words and came to a standstill.

The sheet of ice which Laydon felt between himself and all the world thinned for a moment. Elizabeth's warm colour, her shaken voice, her real distress, touched him humanly.

"Mrs Thursley," he said, "please don't. I don't mind. Please don't think that I do."

"Yes, but you ought to," said Elizabeth. "You ought to mind frightfully. That's what I meant. You ought to mind—and you don't."

Laydon nodded.

"Why don't you?"

He felt at once the impulse towards confidence and the complete impossibility of giving way to it. An icy loneliness that sheltered behind indifference; the sense of irreparable loss, of unnatural aloofness; the dream-like quality of all the relationships over which ten empty years had passed—these were things not to be put into words. He did not resent Elizabeth's touch; he even welcomed it. It was warm and kind; and it was meant for him, the Laydon of to-day, and not for some half-remembered shadow of long ago.

The music of the next dance blared out, racing violently from one discord to another. Laydon stood up and held out his arm. They passed into the ball-room, and came face to face with Tommy and Evelyn.

Elizabeth, still a little tremulous, broke into a flood of teasing nonsense:

"I won't have my dance cut, Tommy—I give you fair warning—not for anyone. I've got a perfectly frightful bone to pick with you, and I'm going to pick it without stopping till the next dance begins. This crash-bang thing they're playing is most appropriate. If it isn't called the *Dentists' Drill*, it ought to be."

"None of the best dentists use drills that crash and bang. My dear girl, who *do* you go to?"

Tommy swept her into the circle of dancers, and Laydon found himself standing with Evelyn. He had not meant to speak to her. He certainly had not meant to dance with her; but without a word being spoken, he found himself holding her, moving with her over the smooth, polished floor. The strident strains of the best jazz band in London softened into a sudden reminiscence of a Grieg melody.

The astonishing irony of the situation brought a bitter smile to Laydon's lips. After all the years, to hold Evelyn in his arms again, not in a lover's embrace, but in this light, conventional clasp as he had just held Marcia—Barbara—Elizabeth! He moved with her, not in a lovers' solitude, but in this brilliant thronging crowd under a glare of lights. The Grieg melody mocked him with its echo of streams, and trees, and birds; through it a jazz nightingale uttered a brassy, syncopated trill.

They made the round of the room once, and neither had spoken a single word. Evelyn had as little intended to dance with Laydon as Laydon had intended to dance with her. Since his return he had touched her twice. Once she had given him her hand, and he had taken it as any stranger might have taken it. Once he had caught her wrist in anger. Now his arm was about her, and memory drove the touch of it deep into her consciousness. She did not speak, because she could not speak. Her feet moved to the rhythm of the dance, and, like Laydon, she felt the glare of lights in the golden room, the noise, the intolerable pressure of all these people.

Then suddenly the strange thing happened. It had happened before in the library at Laydon Manor, and it happened again now.

The crowd, the noise, the jarring music faded. They were gone; there was no crowd; there was no sound. She and Laydon were alone in a great solitude and a great silence. And in this solitude and this silence she was so near to him that his pain was her pain, and his loneliness her loneliness.

Laydon, looking down, saw that she was as pale as her pearls. The music crashed into louder discords, shrieked, brayed, moaned, and stopped. As it ceased, Evelyn raised her eyes for a moment to Laydon's face. A while ago Barbara had done the same thing—with a difference. Evelyn's eyes, very dark, very blue, had the look of a child who has wakened suddenly out of a dream; they were full of an innocent trouble and bewilderment.

Without speaking she dropped her hand from his arm and left him. She walked slowly through the mirrored archway and passed out of his sight.

Chapter Twenty-Four

"How do you do? So pleased not to have missed you after all." She delivered this after the manner of stage duchesses, head well up, hand raised, voice pitched for Ponson's ear.

Then, as the door shut, she let herself go in a chuckle.

"Lord, dear, I'm so glad you've come. The woman that let me in had me frozen stiff—made up her mind I was after the forks, I should think. The cheek of her! Not but what you have to be careful in London. Why, a lady I know very well—very nicely connected she is too—well, she had a young man come to take the electric meter, and next thing she knew, she'd lost a silver christening spoon she set a good deal of store by, and a watch and three rings off her dressing table. One of them was only a Mizpah, to be sure; but the others were real garnets and a single-stone diamond that her husband gave her for their silver wedding. So I don't blame anyone for being careful."

"Won't you sit down?" said Evelyn.

"Thanks, dear, I will."

Miss Palliser proceeded to make herself comfortable by pushing one of the large chairs nearer to the fire. She then sat down, crossed her legs—a proceeding which brought the edge of her black velvet skirt rather above the knee—, and loosened her fur.

"I expect you wonder why I've come," she said with engaging frankness. "Well, dear, I wouldn't have, but you've no idea the things that have been happening. I only wonder it hasn't turned my hair, which would have been a pity though I say it myself, for it's the best thing I've got left me barring my teeth—and all my own too, though that doesn't go for so much as it used to. Oh Lord, I should hate to come to hair dye—or false teeth either, for the matter of that." She showed an even row in the best professional manner "Nice, aren't they? My dentist says they're good for as long as I am."

"Did you want to tell me something?" said Evelyn.

Miss Palliser stopped smiling and nodded vehemently.

"That's right," she said. "I should think I *had* got something to tell you. The extraordinary part is that it should come out now after all these years, just in the nick of time as you might say Funny how things happen, isn't it?" She pushed her fur right back as she spoke, revealing some drabbled folds of purple tulle. "All the same, I don't know that it's funny for me. Fact is I can't make up my mind about it. You see, dear, when you've been married as often as I have, you get sort of used to it. But then, on the other hand there's no doubt that if you're free, you're free and if a gentleman gets in a temper and uses language, you can send him about his business, which it isn't so easy to do if you've married him."

"What has happened?"

Evelyn held her cold hands to the fire, and wished she found it easier to keep her head among these tangled irrelevances.

"You may well ask. Well, I said to my friend—you know, dear, the gentleman I told you about—whatever happens, I said, I'm bound to let Mrs Laydon know. So I came right away to find you. And you can't say I've lost much time about it, when you think it was only yesterday I came across the papers."

"What papers?" Evelyn looked up startled. What was coming? She shivered a little, and shrank from the thought of what this new development might be.

"Don't look like that," said Miss Palliser. "It's nothing to hurt you. I'm the one to look, if anyone's going to. But I made up my mind right away that I wouldn't let it worry me, though I don't say it didn't give me a turn after all these years."

"Miss Palliser, won't you tell me what you mean?"

"I'm telling you as fast as I can. Now let me see—perhaps I'd better begin at the beginning. What d'you think?"

Evelyn nodded.

Pearl Palliser removed her fur altogether, and hung it over the back of her chair.

"Nice and hot you've got it in here, I must say." She pulled at the battered strands of tulle round her neck. "Well now, where was I?"

"You were going to begin at the beginning."

Miss Palliser laughed good humouredly.

"So I was. Well, you know the mess you found me in the other day, dear: I'd been having a good old rummage out. As I said to my friend 'What's the good of keeping a lot of stuff you don't want, when a little extra in the way of cash wouldn't come amiss?' So I had a good turn out; and right at the bottom of my box I came across a lot of letters. Well, I threw 'em back. But yesterday I took 'em out again and had a good old read and a good old cry. Some of 'em were from boys I'd forgotten all about; and they made me feel a bit soppy, I can tell you."

She produced a greyish handkerchief and dabbed her eyes, more in the manner of one who performs a rite than because there were any actual tears to dry.

"Well, right at the last, I came across the papers that the parson had sent me from Australia—the one that wrote and told me that Ted was really dead at last—Ted Edwards, you know, dear, my first husband that I told you about. There was the letter from the parson, and there were a lot of other letters and papers that I'd never bothered to read."

Evelyn said, "Oh!"

Miss Palliser heaved a sigh.

"Don't you be in such a hurry to be shocked," she said. "Bothered wasn't the right word. They were letters from other women, and papers about other women. And when I saw that, I thought it was just one of Ted's dirtiest tricks to get the parson to send them off to me; and I wouldn't read them. See, dear?"

"Yes, I see. I beg your pardon."

"Granted," said Miss Palliser with cheerful affability, "Well, I took them out and I thought I'd burn them. And whilst I was turning them over, a photograph dropped out; and when I picked it up, it was a nice little girl with ringlets and a look of Ted, and written on the back was 'Little Nellie from your loving wife, Ellen, July 5th, 'OI.' What d'you think of that?"

Evelyn hesitated.

"I don't know—I'm afraid—"

Miss Palliser tossed her head.

"I married Ted Edwards in '99. What was he doing with a loving wife Ellen and a little girl of five or so in 1901? You see what I mean, dear?"

Evelyn saw. She said "Oh" again rather faintly.

Pearl Palliser nodded.

"Well, after that I read the papers all right through. There were a couple of letters from his loving wife, Ellen; and a poor, miserable, downtrodden, meek-spirited creature he seemed to have got hold of, for it was nothing but she knew he'd got good reasons for not writing, and she'd go on loving him for ever and ever, no matter where he went or what he did. Lord!" said Miss Palliser, "I can tell you it made me sick. I'd never wished Ted back before, but I'd have liked to have had him there for half an hour or so yesterday so that I could tell him just what I thought of him. Well, there were the letters, and there was a marriage certificate."

She stopped abruptly and gazed at Evelyn in an odd, frowning silence. When it had lasted about a minute, Evelyn said,

"Then you—then he—"

"I'd never been married to him at all. The certificate said that he'd married Lucy Ellen Love-grove at St. Barnabas' Church, Chiswick, on the eighteenth of January, 1895—four years before he married me and never suggested anything but a registry." Miss Palliser's fine eyes were very angry. "There's a sort of satisfaction in feeling that I wasn't married to him; and I'm sure I'm heartily sorry for that poor Lucy Ellen creature that *was*, for a worse lot than Ted Edwards I've never met, and don't wish to." She dabbed at the bright, angry eyes, straightened her hat, which had fallen rakishly over one ear, and resumed her ordinary appearance of good nature. "Well, dear you see what a fix I'm in, of course."

"A fix?"

"Yes, dear. Just you think a bit, and you'll see it as plain as I did when my friend put it to me. I went round to him, of course—we're engaged or as good as—and he pointed it out at once. Gentlemen have such a grasp of these things. He said as quick as quick, 'But if you weren't married to Ted Edwards, then you *were* married to Albert Laycock. You're Mrs Albert Laycock,' he said—'that's what you are. And, for all you know to the contrary, Albert Laycock's still alive, waving ladies and shaving gents in Ontario.' 'Oh mercy, Henry, don't!' I said; and I sat down and had a real good cry."

"You poor thing!"

"Well, I don't know. At first I thought I was; and then I wasn't so sure. I'd like to settle down and be comfortable. But there's always the chance that I'd get bored, Henry being one of the respectable ones. Why, what do you think of his telling me not to call him Henry any more till we were sure I was a widow? '*Mr Cowdray* till the cable comes,' were his last words; and I began to think to myself whether I could do with a man that was as proper as all that."

"What cable?" asked Evelyn.

"Oh, I'll say that for Henry, that he doesn't spare expense. He cabled straight away to Albert's brother to know if Albert was alive. It gives one a very uncertain feeling waiting to know whether you're a widow or not."

"It must be horrid."

"But of course, dear, there's always a cheerful side—and I'm not going to mope whichever way it turns out. If Albert's living, well, he's living; and maybe I'd like Ontario well enough. And if he isn't living, I can just take Henry and settle down like I meant to."

Evelyn had been struggling to order her thoughts. Talking to Pearl Palliser, or rather, being talked to by Pearl Palliser, was like trying to walk on a feather bed; there was so little foothold and such vast billowing masses of words.

"But if you really were married to Mr. Laycock—" she began.

Miss Palliser nodded triumphantly. Her hat slipped over the other ear and hung there unregarded whilst its enormous ornament winked in the fire-light.

"I knew you'd get there! It just knocked you off your balance at first like it did me. But I knew you'd tumble to it when you'd time to get your breath, so to speak. If I wasn't married to Ted Edwards, then I *was* married to Albert Laycock; and that knocks out Jim Field and Jack Laydon—knocks 'em right off the map. For whether Albert's alive or not at this moment, he was alive and doing well in 1916, a year after I married Jack, and a good bit more than a year after I married Jim Field; for I met a cousin of his in the street and she told me so. And I told her"—here Miss Palliser became vehement—"that it was a scandal and a shame if he *was*, for he ought to be out in the war like the other poor boys, or at the *very least* in hospital with an arm or a leg off. She didn't like it, and we had words—a nasty, bony cat of a woman with a what-have-you-got-in-the-larder kind of an eye, something like this dear."

Miss Palliser sat bolt upright, folded her hands on her knees, drew in her plump cheeks, pinched in her nose, and pursed her lips. She certainly produced a vivid, if momentary, impression of a sharp-nosed female with a gimlet eye. It was momentary because she broke suddenly into a rich, deep gurgle of laughter.

"Well, well, it takes all sorts to make a world, even if there's some of the sorts you feel you could do without and welcome. Ah, dear, now that reminds me, that Nosey Abbott fellow—you said he *wasn't* a friend of yours—he's been bothering me again, and I can see he means to go on. He's that sort."

Evelyn nodded appreciatively.

"Yes, he is."

"Well, dear, sooner or later he'll bother me into doing what he wants. You see, it's this way—I'm one of those that can't keep on saying no. It's always gone against me, and I don't suppose I shall get the better of it now. I can start off all right; and I said to him the very first time he came, 'Look here, you Mr. Abbott, or whatever your name is, it's not a bit of good your coming here and worrying me, because I don't know *who he is*, and if I did, I'm not going to say. And anyhow I don't see it's any business of yours. And I won't sign any papers, not if you were the King.' *There!* I couldn't have put it any plainer than that, could I?"

Evelyn laughed.

"No, you couldn't."

It was a relief to be able to laugh.

Miss Palliser sighed, but with undiminished cheerfulness of aspect.

"Sounds all right, doesn't it? But I can't keep it up. That's the bother with me. Next time he came with his 'Don't you think this, and don't you think that, and can't you remember about the other?' he got me to say that as like as not Laydon was Jim Field. And for all I know, he'll be back again in a day or two and talk my head off, and I shall come round and find I've put my name to something."

"Oh, you mustn't—you wouldn't do that!"

"Well, I wouldn't unless he bothered me into it. But I might if he did." Miss Palliser rose and picked up her fur. "Well, so long, dear—and if anything more turns up, I'll let you know."

Chapter Twenty-Five

SIR HENRY PROTHERO came in as Evelyn was finishing tea. Miss Palliser had refused to stay, though obviously much gratified at being pressed to do so. It would have given her a good deal of pleasure to recline gracefully in one of Evelyn's arm-chairs and watch the supercilious Ponson bring in the tea; but she felt herself obliged to forgo this pleasure.

"Fact is," she explained, "Henry's waiting. He said he'd take a turn and come back, and I expect"—she straightened her hat and giggled—"I expect his temper will be a bit the worse for wear as it is."

Sir Henry let himself down rather wearily into a chair, took a cup of tea with a "Thank you, thank you, my dear," stirred it, sipped from it, and then began to sniff.

"Evelyn, what an extraordinary—er—scent!"

"Isn't it awful?" said Evelyn. "It's like a sort of nightmare compound of all the cheap scents I used to love when I was a child. I remember one of the housemaids giving me a bottle of Cherry Blossom, and how furious old Nanna was. Could you bear it if I opened the window for a moment?"

She didn't wish to tell Uncle Henry about Pearl Palliser's visit. As she stood by the open window holding back the curtain, she plunged into talk of the Mannings, and to her relief, his attention was diverted.

"Lacy seems very pleased about the flat you've been able to get for them. She says it sounds absolutely 'It.' By the way, have you heard from her? She said she was writing, but she usually says that at least three times before she gets any farther."

"No, she hasn't written."

"Or Monkey? My dear, I think that window might be shut now."

She shut it and came back to the fire.

"No, I haven't heard from Monkey. He doesn't write unless he's got something to say."

Sir Henry ran his hand over his chin.

"I heard from him this morning," he said.

"Did you?"

"Yes. He'd just seen the man they sent down to make inquiries about that identity disc."

"Oh!" Evelyn drew in her breath very sharply. She looked, but did not speak.

Sir Henry raised his hand and let it fall again.

"It's a case of *spurlos versenkt*—not a trace of it, not a single trace. And the extraordinary thing is that not only can he not trace the disc itself, but he can't trace anyone who ever saw the thing or heard of anyone else seeing it."

"Oh," said Evelyn. The breath that carried the sound was so soft that Sir Henry wondered whether he had really detected a tone of relief.

He said, "A little more tea, my dear—it's one of the coldest days I can remember." Then when he had taken his cup again he harked back: "It's a most extraordinary thing, because Anna Blum particularly says in her deposition that she left the identity disc lying on the top of the clothes by the waterfall. Well, the man—his name's Müller, by the way, and he's half German—Müller says he interviewed and cross-examined six people who saw and handled the clothes, and they all swear positively that there was no identity disc. The local authorities gave him every facility. The records speak of a British officer, name unknown; and there is a rough wooden cross on the grave with a similar inscription. It appears that the clothes were found, in the first instance, by two boys of twelve and thirteen. They swear that they didn't touch them; they said they were very frightened and ran away. The father of one of them, the grandfather and uncle of the other, and a woman who seems to be the village busybody, returned with the boys to the waterfall. They all swear that the clothes were lying in a pile, and that there was no disc. Now, my dear, we've all been building very much on the belief that the disc would be recovered. It would naturally have settled the question of identity once and for all. Well, it hasn't been recovered."

Sir Henry put down his cup and leaned forward, speaking very earnestly.

"It hasn't been recovered, and I can now see no prospect of its being recovered. My dear, I don't want to distress you. But you must really consider whether you are justified in withholding any information you possess."

Evelyn slipped out of her chair and knelt in front of the fire. All that Sir Henry could see of her face was the line of cheek and throat. She put a log on the fire, and stayed kneeling, with her hands held to the glow.

"Do you want me to justify myself?" she said at last.

He was pained, and his voice showed it.

"No—no—not to me—certainly not to me. But you know, Evelyn, there are others to consider. Cotterell now—he's feeling the strain very much. Cotty doesn't give him much peace."

"Oh—Cotty—"

"I know. But he has to be reckoned with. Cotterell's a hasty man. I think myself he ought to have waited a little before he altered his will. I think we all wanted a little time. Well, he wouldn't wait; and now he's beginning to wonder whether he oughtn't to have waited. You see, there's no doubt we all allowed ourselves to build a good deal on the identity disc turning up. It hasn't turned up. That means there's no definite proof—nothing that would hold in a court of law. And Cotty declares that this woman, Pearl Palliser, has admitted to him that she recognized Laydon as Jim Field."

Evelyn went on warming her hands, but she looked round for a moment with rather a strange little smile.

"I shouldn't worry about that, darling. She'd say he was King Edward, or Napoleon, or George Bernard Shaw if you pressed her. She told me Cotty was bothering her to death, and she supposed she'd end up by signing anything he wanted her to. She's like that, you know,—a sort of moral jellyfish."

"You've been seeing her again?"

She nodded, and settled herself on the hearthrug in a sitting position.

"Gregory ought to see her. Unfortunately he's had to go away for a change. I'll put him on to her as soon as he gets back. But meanwhile, my dear, don't you think it would be wiser to share your knowledge with us?"

Evelyn locked her hands about her knees. She looked down at her emerald ring.

"Don't you see?" said Sir Henry—"my dear Evelyn, don't you see that the disappearance of the identity disc means that there will be no external evidence such as would settle the case? We're thrown back on the possibility that Laydon may recover his memory or, alternatively, may declare himself. Now, the longer this is delayed, the harder it will be to convince everyone concerned. Cotty Abbott will point out with perfect truth that the interval—even such an interval as has already elapsed—might quite easily be used to bolster up a fictitious claim by acquiring detailed information about the family affairs. He would point out that Sir Cotterell has himself placed Laydon in a position to acquire this information. He's living at the Manor; he has access to the family papers; and he's in touch with old servants like Lake. You see, it's very difficult to answer. And the longer it goes on, the harder it will be for Laydon to make out a convincing case. If he knows who he is, he ought to say so at once. And if you think you have recognized him, you ought at least to tell Cotterell and myself what grounds you have for this recognition."

Evelyn went on looking at her ring. There was a slight smile about her lips. If she had been moved by emotion the other day, she showed no traces of it now. Her thought was calm and tinged with affectionate amusement. Darling Uncle Henry was addressing her as if she were a deputation or a legislative council—he really did it awfully well. When he had finished, she said in her gentlest voice:

"Yes, I know, darling. But I can't."

Sir Henry sighed. An angry woman may come round. A tearful woman will certainly give way in the end. But the woman who smiles and speaks gently means what she says, and a wise man does not waste good arguments upon her.

"Well, well," he said, and left it at that.

Evelyn jumped up, sat on the arm of his chair, and kissed him.

"Angel!" she said. Then she kissed him again. "I'm crossing to Cologne to-morrow. Have you any messages for Lacy?"

Chapter Twenty-Six

EVELYN STOOD at Anna Blum's door and knocked. The sun shone hot upon the door and the doorstep, and upon Evelyn herself. The stone was warm under her feet, and the air was full of that strange, gentle, spring sound which some people cannot hear at all, the sound of all the green things upon the earth beginning to stretch themselves and grow. Evelyn looked up at a little patch of heavenly blue right overhead. Then she knocked again. This time there were footsteps. The door opened, and Anna stood there, looking at her with that grave, considering look of hers which told nothing.

Evelyn put out her hand with a friendly smile.

"I've come back. May I come in?"

"Certainly." Anna's tone was neither friendly nor unfriendly.

She shut the door, set a chair, took one herself, and picked up her knitting, a sock that was almost finished. The room was warm; the sun shone in through a tightly closed window and made a bright patch on the floor between Evelyn and Anna. It touched Anna's shoulder as it passed, and showed how shabby the stuff of her afternoon dress had grown. It had been a rather bright blue once, and twenty years earlier when Anna had first inherited it from her aunt and godmother, Anna Strohmacher born Müller, she had been very proud of it. As Anna knitted, her arm moved in and out of the slanting sunbeam. Just at the elbow-there was hardly any blue left in the stuff at all, and there was a neat square darn.

It was not Anna's custom to begin a conversation. She knitted in a composed silence until Evelyn leaned forward and said,

"Major Manning came to see you the other day, didn't he?"

Anna nodded.

"It was on Tuesday. I remember because of the baking. I bake on Tuesdays and Fridays, just as my mother did. Everyone to his own liking is what I say; but as far as I am concerned, my mother's ways are good enough for me."

Evelyn found herself obliged to start all over again.

"You saw Major Manning, and he told you that the identity disc could not be found."

"Yes, he told me—and I am sorry. But what would you have?" She shrugged her broad shoulders. "Ten years is a long time, and a little thing like that may very well be lost when you think of all the things that have been lost in ten years."

Her tone was dry and unconcerned. But Evelyn had a quick vision of lost crowns, lost causes. Truly in the ten years between 1915 and 1925 too many things had been lost in Germany to make the loss of one small disc a matter of importance. She had to make an effort to recover her sense that it was important.

"I think Major Manning told you that he had had a report from the man who went down to make inquiries for Mr Laydon's family."

Anna shrugged again.

"*Ach!* Inquiries—after ten years!"

"It's a long time; but the people who found the clothes seemed to remember everything very clearly. I expect they would have told the story a good many times in the ten years, and that would fix it in their memories."

"Perhaps," said Anna politely.

"I saw Mr Müller myself yesterday, Frau Blum."

"Yes," said Anna, "I also saw him—not yesterday—no, it was on Wednesday that he came, the day after I had seen the *Herr Major*."

Evelyn admired her composure; if she did know anything, it was extraordinary. "My dear girl, you won't get a thing out of her," Manning had said. "I've tried, and Müller's tried. If she does know anything, she means to keep it to herself. But go along and have a shot if you want to. You can't do any harm." She bit her lip and began again. Anna's end of the conversation seemed always to be falling to the ground. When one tried to pick it up, there was nothing to take hold of, and one had to begin all over again.

"Mr Müller said that he thought the two young men were speaking the truth. They declared most positively that they were much too frightened to touch anything or to go near the clothes. They were only little boys at the time, and when they saw the clothes they were dreadfully frightened and thought a savage Englishman would spring out on them and kill them. They said they ran as fast as their legs would carry them, and never stopped until they got home."

Anna shifted the sock she was knitting.

"Boys are very untruthful," she observed. "If one of them had taken the disc to look at, and it had dropped into the water, that is what he would say without doubt. He would be frightened, and he would run away; and afterwards, if anyone questioned him, he would say that he had never seen any disc. Boys are like that; they have no conscience. I have had five brothers, besides nephews and cousins, and I know what I am saying."

This was a long speech for Anna to make. It contained, however, so much common sense that Evelyn found it difficult to answer. It was whilst she was wondering what she would say next that Anna looked at her searchingly and asked:

"Why do you so much wish that the disc should be found?"

Evelyn met the look, and was a little puzzled by it.

"I think Major Manning told you why we are anxious to find the disc. Didn't he tell you?"

Anna nodded.

"Something he told me. There were two cousins, and Anton, it seems, is one of them. But he does not know which of the two he is. And the *Herr Major*, who was the friend of both, does not know, nor the old grandfather to whom the estate belongs, nor you, *gnädige Frau*, who are the wife of one of them. That," said Anna, still placidly knitting, "that to me seems a very singular thing. *Ach, ja—sonderbar.*" She shrugged her shoulders, and a very slight, ironic smile played about her lips.

Evelyn's colour rose sharply.

"Frau Blum!"

She sprang up.

"*Ach ja—sonderbar,*" murmured Anna.

"Frau Blum!"

Anna raised her eyes, saw the brilliant flush the quivering lips. She spoke gently, as if she were addressing a child:

"Sit down, and do not be angry. I meant no harm."

Evelyn's flush died away.

"If you cannot tell me anything, it's no use for me to stay."

"Sit down," said Anna.

"No." Evelyn shook her head. "But I want to say one thing. I want you to understand that it is for Mr Laydon's sake that we want to find the disc. Even if I knew who he was a hundred times over, it would not help. You see, people would say that I was mistaken, or deceived, or that I wanted to make out a case in order to help him. We want to find the disc because we want a proof that will stop everybody's mouth and put him in his right place."

Anna went on knitting.

"Why does he not come himself?" she asked. "Why does he send you?"

"He doesn't send me."

"Does he know you have come?"

"No, I don't think so."

"*Ach, so—*"

There was a pause. The little triangle formed by the stitches at the toe of the sock had diminished until Anna seemed to be continually turning her work and putting in a fresh needle; the sock was almost done.

"Then why have you come?" said Anna at last.

"I have told you why."

"He is a man. It is his affair. Why do you concern yourself?"

Evelyn laughed, a queer, involuntary laugh that left her rather shaken.

"I think you know quite well why I have come."

"Perhaps," said Anna, "you wish to be sure that you are a widow. *Ach*, yes, that understands itself. You are young and beautiful, and you wish, no doubt, to marry again."

"No, you don't really think that," said Evelyn gently. "You know very well that I love him."

"Love?" said Anna. "What sort of love is it that doesn't know a man because his shoulders have grown broad and his face has changed? I would not call that love."

Evelyn stood looking at her. She was pale now, and her voice was not quite steady. She was saying things to Anna that she had never said to anyone. She was saying them to Anna because Anna loved him too.

"Frau Blum, have I said that I do not know him?"

"You have not said it."

There were only two needles left in the sock. Anna knitted the few remaining stitches, drew the needles out, and pulled her thread tight through the last loop. Then she got up.

Evelyn turned to the door.

"I'll go. What's the good of our talking this?"

"There is no hurry," said Anna. "You say that you love him?"

Evelyn looked at her without speaking. She was proud, but there was no pride in the look. Her eyes were dark with unshed tears.

"Does he love you?" said Anna.

"I don't know—I don't think so—he doesn't say."

"He will love you. You are beautiful."

Evelyn flushed to the roots of her hair.

"I don't want that sort of love."

"*Ach, was*—one takes what one can get. It is the giving that counts. For the rest, men are as they are made."

Evelyn felt that she could bear no more. She put her hand on the door and groped for the latch. The tears began to run down her cheeks. She felt that she had been weighed and found wanting, judged and condemned. A cold unhappiness welled up in her. A line once familiar came into her mind and stayed there:

"The unplumbed, salt, estranging sea."

It was such a sea, strange, oblivious, that stretched between her and Laydon.

Anna's hand fell on her arm.

"You are in a great hurry all at once. Will you not take the disc before you go?"

Evelyn's hands pressed against the door. She stayed like that, quite still. There was a silence.

"*Na*, I will get it," said Anna.

She let go of Evelyn's arm, crossed the room, and went up the stair, all in her usual slow, deliberate manner.

When Evelyn heard her moving about in the room above, she made an effort and turned. She still leaned against the door; but she faced the room now. She could see the finished sock lying on the edge of the table, the chair in which Anna had sat and knitted, her own chair pushed hastily back, and the patch of bright sunshine on the clean floor. She could hear Anna coming down the stair, and quite suddenly she wanted to run away. She wanted to wrench open the door behind her and run as fast as flying feet could carry her, down the path to where Monkey was waiting with the car. She did not want to see the disc, or to touch it, or to read the name on it.

Anna came in, and Evelyn straightened herself. She did not want to look at Anna; but she made herself look, and saw her come forward with her hand out—and on the palm of it something wrapped up in a square of yellowish paper. One of the corners of the paper was torn. She raised her eyes to Anna's face, and found it calmly expressionless.

"You had it all the time!"

Anna came up to the table and stood there.

"And you are thinking that I lied to you. But"—the broad shoulders lifted a little—"that I did not do." She laid the little packet on the top of the Bible, and just touched it with one of her work-roughened fingers. "No, I did not lie. What I told you was true, only—I did not tell you all."

"Will you tell me now?"

"Yes, now I will tell you. Perhaps you will understand me—perhaps not. But I will tell you."

"You said you put the disc on the top of the clothes."

Anna nodded.

"That is true. All that I told you is quite true. I put the disc on the top of the clothes, and I did not look at it or read the name. I thought I had meddled enough. Then I went home; and in the night, when I was sitting there watching the Englishman, I began to think about Anton, the real Anton. I did not love him, you understand; he was a burden to me, and he was rough and violent. But, after all, he was my husband's nephew, and I thought of him a little. I did not weep, but I tried to think good, pious thoughts. And then it came to me that Anton would be buried in an Englishman's name, and that perhaps he would be buried with that disc about his neck. I did not know what they would do with it, but I thought perhaps they would bury it with him; and it came over me that Anton had hated the English very much, and what would he say if he rose on the Judgment Day with an Englishman's name about his neck? Perhaps it seems foolish to you. Sometimes it has seemed foolish to me; but that night it did not seem foolish. I thought of Anton rising *am Jüngsten Tag* and being very angry; and at the last I could bear it no longer. I put on my things and went up through the wood, and took the disc from the top of the clothes and brought it home. I did not look at it. I folded it up in a piece of writing paper, and I hid it in a safe place."

"You didn't look?" said Evelyn.

Anna touched the little packet again.

"No, I have never looked. Why should I want to know his name? I thought I knew too much. I did not want to know any more. If one does not know a thing, one can swear that one does not know it, and there is no lie on one's conscience. I was brought up to speak the truth, and I do not like to tell lies."

"But why," said Evelyn, "Frau Blum, why didn't you say before that you had the disc?"

Anna laughed.

"Why should I say?"

"Why shouldn't you?" said Evelyn.

"Do you really ask that? Think a little. Already I have trouble enough for what I have done. I do not complain. But I do not wish for any more trouble—and in Germany one may get into very bad trouble indeed over such a thing as keeping back papers, or certificates, or such-like. Also I had the thought that if I kept the disc—" She paused and looked at Evelyn. "*Na*, that was nothing but foolishness."

Evelyn came a little nearer.

"What did you think?"

"I thought that perhaps he would come back," said Anna Blum. "I thought I would keep it. I thought he would come back and ask for it himself."

She picked up the disc in its yellow paper and held it out.

"There you have it. Open it and read the name."

Evelyn made no movement to take it. She lifted her head and spoke very gently, but as if from a distance:

"I don't want to open it. I don't want to read the name."

Something in Anna responded. She nodded.

"What then do you want?"

"I want it for his family—for Sir Cotterell Laydon. I don't want it for myself at all; I want it to use if there is trouble about the succession."

"Take it then. It has never been unwrapped."

Still Evelyn did not put out her hand.

"I don't want to take it like that. I want you to do something for me. I want you to sew it up in a piece of stuff. Will you do it?"

A curious look of comprehension came into Anna's eyes. She nodded slowly twice and put the disc back on the Bible. Then she opened her work-box and produced a scrap of linen.

"With this I have been patching the last of my grandmother's sheets. It is good old linen; now there is none like it any more."

She pressed the paper close about the disc, set it on the linen, and cut a square. Then she threaded a needle, turned the edge of the linen in neatly, and ran a draw-string of stout thread all round it. When the disc was in its linen bag, she fastened it with a few strong stitches and put it into Evelyn's hand.

As their fingers touched, Anna said sharply,

"Is he well? Is he happy? You have told me nothing."

Evelyn held the disc. The linen was cold against her palm.

"He is well."

"And happy?" Anna's round blue eyes accused her.

"No, he isn't happy."

"Why?"

"I don't know why."

Something fierce came into Anna's voice.

"He was happy here where he had nothing. Now he has everything, and he is not happy. Whose fault is that?"

"No one has everything, Frau Blum."

Evelyn turned to the door and opened it. The sun streamed in. It dazzled her, and she turned back. Anna had not moved. There was a great sadness in her face.

"Some of us have nothing," she said.

Evelyn had an extraordinary impulse of understanding and pity; her heart went out to Anna. She kissed her quickly on the cheek and ran through the open doorway into the sunshine and down the winding path among the trees.

Chapter Twenty-Seven

"Monkey, I think you're absolutely *weak* about Evelyn."

Lacy's flute-like voice was a little plaintive. She felt herself justly aggrieved. To begin with, it was a very fine day and she would have enjoyed the drive. Why then should Monkey have insisted on her remaining at home—really *insisted*—when all she had ever suggested was that she should sit in the car and keep him company whilst Evelyn went to see Frau Blum?

"You can say what you like, Monkey, but it would have been much better if I had come with you as I *suggested*. Suppose Evelyn had *fainted*, or anything like that?"

"She didn't faint, thank the Lord."

"She might have fainted—you never know. And if she *had* fainted, why, then I should have been *there*. And *anyhow* I should have *insisted* on hearing what had happened, whereas, as far as I can make out, you let her come back looking like a ghost, and didn't ask her a single question."

"My child, what a dramatic mind you've got! I didn't say Evelyn looked like a ghost; I said she looked as if she'd had a trying scene with Anna. And when she got into the car and said, 'You won't ask any questions, Monkey,—will you?', well, I naturally didn't ask any. And what's more, Lacy, you're not going to ask any either."

Lacy smiled and dropped him a little curtsey.

"Really?" she said. "And how are you going to stop me, Monkey darling?"

Manning put a hand on her shoulder. All the lines on his face deepened.

"I'm serious."

She twisted away from him with a pettish laugh.

"And so am I serious. Evelyn's my very own cousin, and I shall ask her as many questions as I like."

Manning went out of the room and banged the door behind him.

A little later Lacy had an opportunity of putting her questions. She spent the whole of the evening alone with Evelyn, but she did not get much farther than:

"I hope your visit to Frau Blum went off all right."

"Oh, yes, quite all right," was the very composed reply.

"You won't want to go again now, will you?"

"No, I don't think so."

"Did you get anything out of her?"

There was a little silence. Evelyn looked up from the letter she was writing.

"I'm so sorry—what did you say?"

"I asked whether you got anything out of her. Monkey says she's as close as wax."

"I'm frightfully sorry for her," said Evelyn.

She went on writing, and Lacy began to realize that her question had been left unanswered for the second time. She returned to the charge with obstinate sweetness:

"You didn't get anything out of her, I suppose?"

"Her? Oh, Frau Blum. Sorry, Lacy, I'm rather in the middle of this letter." Then, after a pause, "Do you mind if we don't talk about it?"—after which there was really no more to be said.

Evelyn returned to town with the Mannings. Manning had leave before taking up his appointment, and he and Lacy went straight to Laydon Manor in response to a rather urgent invitation from Sir Cotterell.

Evelyn went back to her flat to pick up a few things. She had spent a fortnight at Laydon Manor in May every year for the last nine years. This year's visit loomed rather terrifyingly in her thought, since Laydon would as a matter of course be there, and to live under the same roof with him, move with him amongst the old remembered places, was an ordeal from which she shrank. The Mannings had been asked in order to make the situation a little easier. Lacy, gratified and important, was already very much the chaperone.

"Because, of course, Evelyn darling, it's a very, very delicate position; and I'm not at all sure it wouldn't be *wiser* for you to give up your visit this year."

Evelyn surveyed her with a smile.

"Lacy, or the dragon!" she observed. "It's frightfully edifying, but it'll give you lines and turn you into a frump if you go on with it."

"All the same, Evelyn darling,—"

"Come right off it," said Evelyn. "I'm not taking any."

It was whilst Evelyn was considering whether she would pack her green tea-gown that the front door bell rang. Ponson, pausing at her door, inquired whether she was at home, and Evelyn, after saying "No," suddenly changed her mind and said "Yes."

It might, of course, be Cotty or Mrs Cotty. But on the other hand it might be Marcia Lane, whom she really wanted to see—or it might be Laydon. The bare possibility was enough to make her revoke her "No."

She went into the drawing-room and waited, furious with herself because her cheeks were hot. She bent over the fire to provide them with a legitimate excuse, and heard behind her the sound of the opening door and Ponson's voice, very carefully restrained:

"Mrs Albert Laycock."

The door was shut again, and Evelyn found herself gazing spellbound at Pearl Palliser in mourning garb so deep that it fairly took her breath away. She had on a dress which was almost covered with rustling crape and a long widow's veil. Her hands were encased in black kid gloves, and she wore the widest and most noticeable of lawn collars and cuffs. A jet chain hung to her knees.

Evelyn found herself shaking hands.

"Well, dear," said Miss Palliser, "you see how it is."

"Mr Laycock?"

"Gone," said Miss Palliser. Her voice was cheerful, but she raised her eyes perfunctorily to the ceiling. "The cable came whilst you were real away. Very prompt, I'm sure, and only goes to prove what I've always said, that it's a real blessing to be living in up-to-date times, where you're not kept waiting months and years to hear a bit of news."

She paused to take breath, and settled herself comfortably in a chair by the fire.

"Well, dear, I'm a widow *this* time, and no human doubt about it. And you'll be pleased to hear that my banns are put up to marry Henry Cowdray a month from to-day."

"Oh, I hope you'll be happy," said Evelyn. She tried to keep her fascinated gaze from the black kid gloves and the folds of the widow's veil.

Miss Palliser nodded comfortably.

"You're looking at my mourning. Nice, isn't it? Makes me look slim too. A bit extravagant perhaps, but I said to Henry straight away when the cable came, 'All right, Henry,' I said, 'poor Albert's gone, and I'll marry you as soon as you can get the banns put up; but I'm not going to be done out of my weeds for you, or for anyone else either, and that's that.' You see, dear, I never got a chance to wear them for Ted Edwards, because he just kind of faded away, and when I did really hear from that Australian parson—well, I was married to Jim Field, or thought I was, and it'd have looked a bit queer if I'd come out a widow—a bit sudden as you might say. Then when Jim Field and Jack Laydon were missing—I don't know, I didn't seem to have the heart to bother about it. You may believe me or not just as you like, but I did cry my eyes out over those two boys, and I didn't seem to have the heart to think about being dressy." She took a stiff new handkerchief with a black border and applied it to her eyes.

Evelyn found herself unable to think of anything to say. She gazed sympathetically at Miss Palliser, and after a moment the black-gloved hand withdrew the handkerchief and disclosed Miss Palliser's naturally cheerful expression.

"Well, I'm a fool to cry, to be sure,—and when a drop of water's ruin to crape and all. Well, where was I? Oh, I was talking about being extravagant. Henry had a lot to say about it. But don't you think I was right, dear,—not to give way I mean? It isn't as if it'd all go to waste either. The gloves, and the collar and cuffs, and the crape I grant you; but there's a friend of mine that'll be glad enough to have them. And as to the rest, I told Henry he didn't know what he was talking about. I can put a touch of colour on the dress and wear it out in the afternoon as easy as easy. And I rather thought of putting that nice large paste ornament I had on the other day right across the front of the hat. But there, dear, men are obstinate, and the less they know about a thing, the more fuss they kick up."

She stopped, displayed a momentary embarrassment, fidgeted with her handkerchief, and then said rather abruptly,

"I suppose now, you wouldn't come and see me married, would you?"

"Oh, yes, I would," said Evelyn. "I will if I'm in town."

"Of course if it hadn't been for a kind of accident, as you may say, you might have been coming to my wedding as a connection so to speak. But as I *was* married to Albert Laycock, why, then of course I never was Mrs Jack Laydon, though I thought so at the time and for ten years after. But of course I'm not asking you to come for that because I'm not a family connection any more, and never was. It's just a fancy I've got, to have you there, dear. And it'll be in church, as I told you, and all very proper and respectable, Henry being a sidesman and taking round the bag on Sundays." She went off into deep chuckling laughter. "Now, dear," she said, "I'm coming to business. I didn't come here to talk about myself, but to tell you I'd had Nosey Parker round again."

"Mr Abbott?"

"Mr Nosey Parker Abbott. Oh, Lord, he *is* a nosey one too! And I'm afraid you'll be angry with me, dear; but he worried me into it."

"Into what?" Evelyn's tone was alarmed.

Miss Palliser nodded ruefully.

"He worried me into it. I told you as like as not he *would*. And he did. First thing I knew, I had a pen in my hand signing my name."

"Oh, Miss Palliser, *don't*! What did you sign?"

"A paper," said Miss Palliser in tones of gloom. "He took it down, and wrote it out, and put the pen into my hand, and next thing I knew I was signing my name. And he asked me as sharp as a ferret, 'Is that your legal name?' and I said 'Lord knows,' for the cable hadn't come."

"Oh, Miss Palliser, what did you sign?"

"Well, seeing it was all so uncertain, I put Pearl Palliser."

"No, no. I mean what was in the paper?"

"Don't ask me, dear."

"But you must know."

"Can't say I do. But it was something about recognizing you know who, and being sure he was Jim Field the first time I saw him."

Evelyn bit her lip. It was no good being angry.

Miss Palliser got up reluctantly.

"Well, so long," she said. "Henry's waiting for me to go and choose a carpet with him, and I'd rather he was in a good temper for it. It might make as much as five pounds difference in the price— you never know. I'll send you a card about the wedding. And here's luck to you."

She went towards the door, but turned as Evelyn touched the bell.

"Look here, dear," she said, "I don't mind telling you now that, honest, I don't know which he is. Sometimes I've thought he was one, and sometimes another. That's the gospel truth. And now, as far as I'm concerned, I don't *care*. See? He may be Jim Laydon, or he may be Jack Laydon, or he may be Jim Field, which I've put my name to. Whichever of the three he is, he's not my husband, thank goodness, for I want to settle down comfortably with Henry. And you're free to take your pick, dear. Well, cheery-o!"

She opened the door, waved affably, and, encountering Ponson, became with startling suddenness a figure of majestic woe. Even the fact that the coat which she had left in the hall was both old and shabby did not impair her dignity. She assumed the garment after the manner of a tragedy queen, and departed full of inward satisfaction.

Evelyn stood in the middle of the room, quite still. "You're free to take your pick." An anger that was like ice and a pride like fire fought in her.

Chapter Twenty-Eight

EVELYN DROVE HERSELF down to Laydon Manor next day, arriving in time for tea. Laydon did not appear, and after tea she went for a long solitary ramble through the woods behind Laydon Sudbury.

Primroses lingered in the shady places, but on the open grassy slopes cowslips, cuckoo-pint and purple orchises were flowering, whilst in any open glade the bluebell buds were almost out. After a very long, cold winter, which had left no room for spring, just to see blue sky, to walk in the open without furs, and to feel the warmth of the sun and the softness of the May air was pure delight.

Evelyn came slowly up the gardens with the sun low behind her, and fell in with Lacy in the beech walk. She had had her solitary hour and was feeling at peace with all the world, not wanting to plan or to think, but just to be with people whom she loved, in this lovely green place where the light was golden and birds were singing.

"Where have you been?" said Lacy. "I think you might have told me you were going for a walk." This from Lacy who hated the country, and walking, and wet grass and muddy shoes.

Evelyn laughed at her.

"It's all very *well*, Evelyn, but you've no idea how bored I've been. I don't *like* walking, but I'd rather walk than be bored to death. Uncle Cotterell's in one of his very worst tempers, shut up in the library with Monkey. And nobody's brought a novel into the house since Aunt Catherine died about forty years ago."

"Poor old Lacy!"

Evelyn slipped an arm through hers. The beech walk was a grassy lane smoothly mown and guarded by tall beech hedges still brown and bare, with some of last year's copper leaves clinging to them. It took a right-angle turn at the top of the long, gentle slope, and thence led to the terraces below the house. Just where it turned, in the far angle, the hedge was interrupted, showing an old brick wall with a heavily clamped oak door.

Lacy stopped, looked at the door, hesitated, and then said,

"Do they still keep it locked?" Evelyn nodded. "But you've got your key—I know Uncle Cotterell gave you one."

"Yes."

Evelyn was remembering her wedding day, and Sir Cotterell's words: "The key of the Lady's Garden, my dear. You know the story. No one goes into it unless the lady of the house takes them. And if you care for old customs, you should go there for the first time with Jim."

Lacy's high, sweet voice broke in:

"I wish you'd take me in, Evelyn—I've never been."

"Nor have I." Evelyn's tone was dry.

"Never been? How extraordinary! You've never used your key?"

"No."

"Evelyn, darling, how weird of you! I've always wanted to go in so dreadfully. Do they keep it up?"

"Oh, yes. McAlister always asks me about the flowers."

"Oh, he goes in?"

"Yes, the head gardener has a key—and Sir Cotterell. But Sir Cotterell never uses his."

"Evelyn, *do* take me in. I wonder if the story is true."

"Yes, I think so. I don't know why it shouldn't be. They used to do things like that in the fifteenth century. It was a vow, you know,—she swore no one should see her face till her lord came back from the wars. She was frightfully beautiful, but she wore a veil always, except when she walked in this garden. She had the wall built all round it, and she used to walk up and down, and pray for him to come back."

"I forget if he came—and I forget her name," said Lacy.

"Her name was Aveline de Waveney, and she was married to Sir Cotterell's twentieth great-grandfather. He came back when they were both quite old. But she went on wearing her veil—I expect she'd got used to it."

"Oh, *do* take me in. Evelyn, you will, won't you?"

"No, my child, I won't."

Lacy maintained an offended silence for about two minutes. Then she said in an injured voice,

"I wish I hadn't come. You're horrid, and Uncle Cotterell's wild, and the Gaunts are coming up from the Vicarage to dine, and they've got a perfectly awful cousin staying with them, and of course they've got to bring her."

"Don't be cross, Lacy. Why is Sir Cotterell wild?"

"Oh, Cotty Abbott, of course. I don't *blame* Uncle Cotterell. Cotty's enough to drive anyone out of their senses—even without being married to that perfectly awful Sophy!"

"What's Cotty done now?"

"Well, he rang up just after you went out, and Uncle Cotterell came back foaming at the mouth, and said that Cotty said that he and Sophy were coming down to-morrow with *documentary* evidence to prove that Uncle Cotterell had been imposed on. We *shall* have a cheerful dinner tonight and no mistake. The Gaunt cousin is the most *awful* woman. I think I shall put on that tea-gown I got from Toinette. It cost the most frightful amount—I simply *daren't* tell

Monkey how much—and if a party's going to be *extra* dreadful, I do think it helps one through to know that your clothes have cost a *great* deal more than they ought to have."

Laydon was the last of the family party to come into the drawing-room that evening.

It was a delicately proportioned room panelled in white, with recessed windows that looked upon the terrace; but it was rather obviously a room without a mistress. A portrait in water colours of the last Lady Laydon smiled archly from the centre panel above the hearth. Her husband stood just below, talking in vehement tones to Manning and Sir Henry Prothero. Lacy in black and gold—a great deal of gold and very little black—was standing on tiptoe, trying to catch the effect of her new tea-gown in the long Empire mirror whose scroll work had gone a little dim with age.

Laydon's thought as he came in was a quick: "She hasn't come!" Then something white moved in the farthest recess, and Evelyn dropped the pale blue curtain behind her and came down the room.

"Such a lovely night! There'll be a moon too," she said. Then she gave Laydon her hand and a sweet, strange smile, and passed on.

"Mr and Mrs Gaunt—Mrs Weatherby," said Lake at the door; and Evelyn became involved in greetings and a long explanatory introduction.

"Evelyn, my dear,"—this was the Vicar—"it is good to see you again. I feared, we all feared—at least Marion says 'No', but I was very much afraid—that we should not have the pleasure of seeing you here this year—Marion, my dear, why do you pinch me? It is all the greater pleasure. And let me introduce our cousin—or at least Marion's cousin—who is staying with us, we hope, for quite a long visit."

He had got as far as this, when Mrs Gaunt interposed briskly:

"Mrs Weatherby—Mrs Laydon."

Evelyn shook hands with a tall, dark woman in an extravagantly fluffy garment composed of bright pink beads and bright blue tulle. The lady showed a good many bones, and waved a large feather fan in rainbow shades of pink and blue and green. She had a hard eye, a loud voice, and an over-assured manner. Nothing short of a lifelong affection for the Gaunts could have infused any cordiality into Evelyn's manner.

At dinner, up to a certain point, Mrs Weatherby proved a God-send, for she talked with so much sustained energy as to save everybody else a great deal of trouble. She had been to all the latest plays; she had read all the latest books. In the world of politics she knew exactly why So-and-So had failed of a Cabinet post, and why Somebody Else had applied for the Chiltern Hundreds. She sat between Laydon and Sir Henry, but her conversation was by no means confined to them. If she dropped her voice a shade in order to acquaint Laydon with the true scandalous history of *Mlle Une Telle*, who had recently been gracing the London stage, she did not drop it so far as to deprive anyone else of a single interesting detail.

Mr Gaunt, vaguely benign, began to feel his vagueness invaded by a shade of embarrassment. Mrs Gaunt, small, brisk, precise, made two or three attempts to stem the flood. Her little dry cough and her "Are you quite sure, my dear Millicent, that your information is correct?" had no other effect than to induce a yet more copious flow from dear Millicent's lips. Evelyn caught Lacy's eye once, and it said *"I told you so"* with so much poignancy that she did not dare to meet it again.

It was with the savoury, however, that the worst moment arrived. Dear Millicent, having pilloried a Bishop, given reasons why at least two Deans should be unfrocked, and left a Judge, three Actresses, and a very prominent K.C. without a vestige of moral support, suddenly flung Chris Ellerslie's name into the arena:

"I adore his books, of course, though they say he'll gamble away whatever it is he makes out of one, in a single night. He's a Mah Jong fiend, and they tell me—of course I don't play myself—that you can drop an absolutely unlimited amount. Not that that matters to Chris, because I hear he's frightfully well off—outside his books, you know—and he's going to marry a pretty widow with pots of money. Some people have all the luck. I don't know her name, but the man who told me declared she was quite pretty—the golden-haired, blue-eyed type, if you admire it; I can't say I do myself."

Her hard, restless eyes challenged a compliment from Laydon. She fingered the large false pearls at her throat, and paused for him to take his cue. When he did not take it, she went on talking with the comfortable conviction that she was being very brilliant and entertaining, and waking up these dull country people for once in their lives.

It was not to be supposed that the man-less half-hour in the drawing-room after dinner would pass easily. Mrs Weatherby smoked one cigarette after another and looked bored, whilst Lacy talked about her flat, its curtains, its carpets, the probable condition of furniture which had been stored for six years, and a few more equally exciting topics. She was quite determined not to give "that appalling person" any further opportunity of displaying her conversational talents; and as she was herself no mean performer, she held the stage until the men came in.

"Evelyn, my dear, will you give us a little music?"

Sir Cotterell's old-fashioned phrase brought the suggestion of a sneer to Mrs Weatherby's face. She looked invitingly at Laydon, but it was Sir Henry Prothero who seated himself beside her whilst Evelyn moved to the piano.

Laydon watched her. She had on a white dress with long, soft, floating sleeves. Her arms showed through them, and they fell away like a mist as she lifted her hands to the keyboard. He wondered if it was the white dress that made her seem so pale. Her eyes were like deep water. He could make nothing of their look. On the surface, colour, sparkle, beauty; but in the depths, what? He could not tell. The depths might hide a shipwreck, or a treasure. She wore her pearls—Jim Laydon's pearls, and on her left hand, dark against its whiteness, was the emerald of Jim Laydon's ring. She wore the pearls; she wore the ring. What was in her heart? What image? And what memories? A burning fire of jealousy rose in him; the flame of it consumed him. He watched her hands move on the keys, and listened to the singing, rippling notes. She played something that was like bright water. He looked back into the lost years and saw bright water run beneath dark trees. Here the sun shone on it and it was bright; and there the low black branches shadowed it and it was dark. Anton Blum had known that water well.

Chapter Twenty-Nine

THE NIGHTMARE EVENING was over at last. Mr Gaunt had said good night with such an affectionately troubled look that Evelyn was moved almost to tears. Mrs Gaunt wore the air of a woman who has made up her mind. She had. She had decided not only that dear Millicent was to go without delay, but that dear Millicent must never be asked again.

"She has changed very much—very painfully. She behaved atrociously. Yes, Matthew, she did." This in the seclusion of their bedroom.

"We must try to be charitable, though I admit—"

"I was *horrified* at her behaviour. She must go."

"But, my dear, we asked her for a month. We mustn't be inhospitable, or uncharitable, or—in fact, Marion, I don't see how—"

"There are *ways*," said Mrs Gaunt darkly.

Laydon flung out of the house as soon as the guests had departed. Darkness, space, silence—these were his needs. The house smothered him.

Evelyn went to her room, but she did not undress. Instead, she locked the door, put out the light, and threw the window wide. She had the set of rooms which had been Lady Laydon's, and which would have been her own if she had come here as Jim's wife. There was a bedroom, and next door to it a sitting-room opening through long French windows on to a stone-railed balcony. The bedroom windows looked out towards Laydon Sudbury.

The village lights were out; there was not one yellow twinkle left. But in the moonlit dusk she could see the square tower of the little church, and above and around the village a blackness of mysterious woods. She had walked in them that afternoon when they were full of scent of flowers and the spring sunshine. Now they looked strange and formless like the forests of a dream. Everything was still and silent under the moon. She leaned out, and wondered at the soft warmth of the night air.

She stayed like that for a long time, half kneeling, half sitting, letting her thoughts drift. Cotty was coming down to-morrow. Well, it didn't matter. Lacy had been rather a brick after dinner. That awful woman! The poor darling Gaunts. Lacy could be a brick sometimes. It was extra nice of her, because she really was put out about the Lady's Garden. Impossible to take her there; impossible to take anyone there. Sir Cotterell was a dear; he never asked her if she used her key, never showed by word or look that he remembered that she had one. Well, she had never used it.

She began to wonder what the garden was like. It seemed so strange that she had never been into it, when every year she was consulted about the flowers by old McAlister, who after all generally had his own way. Last year they had planned a drift of star narcissus. She wondered how it looked under the moon. Vaguely and slowly there came into her mind the desire to go to the garden and stand among the flowers. She felt a drawing and a compulsion, and then sharp reaction. What nonsense! Of course she couldn't go at this hour.

She drew the curtains, switched on the light, and missed the wild, fresh sweetness of the night air. After a moment she went to her jewel-case, unlocked it, and lifted out the tray that lay uppermost. Underneath, in a long velvet-lined compartment, lay the key—a large old-fashioned key beautifully wrought with iron tracery. She looked at it. It had lain there for nearly ten years. Why should she not use it? Why be within four walls and under this glare of light, when the May night waited outside, beautiful, comforting, serene, in a silver dusk?

She threw a loose black satin wrap over her white dress and went down through the still house to the library. The French window opened easily. She passed the Dutch garden and went down the steps beyond.

Laydon came up the long slope of the beech walk between the bare hedges, and saw something move in the shadowed angle by the door of the Lady's Garden. He stood still, and in a moment the door creaked and swung open, letting the moonlight through. A dark figure stood out against the light. He saw the moon on Evelyn's hair, and the flutter of a long white sleeve as she turned to close the door behind her. Then everything was in shadow again. He did not move at once. Evelyn—here—alone like this! Strange! But perhaps she was only doing what she had done a hundred times before. And the garden was hers. It was not hard to imagine the lure of its peace and stillness on such a night as this.

He began to walk on slowly, and as he walked he thought about the garden. It had been the centre of their games when they were children, a secret place, remote and hidden. The games centred about it, but it remained unknown, untrodden. He could remember Lacy's "But why can't we go in? I want to go in. Oh, do make him let us go in just *once*!" He could see the little flushed face and the long floating hair. He could hear her stamp her foot and cry out pettishly: "But I *want* to go in!" And he could hear McAlister's answer: "Then want'll be your master, Miss Lacy." None of the children had even been into the garden—not big Jim Field, though he had once sworn to climb the wall and failed, nor little Lacy, nor the two Laydon boys, nor Evelyn. None of them had ever been into the garden. But Evelyn was there now.

He walked into the shadowed corner, pushed gently at the door, and stood on the threshold, looking in. The garden was small, and the middle of it was sunk and paved. Laydon stood at the top of half a dozen steps and looked down on a paved walk with a pool in the middle of it. A very sweet scent came up to him, and he saw that the sloping sides of the garden were thickly planted with white narcissus. He came down the steps and stood by an old, crooked hawthorn which grew at the foot, its branches hidden in a drift of white blossom.

On the moss-grown steps his feet had made no sound at all. He stood amongst the white flowers and saw Evelyn quite close to him, sitting motionless on the low stone wall that guarded the pool. She had thrown back her cloak; her head was raised; her eyes looked far. There were yellow irises growing in the pool; the moonlight blanched them almost to silver. There was such a stillness that it seemed impossible to move or speak. To Laydon the moment was almost one of peace. For the first time he could look at Evelyn and know that no one was there to weigh his look or to find a meaning in it.

He did not know how long a time went by, but at last she moved. It seemed to Laydon that she came back. She had been away in some far off place of dreams.

She came back with a little shiver, dropped her eyes from the glory of the night sky, and put out her hand. Laydon moved too, and at once her face changed. She said "Who's there?" in a soft, fluttered voice, and put her hand to her throat in the way she had when anything startled her.

He took a step forward.

"It is I. Did I frighten you?"

Evelyn did not speak. She could not say to him any of the things that were in her mind. Her thought was full of him, so full that she could not find words. After that one startled instant, it seemed the most natural thing in the world that he should be there. He came forward slowly and looked down into the water.

"Do you come here often?" The words came in spite of himself. They were part of his hunger to know what lay behind that still look of hers.

She answered in her lowest, gentlest voice:

"I've never been here before."

That touched the old boyish romance, the secret dream. This was the garden of the dream; and they were here together.

"Why did you come to-night?"

Evelyn lifted her eyes, and the dream was chilled. He thought they said "What is that to you?"; yet after a while she said, speaking very slowly,

"I think I came—to say good-bye."

She looked into the pool as she spoke, and saw her own face dimly. She saw Laydon as a dark and formless shadow.

"Good-bye—to what?"

She did not answer at once. The dark came closer to them both. At last she moved; her lips moved.

"To the past, I think, Tony."

The soft, low-spoken words pierced his heart. So it was like that? Irrevocably the past was gone. She was letting it go, saying farewell to it; and he had no power to bid it stay. She was gone from him—Evelyn—Evelyn—lost—lovely—beloved—Evelyn!

Evelyn looked into the water. Her heart beat hard; a passion of thoughts beat with her heart. "Let the past go. What does it matter? It's now that counts. It's you and I, and this moment—*this*. Tony—Tony—*Tony*! Don't you care at all? Can't you let the past go?" The clamorous thoughts went on. Her lips were cold and silent.

Laydon was conscious only of his own crying need. If he could know. If he could be sure. If he could bridge that ten years' gap and know which of them had had her heart. And yet, if he knew, how would it help the man he was to-day? To trade on a long-ago romance, to take what had belonged to one of those young lovers—how would that help him now? If she had cared for the boy he was no longer, would that content him? If she had cared for the other boy, if she still cared for him—

If only they could have started clear of all these cross-currents of memory, with their cold, confusing touch. If they could get clear of them now,—

There was still Chris Ellerslie.

An ugly stab of jealousy ran deep into his mood. He turned from the past to the present with a jerk. There was a bitter smile as he looked at the silver-golden irises, the moon-flecked pool, and the mysterious drifts of blossom that surrounded Evelyn and himself. The place, the hour, the exquisite breath of the flowers—these were pure romance, or a boy's dream of it. Once, in a dream, he had stood in such a place as this and held her to his heart, wordless because no words would come and none were needed. Now romance was in the dust of the dead years. There remained the strange irony that had brought them here—*here*, to realize how far apart they were. The silence that might have been so sweet became thing intolerable.

As if his thought had touched her, Evelyn moved. She made a little groping motion with her hand and rose slowly to her feet. Her cloak had dropped across the low stone wall; her white dress was uncovered. Laydon's heart cried out in him. He saw, not Evelyn, but lost love itself, unearthly, blanched, withdrawn. He made a step forward, and as he did so, the door at the top of the steps swung in. There was a rustling sound, and Lacy's voice with a catch in it:

"Evelyn—are you there? Evelyn—oh!"

Lacy stood on the topmost step, bending forward, clinging to the door. From where she stood she could see the pool and Evelyn standing white above it. She cried out, an involuntary, frightened cry:

"Evelyn!"

Evelyn did not speak. She bent down, took up her cloak, and put it on. To Laydon she seemed to become a shadow amongst the shadows, a shadow crowned with a nimbus where the moonlight caught her hair. She went up the steps, and he followed her. The moment with all it might have held was gone.

Lacy Manning caught at Evelyn's arm.

"Evelyn!"

But Evelyn walked past her and stood outside in the deep shadow, waiting. When Laydon and Lacy had crossed the threshold, she shut the door and turned the key. All the beauty and the fragrance were shut away. She drew the key from the lock, and went by so close to Laydon that her cloak touched him with a light, fluttering touch as if a leaf had blown against his hand.

He stood and watched her go, walking with a strange swiftness and energy. He turned with a start to find Lacy pulling at his sleeve.

"I wanted to see the garden so badly. I've always wanted to see it—and now she's angry. I've never seen her like this."

"Why did you come?" His voice was harsh, and she recoiled a little.

"I wanted to see the garden. I've *always* wanted to see it. I asked her this afternoon if she'd take me there. I wanted to see it so much. And I was looking out of my window, and—and I saw her come along the lower terrace, so of course I knew she was going to the garden, and—oh, I've never seen her quite like this!"

"You'd better go in," said Laydon.

Lacy flared up.

"I think you're frightfully unkind—and when I only wanted to help. Yes, I *do*. And I don't care how angry Evelyn is, I *do* love her more than anyone else in the world except Monkey and Don. And if that doesn't give you a right to be *interested* and to help, I don't know what does. And I don't care what Monkey says!"

Lacy's fright was passing. She was not very brave in the dark, and nothing but the most urgent curiosity would have given her enough courage to follow Evelyn. But with Laydon at her side the beech walk ceased to be terrifying and became pleasantly romantic. A sense that here was Opportunity came upon her with irresistible force, and she turned to Laydon with an impulsive gesture.

"You *won't* be angry—will you? It's because I care, because I *really* care. Have you—have you made it up?"

Laydon felt a desire to shake Lacy as he had once shaken her when she was a little girl. He wondered if Monkey ever shook her. He restrained his impulse, and said drily,

"Not exactly."

"Oh, why *don't* you? I know you're unhappy. *Any*one can see you care. And as for Evelyn—it was always *you* she cared for—always, always, *always*."

There was a short, intense silence. Then Laydon said,

"What exactly do you mean by that, Lacy?"

They had reached the end of the beech walk. Lacy turned so as to face him.

"I mean she cared—for *you*—that she's never cared for anyone else. It's always been you. Those three days that you were engaged—why, she was quite different—like another person. I don't know what came between you, but whatever it was, it broke her heart.

Why, there's never been a time since then that there haven't been any number of people who'd have been only too frightfully proud and happy if Evelyn would have looked at them. But she never would. I honestly believe she's tried. I think she would have liked to have been able to care. I think she would have taken Chris Ellerslie if she could have brought herself to do it. But she *couldn't*. I told Monkey all along that she'd never cared for anyone but you."

"Me!" Laydon's voice took an extraordinary inflection. It suggested a certain savage humour.

"Yes—*you*. It was always Jack with her, and never anyone else. And I knew—oh, I knew from the very beginning that you were Jack. Monkey may say what he likes, but I did know; and I told Evelyn the first time she came to Cologne."

"You—told—Evelyn." His voice was expressionless and slow.

"Yes, I told her. So you see there's no need *at all* for *either* of you to go on being unhappy. She's cared for you all along—she really has. So you see there's nothing to prevent your both being perfectly happy."

Laydon said "I see," and then said nothing more. He stood aside for Lacy to climb the terrace steps, but when they had reached the top, he went on ahead of her to where the library window stood open. There was no sign of Evelyn. The room was dark. Lacy put her hand on the switch and flooded it with light.

When she turned, Laydon was gone. She heard his steps receding. She ran to the window and called him softly:

"Jack—Jack—aren't you coming in?"

There was no answer.

Chapter Thirty

SIR COTTERELL TURNED from the library window. The Dutch garden was ablaze with tulips; each formal bed sunk in the grey stone paving was jewel-bright in the sunshine. The tulips were opening in the warmth—white, scarlet, orange, purple, and gold. The sky overhead was purest turquoise. No greater contrast could possibly have been imagined to that day of dark cloud and soaking rain in which Laydon had come home.

"Where is he?" said Sir Cotterell; he spoke with an angry impatience. "I haven't set eyes on him this morning. He ought to be here. I want him here when Cotty comes. He ought to be here. If he isn't, and I've to send for him, it'll look—No, he ought to be here, and not give Cotty any handle." He spoke to his brother-in-law, who sat half hidden by *The Times*; but it was Manning, just come into the room, who answered him:

"I'm afraid, sir," he began.

Sir Cotterell swung round.

"Well, what's up? Come, out with it, man, out with it! Can't you find him? He's not gone off, I take it." He laughed angrily. Everything about him betrayed strain.

Manning grimaced.

"Did he know Cotty was coming?"

"Know? Why, of course he knew! Everybody in the house knew. I should think the scullery-maid and the boot-boy knew. No one's got any private affairs nowadays—everybody knows everything—everybody's got to know everything. That's democracy—and a precious muddle it'll make of things before it's through."

Sir Henry Prothero let his paper rustle down upon his knee. He caught Manning's eye, and inquired placidly:

"Did you tell him Cotty was coming?"

"I?" said Sir Cotterell sharply. "I?—tell him? Well—"

"I just wondered whether you'd had the opportunity—Cotty rang up so late. But perhaps you had a talk after the Gaunts had gone."

"Perhaps I'd nothing of the sort," snapped Sir Cotterell. "Considering he made off almost before they were out of the house, I don't quite see when I could have this 'talk' of yours. I suppose I *might* have sat up till all hours; but I didn't. No doubt I *ought* to have done so; but I didn't."

"And you haven't seen him this morning?"

"I've already told you I haven't."

"Well, sir," said Manning, "if that's the case, it's pretty clear he didn't know Cotty was coming, and he's gone off somewhere. Lake says he's taken a suit-case."

Sir Cotterell's face changed painfully. He put a hand on the back of the tall chair by which he stood.

"Treats my house like an hotel," he muttered—"like a damned hotel. Goes off without a word—goes off when he knows that Cotty's coming down." There was a short, trying pause. "Cotty'll say he funked meeting him—he'll say he funked this new evidence—he'll say—"

Sir Henry glanced at him with concern.

"I think we may take it that he didn't know Cotty was coming."

Sir Cotterell stared back at him angrily:

"Tell Cotty that! Tell him—and go on telling him. Do you think he'll believe you, Henry? Do you think he'll believe any of us? I tell you he'll believe the fact—and so would anybody else. And the fact is that he's gone. Cotty's coming down with fresh evidence—and he's gone."

The hand that rested on the chair pushed it so violently that it fell forward and struck the table. With a sharp oath Sir Cotterell went back to the window and stood there drumming on the pane. Presently he said,

"Where's Evelyn?"

"I don't know," said Manning.

"Have you seen her? Has she vanished too?"

"She had breakfast and went out before any of us were down. Lacy went to look for her I'll see if they're back."

Manning was glad enough of an excuse to leave the room. Scenes were abhorrent to him; and life at present appeared to be one long succession of scenes endured, just averted, or impending.

He met Evelyn coming up the garden, bareheaded in the sunlight. She looked pale, and young, and rather pitiful. He was reminded, without knowing why, of a child who has received an unjust punishment. She smiled at him, and he was aware of effort. The child was trying to be brave, and finding it hard.

She said "Has Cotty come?" And when he shook his head the line of her lips relaxed a little, and she slipped a hand inside his arm.

"Monkey, I'm so nervous. Pinch me, or beat me, or something. I don't want to disgrace myself before Sophy."

"You won't."

"I'm not so sure."

"I am. Buck up, old girl!"

They met Lacy in the hall. Evelyn walked past her into the library. Lacy stopped short, flushed scarlet, and met her husband's searching look with an indignant,

"Monkey, she's furious with me."

"So I see, my child. Perhaps you'll explain why."

Lacy dabbed at her eyes, which were very bright and not at all wet.

"She's furious."

He nodded.

"You've said that already. Besides I can see it for myself. The question is, why is she angry? What have you been doing?"

"Of course it's *me*."

"Well, isn't it? What have you been doing? Butting in?"

"I didn't b-b-butt."

"What did you do?"

"I only told him—I mean—"

Monkey's hand shot out; his very strong, lean fingers took Lacy's shoulder in a most compelling grip.

"You butted in after I told you you weren't to."

"I d-didn't."

"Yes, you did. Out with it! What did you say to him?"

"I only s-said—Monkey, you're hurting me *dreadfully*!"

"What did you say?"

"I s-said she'd always cared for him."

"The dickens you did!" His grip relaxed a little. "Well, you'd no business to butt in; but I don't know why that should make him stampede."

"Monkey! He hasn't!"

"He has. Packed up at dawn and trekked into the blue."

"Monkey!" Lacy's tone was frankly horrified.

He pulled her round to face the light.

"Look here! You haven't told me everything. You must have said something to make him go off like that. What did you say?"

Lacy looked scared; her colour flickered.

"What did you say? What's the good of not telling me? You know you'll have to."

He bent a horribly frowning gaze upon her, and all of a sudden she pressed nearer to him.

"Monkey—Monkey darling—I didn't mean any *harm*—I only wanted to help—I can't *bear* it when Evelyn looks unhappy."

"What did you say?"

"I said—she'd always cared for Jack—and I knew he was Jack—and why didn't they make it up—and be happy?"

Manning's frown disappeared before a look of such cold anger that Lacy for once in her life really feared him. She said "Monkey!" with a little gasp, and then voice and face changed suddenly. "The Cottys!" she said, gave him a violent push, and turned to meet Sophy Abbott. Even in the midst of his anger, Manning felt a spasm of admiration for her presence of mind.

"What a lovely day for a drive! But, my *dear* Sophy"—Lacy's voice was most sweetly flute-like—"my dear Sophy, aren't you boiled? I've been turning out cotton dresses, and Monkey's in a most frightful temper because he's only brought winter things." She shook hands smilingly with Cotty as she spoke, and ignored Sophy's offended stare.

Both the Abbotts wore an air subtly blended of stiffness and triumph. Sophy was wrapped in the massive sable coat which formed part of every Mendip-ffollinton trousseau. It reached to her ankles and, perhaps mercifully, concealed them. As a concession to the May sunshine, she had assumed a small close toque composed entirely of Parma violets, and wore over it an ample dark green motor veil, which was tied in a very large bow under her second chin. Cotty carried a despatch case.

The whole party came into the library together. Sir Henry put down his paper and came round the table. His pleasant greeting was in contrast to Sir Cotterell's irritable "How do, Sophy?" followed by "Well, Cotty? Another mare's nest, eh?"

Evelyn was standing by the hearth, her back to the empty fireplace. She nodded, and smiled rather vaguely.

Sir Cotterell went to the head of the table, pushed back a chair, and sat down.

"Let's get it over," he said. "I take it from what you said on the telephone last night that you think you've got something definite to show me. All right, Cotty, let's have it. Only I warn you now, as I warned you the last time you came down, that I won't have the matter harped on and raked over continually, and nothing but suspicions and gossip and a lot of hearsay tales to show for it. I just want to make that quite clear to everyone. Sit down, Sophy, won't you? Evelyn, my dear, have a chair. Sit down, everyone. Now, Cotty, whatever it is, get it off your chest and let's have done with it."

Sophy Abbott sat down stiffly. She unfastened her coat and let it trail a regal length upon the floor. Her cheeks were unwontedly flushed; her pale eyes bulged a little more than usual.

Lacy took a chair between her father and her husband. Every now and then she stole a look, half daring, half frightened, at Manning's grim face. He was still angry, he was still dreadfully angry. But perhaps he was angry with Cotty, and not with her. She looked past him at Evelyn, who sat at the foot of the table leaning back in her chair. Evelyn was angry too. It was simply *dreadful* to have Evelyn and Monkey both angry at the same time.

Cotty Abbott opened his despatch case and took out a folded paper. He opened it, tapped it, took out a pair of pince-nez, cleared his throat, and tapped the paper again.

"Before I pass this paper round," he began, "I would like—er—to protest against the manner in which my efforts to elucidate this case have—er—been received." He cleared his throat again. "As everyone here is aware, I was not satisfied as to the identity of the person who has claimed to be one of my uncle's grandsons. I was not at all satisfied. I said to Sophy that same evening—I mean the evening of the—er—day, the—er—last occasion that we all met—I said to Sophy on that very evening that I was not satisfied. Sophy was not satisfied either, and Tom Mendip-ffollinton, who was present, agreed with us that the evidence as to his identity was, in point of fact, not evidence at all. Those were, I may say, his very words. He gave it as his considered opinion that the evidence was not really evidence at all. Sophy and I agreed with him."

Sir Cotterell leaned forward.

"If you've merely come here to repeat your brother-in-law's opinions, Cotty,—"

"He hasn't," said Sophy Abbott, in an unpleasant voice. She opened her coat a little farther, and fanned herself with a fur-lined glove.

"Perhaps," said Sir Henry Prothero, "perhaps we could cut out these preliminaries." His tone was very urbane. "What's this paper you've brought down, Cotty?"

Sir Cotterell flung himself back in his chair.

"Cut the cackle and come to the horses," he muttered.

Cotty looked about the room, frowning.

"I imagined that the person most concerned would have been present. Is it not intended that he should be present?"

Sir Henry made a bland gesture.

"Laydon is, unfortunately, away," he said.

"He was here yesterday." Cotty's little eyes stared at him suspiciously.

Sir Henry made no answer, and Sophy Abbott thrust in with:

"Most extraordinary! Why, it looks—it almost looks as if—" She paused, coughed meaningly, and added, "Well, perhaps we'd better not say what it looks like."

"Suppose you tell us what's in that paper, Cotty," said Sir Henry rather sternly.

"It's a statement." Cotty rustled it with an air of triumph. They might say what they liked, but he had got the woman's signature. His voice rose a little. "It's a statement signed by the woman, Pearl Palliser."

"A statement!" Sir Cotterell rapped out the words. His hand stiffened on the arm of the chair.

"A statement," said Cotty Abbott, "signed by her in my own presence, and witnessed by Tom Mendip-ffollinton. It declares that she recognized this man as her husband, Jim Field. He went to see her the day after my uncle had accepted him as his heir, and she immediately recognized him to be her husband, James Field. Her exact words were, 'I thought I'd seen a ghost.'" He paused and surveyed the circle of faces—Sir Henry very grave; Manning frowningly incredulous; Sir Cotterell with the look of a man struck hard and unawares. He saw Lacy, brilliantly flushed, her mouth open as if to speak; and Evelyn sitting back in her chair quite still and pale, one hand lightly clasped at her breast and a strange little smile on her lips.

Manning got up, came round to her, leaned over the back of her chair, spoke low and urgently in a tone meant only for her.

"Evelyn, it's gone far enough."

She turned her eyes on him with a slow wonder in them.

"How did you know?"

He shrugged his shoulders.

"It's gone far enough. The old man can't stand any more."

Sir Cotterell was trying to speak. He looked at Cotty, put out a trembling hand, and said—

"Give me—the paper."

Evelyn got up. She rested her left hand on the table and leaned a little forward. She did not quite know what she was going to say, and she found herself repeating Manning's words:

"I think—this has gone far enough."

A look of relief and satisfaction crossed Sir Henry's face. He sat back in his chair. The Abbotts turned and stared at Evelyn. Sir Cotterell said again,

"Give me—the paper."

"Sir Cotterell." Evelyn's voice rose and steadied. "Sir Cotterell, I'm so sorry."

He looked at her then, rather vaguely.

"What is it, my dear? Cotty said—"

"I know. But it doesn't matter."

"Doesn't matter?" This very sharply from Sophy.

"No." She turned to Cotty. "Pearl Pal-User told me all about it, you know. She said you worried her till she didn't know what she was doing. She told me she'd signed something. She didn't really seem to know what she had signed but she said she'd signed something. However none of that really matters, because I've got the identity disc."

Sir Henry pushed his chair back. Lacy Manning gave a little faint scream. Cotty dropped his pince-nez and sat groping for them. Sir Cotterell slowly withdrew the hand which had been stretched out to take Pearl Palliser's statement. He took hold of the edge of the table and got to his feet.

"The identity disc? Nonsense!" said Sophy Abbott at the top of her voice.

"Go on, Evelyn," said Manning.

"I got it from Anna Blum."—Evelyn spoke simply and clearly—"She had it all the time. She gave it to me. Not the first time I went to Cologne, but this time—the other day—a week ago."

"The identity disc?" The words were just an unsteady whisper, but suddenly Sir Cotterell stood up straight; the colour came back into his lips and the fire into his glance.

"That's final!" he said. "That's what I've wanted. Henry, that's final. Even Cotty won't say that the disc isn't evidence. Evelyn—my dear—" He ended on a note of appeal.

Evelyn moved the hand that had been clenched against her breast. She brought it down open on the table, and in the palm was a little bag of gold brocade.

Manning came up to the table and took it from her hand. Nobody moved or spoke whilst he untied the thread that fastened it and tipped out a packet covered with yellowish linen, Evelyn put her finger on it for a moment. She said, "Wait!" with a catch in her voice. Then she spoke across the table to Sir Cotterell:

"I haven't looked at it. Anna gave it to me. But I didn't look at it—I didn't want to look at it."

Sophy Abbott's angry laugh rang out:

"My dear Evelyn, do you really expect us to believe that?"

For an instant Evelyn turned her eyes upon her. They were very darkly blue. They looked in Sophy's direction, but they did not seem to see her. She spoke quite gently:

"Yes, Sophy, I ask you to believe it." She paused, and added with extreme simplicity, "It's true."

Then she turned again to Sir Cotterell.

"It's for you. I don't want to see it. I know." She took her hand from the table. "I won't stay. No, I don't want anyone to come with me—*please*." The last word was for Manning, who had put his hand on her arm.

He let her go, and she went out of the room without turning her head. The door closed behind her. Lacy Manning began to cry softly.

"Open it," said Sir Henry in his quiet, courteous voice.

Manning broke the stitches, took out the paper-covered disc, unwrapped it.

Sir Cotterell came round the table and stood at his elbow. When the last fold of the paper was gone, he snatched at the disc and held it. His other hand pressed hard on Manning's shoulder. The room, the disc, the printed words, swam together.

"I can't see—I can't read it—Manning—*Manning*."

In a dead silence Manning took the disc and read the name aloud.

Chapter Thirty-One

LAYDON LEFT the Manor without any very clear idea of where he was going. His immediate need was to get away; he could no longer bear to be under one roof with Evelyn. A twenty-mile tramp through the night had brought him no farther than this. Laydon woods and meadows, the stream he had fished as a boy, all this spring warmth and burgeoning, were alike intolerable.

He arrived in London, and drove to the hotel at which he and Manning had stayed. The relief of losing himself, of being a casual stranger in the midst of a perfectly indifferent crowd, was very great. Yet with relief there came some prickings of conscience. He must write at once to Sir Cotterell. But after sitting and frowning a long time at a blank sheet of paper, he got up and made his way to the telephone exchange.

It was Manning who answered his "Hullo!"

"I'm speaking from town," said Laydon abruptly, and heard Manning suppress an exclamation.

"Well, so long as you *are* speaking! I don't mind telling you that Sir Cotterell was a good deal peeved at your going off."

A pause. Then Laydon, rather strained:

"Yes, I was afraid he wouldn't like it. Monkey, I *had* to go."

"H'm—Evelyn had to go too."

"Evelyn!"

"*Had to go too.* Is the line bad your end? I can say it louder if you'd like me to."

Silence. Then Manning again:

"Hullo! Are you there?"

"Yes. Monkey—why did she go?"

"Why did you go, for the matter of that? I shouldn't wonder if—no, never mind. Yes, I want another three minutes. Hullo, Laydon, don't let them cut us off—tell the lady your end that you'll go the limit. Hullo! You are there, aren't you? Well, we've had another nice little family party down here—Cotty and Sophy, and a statement signed by the versatile Miss Palliser all complete. You were well out of it."

"A statement! What statement?"

"Oh, the lady said you were her husband—that's all—her husband, Jim Field, And Evelyn—"

"Monkey, what's this nonsense? Evelyn didn't—"

"My dear chap, Evelyn up and cast a bomb into our midst, and having cast it, departed. The last anyone saw of her was the back of her car heading for town at about a hundred miles an hour."

Laydon's hand clenched on the receiver.

"What happened?" he said slowly.

"She cast her bomb, and went. We're still picking up the pieces here."

"What did she do?"

"You'd better ask her. And look here, old man, here's a bit of good advice for you—*Don't be a mug.*"

Laydon heard the click of the receiver. The line went dead. He came out of the box and shut the door behind him.

Evelyn reached her flat to find Jessica Sunning out. She went to her room, took off her things, changed into something thin and cool, and sat down empty-handed to wait. She seemed to have come to a place where everything left off. Fear, doubt, emotion, pain— everything had come to an end. It was as if she had been wandering in a maze, led first this way and then that, until a sudden turn had brought her to the centre. She remembered wandering once in such a maze, and she remembered the blank feeling with which she had come out upon the little open patch of grass in the middle. This was the feeling that possessed her now—blankness, a sense of having come to the end.

She sat quite still, her head thrown back against a dark cushion, her hands lying loosely in her lap palm upwards. Time seemed to flow by her like the flowing of a stream whose murmur is so much one with consciousness that it is no longer heeded. She heard the door open. The sound seemed to come from a long way off. If it was Jessica, it did not matter. If it was Ponson, she would go away again; she did not matter either. The door was closed.

Evelyn lifted her eyelids and saw Laydon standing at the far end of the room. She saw him as one sees someone in a dream. She was so much at the end of everything that she could look at him like that. As she looked, she was vaguely aware of how much he had altered in the last few weeks, even in the last few hours.

The unnatural pallor where cheek and chin had been covered with the thick beard was gone, merged into the general tan. The heavy peasant mask was gone.

Laydon, watching, felt his heart contract. He said, "Evelyn!" And at the sound of his voice, sharp with anxiety, she woke a little from her strange mood and smiled.

"How did you know?"

"Monkey told me."

"Monkey?"

"I rang up. He said you'd gone."

"Did he say anything else?"

He came nearer, and stood looking down on her, one big shoulder just touching the white mantelpiece.

"He said there'd been a scene."

"Yes, I suppose there was a scene." Her voice slid away into silence.

"Evelyn—he didn't say what had happened."

The dream began to fall away. After all, she had not come to the end. She had to speak, to tell him. Up to this moment she had not moved at all. Now she lifted her hands and laid them on the arms of the chair.

"He didn't tell you—what happened?"

"No, he didn't tell me. He said that you would tell me."

Evelyn sighed. The long breath seemed to shake her. Then she got up and stood quite near him, facing him, her eyes on his.

"Anna gave me the disc," she said.

"Evelyn!"

She took hold of the edge of the mantelpiece to steady herself.

"No—wait. She had it all the time. She gave it to me. I didn't look at it."

"Evelyn." He spoke in a voice dropped to its lowest note, shaken, hardly audible.

"I didn't look—I didn't want to look. I left it for them—for Sir Cotterell. I didn't want to look at it."

There was a very, very deep silence. It was broken at last by Laydon.

"Evelyn—do—you—know?"

Evelyn smiled. This was really the end. They had come to the place where they could speak the naked truth. She said in a still, effortless voice,

"I want to ask you something."

And as she said the words, she knew that there was no need to ask. The answer was in Laydon's eyes.

"Evelyn, who am I?"

"I think you know."

"But you? Do you know?"

"Oh, yes. You are—you. Isn't that enough?"

She saw his face become rigid.

"No!" The word was loud and harsh.

Evelyn came a little nearer; her hand touched his arm.

"Why does the past matter? Why do you care about it?"

"It matters."

"Why?"

His hands came down heavily upon her shoulders.

"I must know. You cared—I must know who you cared for. Evelyn—who was it? Was it Jack?"

She felt the strength of his big hands, the iron force with which he steadied his voice. There was pity in her eyes.

"Does a girl of eighteen care very much for anyone but herself?"

"You cared."

"I thought I cared for Jack. I cared for what he stood for—all sorts of romantic dreams. I thought my heart was broken when I woke up and found the dreams were gone."

He said, "Lacy was right," in a dull, toneless voice.

"Was she?"

She felt his grip relax. His hands fell to his sides.

"Yes. I've been a fool. She said you cared for Jack."

"I've told you what I cared for. I married Jim."

"Yes. Why?"

"I think"—her voice shook a little—"I think, because he made me feel so safe."

He made a sharp movement, seemed about to speak, then turned to her,

"Eve—"

Evelyn put out both her hands. She had begun to tremble very much. She said in a whispering, sobbing voice,

"It doesn't matter—it doesn't. Why do you let it matter?"

She felt his arms close round her.

"Are you safe—now?"

She laid her face against his, and did not speak.

"Who am I, Eve?"

"The man I love. Oh, no one but you has ever called me Eve."

"Who am I?"

"Do you love me?"

"Yes. Eve, who am I? Say it! Say it! I want you to say it first, before anyone else does. It's ten years since anyone's said my name. Eve, I thought I'd lost you—I thought I'd lost everything. I saw that damned paragraph, and I thought—What could I think? Ten years—and you—how could I just come back as if nothing had happened? I thought you were gone—I was trying to let you go. I can't believe—" His voice broke for an instant, and then rose to the old eager, boyish note, "I can't believe it's true. Say it, Eve, say it quickly!"

Evelyn put her lips against his cheek.

"Jim!" she said. "Jim!"

THE END